MAO
II

DON DELILLO

MAO II

VIKING

VIKING
Published by the Penguin Group
Viking Penguin, a division of Penguin Books USA Inc.,
375 Hudson Street, New York, New York 10014, U.S.A.
Penguin Books Ltd, 27 Wrights Lane, London W8 5TZ, England
Penguin Books Australia Ltd, Ringwood, Victoria, Australia
Penguin Books Canada Ltd, 2801 John Street,
Markham, Ontario, Canada L3R 1B4
Penguin Books (N.Z.) Ltd, 182–190 Wairau Road,
Auckland 10, New Zealand

Penguin Books Ltd, Registered Offices:
Harmondsworth, Middlesex, England

First published in 1991 by Viking Penguin,
a division of Penguin Books USA Inc.

PUBLISHER'S NOTE:
This is a work of fiction. Names, characters, places, and incidents either are the
product of the author's imagination or are used fictitiously, and any resemblance
to actual persons, living or dead, events, or locales is entirely coincidental.

Portions of this book first appeared in *Esquire* and *Granta*.

PHOTOGRAPH CREDITS:
Pages iv–v—Peter Turnley/Black Star; page 1—UPI/Bettmann; page 17—Syndication International; page 105—© Jean Gaumy/Magnum Photos; page 225—Reuters/Bettmann

LIBRARY OF CONGRESS CATALOGING-IN-PUBLICATION DATA
DeLillo, Don.
Mao II / Don DeLillo.
p. cm.
ISBN 0-670-83904-3
I. Title.
PS3554.E4425M36   1991
813'.54—dc20   90-50917

Printed in the United States of America
Set in Electra
Designed by Francesca Belanger

TO GORDON LISH

AT YANKEE
STADIUM

H ere they come, marching into American sunlight. They are grouped in twos, eternal boy-girl, stepping out of the runway beyond the fence in left-center field. The music draws them across the grass, dozens, hundreds, already too many to count. They assemble themselves so tightly, crossing the vast arc of the outfield, that the effect is one of transformation. From a series of linked couples they become one continuous wave, larger all the time, covering the open spaces in navy and white.

Karen's daddy, watching from the grandstand, can't help thinking this is the point. They're one body now, an undifferentiated mass, and this makes him uneasy. He focuses his binoculars on a young woman, another, still another. So many columns set so closely. He has never seen anything like this or ever imagined it could happen. He hasn't come here for the spectacle but it is starting to astonish him. They're in the thousands now, approaching division strength, and the old seemly tear-jerk music begins to sound sardonic. Wife Maureen is sitting next to him. She is bold and bright today, wearing candy colors to offset the damp she feels in her heart. Rodge understands completely. They had almost no warning. Grabbed a flight, got a hotel, took the subway, passed through the metal detector and here they are, trying to comprehend. Rodge is not unequipped for the rude turns of normal fraught experience. He's got a degree and a business and a tax attorney and a cardiologist and a mutual fund and whole life and major medical. But do the assurances always apply? There is a strangeness down there that he never thought he'd see in a ballpark. They take a time-honored event and repeat it, repeat it, repeat it until something new enters the world.

Look at the girl in the front row, about twenty couples in from the left. He adjusts the eyepiece lever and zooms to max power, hoping to see her features through the bridal veil.

There are still more couples coming out of the runway and folding into the crowd, although "crowd" is not the right word. He doesn't know what to call them. He imagines they are uniformly smiling, showing the face they squeeze out with the toothpaste every morning. The bridegrooms in identical blue suits, the brides in lace-and-satin gowns. Maureen looks around at the people in the stands. Parents are easy enough to spot and there are curiosity seekers scattered about, ordinary slouchers and loiterers, others deeper in the mystery, dark-eyed and separate, secretly alert, people who seem to be wearing everything they own, layered and mounded in garments with missing parts, city nomads more strange to her than herdsmen in the Sahel, who at least turn up on the documentary channel. There is no admission fee and gangs of boys roam the far reaches, setting off firecrackers that carry a robust acoustical wallop, barrel bombs and ash cans booming along the concrete ramps and sending people into self-protective spasms. Maureen concentrates on the parents and other relatives, some of the women done up touchingly in best dress and white corsage, staring dead-eyed out of tinted faces. She reports to Rodge that there's a lot of looking back and forth. Nobody knows how to feel and they're checking around for hints. Rodge stays fixed to his binoculars. Six thousand five hundred couples and their daughter is down there somewhere about to marry a man she met two days ago. He's either Japanese or

Korean. Rodge didn't get it straight. And he knows about eight words of English. He and Karen spoke through an interpreter, who taught them how to say Hello, it is Tuesday, here is my passport. Fifteen minutes in a bare room and they're chain-linked for life.

He works his glasses across the mass, the crowd, the movement, the membership, the flock, the following. It would make him feel a little better if he could find her.

"You know what it's as though?" Maureen says.

"Let me concentrate."

"It's as though they designed this to the maximum degree of let the relatives squirm."

"We can do our moaning at the hotel."

"I'm simply stating."

"I did suggest, did I not, that you stay at home."

"How could I not come? What's my excuse?"

"I see a lot of faces that don't look American. They send them out in missionary teams. Maybe they think we've sunk to the status of less developed country. They're here to show us the way and the light."

"And make sharp investments. After, can we take in a play?"

"Let me look, okay. I want to find her."

"We're here. We may as well avail ourselves."

"It's hard for the mind to conceive. Thirteen thousand people."

"What are you going to do when you find her?"

"Who the hell thought it up? What does it mean?"

"What are you going to do when you find her? Wave goodbye?"

"I just need to know she's here," Rodge says. "I want to document it, okay."

"Because that's what it is. If it hasn't been goodbye up to this point, it certainly is now."

"Hey, Maureen? Shut up."

From the bandstand at home plate the Mendelssohn march

carries a stadium echo, with lost notes drifting back from the recesses between tiers. Flags and bunting everywhere. The blessed couples face the infield, where their true father, Master Moon, stands in three dimensions. He looks down at them from a railed pulpit that rides above a platform of silver and crimson. He wears a white silk robe and a high crown figured with stylized irises. They know him at molecular level. He lives in them like chains of matter that determine who they are. This is a man of chunky build who saw Jesus on a mountainside. He spent nine years praying and wept so long and hard his tears formed puddles and soaked through the floor and dripped into the room below and filtered through the foundation of the house into the earth. The couples know there are things he must leave unsaid, words whose planetary impact no one could bear. He is the messianic secret, ordinary-looking, his skin a weathered bronze. When the communists sent him to a labor camp the other inmates knew who he was because they'd dreamed about him before he got there. He gave away half his food but never grew weak. He worked seventeen hours a day in the mines but always found time to pray, to keep his body clean and tuck in his shirt. The blessed couples eat kiddie food and use baby names because they feel so small in his presence. This is a man who lived in a hut made of U.S. Army ration tins and now he is here, in American light, come to lead them to the end of human history.

The brides and grooms exchange rings and vows and many people in the grandstand are taking pictures, standing in the aisles and crowding the rails, whole families snapping anxiously, trying to shape a response or organize a memory, trying to neutralize the event, drain it of eeriness and power. Master chants the ritual in Korean. The couples file past the platform and he sprinkles water on their heads. Rodge sees the brides lift their veils and he zooms in urgently, feeling at the same moment a growing distance from events, a sorriness of spirit. But he watches and muses.

When the Old God leaves the world, what happens to all the unexpended faith? He looks at each sweet face, round face, long, wrong, darkish, plain. They are a nation, he supposes, founded on the principle of easy belief. A unit fueled by credulousness. They speak a half language, a set of ready-made terms and empty repetitions. All things, the sum of the knowable, everything true, it all comes down to a few simple formulas copied and memorized and passed on. And here is the drama of mechanical routine played out with living figures. It knocks him back in awe, the loss of scale and intimacy, the way love and sex are multiplied out, the numbers and shaped crowd. This really scares him, a mass of people turned into a sculptured object. It is like a toy with thirteen thousand parts, just tootling along, an innocent and menacing thing. He keeps the glasses trained, feeling a slight desperation now, a need to find her and remind himself who she is. Healthy, intelligent, twenty-one, serious-sided, possessed of a selfness, a teeming soul, nuance and shadow, grids of pinpoint singularities they will never drill out of her. Or so he hopes and prays, wondering about the power of their own massed prayer. When the Old God goes, they pray to flies and bottletops. The terrible thing is they follow the man because he gives them what they need. He answers their yearning, unburdens them of free will and independent thought. See how happy they look.

Around the great stadium the tenement barrens stretch, miles of delirium, men sitting in tipped-back chairs against the walls of hollow buildings, sofas burning in the lots, and there is a sense these chanting thousands have, wincing in the sun, that the future is pressing in, collapsing toward them, that they are everywhere surrounded by signs of the fated landscape and human struggle of the Last Days, and here in the middle of their columned body, lank-haired and up-close, stands Karen Janney, holding a cluster of starry jasmine and thinking of the bloodstorm to come. She is waiting to file past Master and sees him with the single floating eye of the crowd, inseparable from her own apparatus of vision but sharper-sighted, able to perceive more deeply. She feels intact, rayed with well-being. They all feel the same, young people from fifty countries, immunized against the language of self. They're forgetting who they are under their clothes, leaving behind all the small banes and body woes, the daylong list of sore gums and sweaty nape and need to pee, ancient rumbles in the gut, momentary chills and tics, the fungoid dampness between the toes, the deep spasm near the shoulder blade that's charged with mortal reckoning. All gone now. They stand and chant, fortified by the blood of numbers.

Karen glances over at Kim Jo Pak, soft-eyed and plump in his nice new suit and boxy shoes, husband-for-eternity.

She knows her flesh parents are in the stands somewhere. Knows what they're saying, sees the gestures and expressions. Dad trying to use old college logic to make sense of it all. Mom wearing the haunted stare that means she was put on earth strictly to suffer. They're all around us, parents in the thousands, afraid of our intensity. This is what frightens them. We really believe. They bring us up to believe but when we show them true belief they call out psychiatrists and police. We know who God is. This makes us crazy in the world.

Karen's mindstream sometimes slows down, veering into sets of whole words. They take a funny snub-nosed form, the rudimentary English spoken by some of Master's chief assistants.

They have God once-week. Do not understand. Must sacrifice together. Build with hands God's home on earth.

Karen says to Kim, "This is where the Yankees play."

He nods and smiles, blankly. Nothing about him strikes her so forcefully as his hair, which is shiny and fine and ink-black, with a Sunday-comics look. It is the thing that makes him real to her.

"Baseball," she says, using the word to sum up a hundred

happy abstractions, themes that flare to life in the crowd shout and diamond symmetry, in the details of a dusty slide. The word has resonance if you're American, a sense of shared heart and untranslatable lore. But she only means to suggest the democratic clamor, a history of sweat and play on sun-dazed afternoons, an openness of form that makes the game a kind of welcome to my country.

The other word is "cult." How they love to use it against us. Gives them the false term they need to define us as eerie-eyed children. And how they hate our willingness to work and struggle. They want to snatch us back to the land of lawns. That we are willing to live on the road, sleep on the floor, crowd into vans and drive all night, fund-raising, serving Master. That our true father is a foreigner and nonwhite. How they silently despise. They keep our rooms ready. They have our names on their lips. But we're a lifetime away, weeping through hours of fist-pounding prayer.

World in pieces. It is shock of shocks. But there is plan. Pali-pali. Bring hurry-up time to all man.

She does not dream anymore except about Master. They all dream about him. They see him in visions. He stands in the room with them when his three-dimensional body is thousands of miles away. They talk about him and weep. The tears roll down their faces and form puddles on the floor and drip into the room below. He is part of the structure of their protein. He lifts them out of ordinary strips of space and time and then shows them the blessedness of lives devoted to the ordinary, to work, prayer and obedience.

Rodge offers the binoculars to Maureen. She shakes her head firmly. It is like looking for the body of a loved one after a typhoon.

Balloons in clusters rise by the thousands, sailing past the rim of the upper deck. Karen lifts her veil and passes below the pulpit, which is rimmed on three sides by bulletproof panels. She feels the blast of Master's being, the solar force of a charismatic soul. Never so close before. He sprinkles mist from a holy bottle in her face. She sees Kim move his lips, following Master's chant word for word. She's close enough to the grandstand to see people crowding the rails, standing everywhere to take pictures. Did she ever think she'd find herself in a stadium in New York, photographed by thousands of people? There may be as many people taking pictures as there are brides and grooms. One of them for every one of us. Clickety-click. The thought makes the couples a little giddy. They feel that space is contagious. They're here but also there, already in the albums and slide projectors, filling picture frames with their microcosmic bodies, the minikin selves they are trying to become.

They veer back to the outfield grass to resume formation. There are folk troupes near both dugouts dancing to gongs and drums. Karen fades into the thousands, the columned mass. She feels the meter of their breathing. They're a world family now, each marriage a channel to salvation. Master chooses every mate, seeing in a vision how backgrounds and characters match. It is a mandate from heaven, preordained, each person put here to meet the perfect other. Forty days of separation before they're alone in a room, allowed to touch and love. Or longer. Or years if Master sees the need. Take cold showers. It is this rigor that draws the strong. Their self-control cuts deep against the age, against the private ciphers, the systems of isolated craving. Husband and wife agree to live in different countries, doing missionary work, extending the breadth of the body common. Satan hates cold showers.

The crowd-eye hangs brightly above them like the triangle eye on a dollar bill.

A firecracker goes off, another M-80 banging out of an exit ramp with a hard flat impact that drives people's heads into their torsos. Maureen looks battle-stunned. There are lines of boys wending through empty rows high in the upper deck, some of them only ten or twelve years old, moving with the princely swagger of famous street-felons. She decides she doesn't see them.

"I'll tell you this," Rodge says. "I fully intend to examine this organization. Hit the libraries, get on the phone, contact parents, truly delve. You hear about support groups that people call for all kinds of things."

"We need support. I grant you that. But you're light-years too late."

"I think we ought to change our flight as soon as we get back to the hotel and then check out and get going."

"They'll charge us for the room for tonight anyway. We may as well get tickets to something."

"The sooner we get started on this."

"Raring to go. Oh boy. What fun."

"I want to read everything I can get my hands on. Only did some skimming but that's because I didn't know she was involved in something so grandiose. We ought to get some hotline numbers and see who's out there that we can talk to."

"You sound like one of those people, you know, when they get struck down by some rare disease they learn every inch of material they can find in the medical books and phone up doctors on three continents and hunt day and night for people with the same awful thing."

"Makes good sense, Maureen."

"They fly to Houston to see the top man. The top man is always in Houston."

"What's wrong with learning everything you can?"

"You don't have to *enjoy* it."

"It's not a question of enjoy it. It's our responsibility to Karen."

"Where is she, by the way?"

"I fully intend."

"You were scanning so duteously. What, bored already?"

A wind springs up, causing veils to rustle and lift. Couples cry out, surprised, caught in a sudden lightsome glide, a buoyancy. They remember they are kids, mostly, and not altogether done with infections of glee. They have a shared past after all. Karen thinks of all those nights she slept in a van or crowded room, rising at five for prayer condition, then into the streets with her flower team. There was a girl named June who felt she was shrinking, falling back to child size. They called her Junette. Her hands could not grip the midget bars of soap in the motel toilets of America. This did not seem unreasonable to the rest of the team. She was only seeing what was really there, the slinking shape of eternity beneath the paint layers and glutamates of physical earth.

All those lost landscapes. Nights downtown, live nude shows in cinder-block bunkers, slums with their dumpster garbage. All those depopulated streets in subdivisions at the edge of Metroplex, waist-high trees and fresh tar smoking in the driveways and nice-size rattlers that cozy out of the rocks behind the last split-level. Karen worked to make the four-hundred-dollar-a-day standard, peddling mainly bud roses and sweet williams. Just dream-walking into places and dashing out. Rows of neat homes in crashing rain. People drooped over tables at five a.m. at casinos in the desert. Progressive Slot Jackpots. Welcome Teamsters. She fasted on liquids for a week, then fell upon a stack of Big Macs. Through revolving doors into hotel lobbies and department stores until security came scurrying with their walkie-talkies and beepers and combat magnums.

They prayed kneeling with hands crossed at forehead, bowed deep, folded like unborn young.

In the van everything mattered, every word counted, sometimes fifteen, sixteen sisters packed in tight, singing you are my sunshine, row row row, chanting their monetary goal. Satan owns the fallen world.

She stacked bundles of baby yellows in groups of seven, the number-symbol of perfection. There were times when she not only thought in broken English but spoke aloud in the voices of the workshops and training sessions, lecturing the sisters in the van, pressing them to sell, make the goal, grab the cash, and they didn't know whether to be inspired by the uncanny mimicry or report her for disrespect.

Junette was a whirlwind of awe. Everything was too much for her, too large and living. The sisters prayed with her and wept. Water rocked in the flower buckets. They had twenty-one-day selling contests, three hours' sleep. When a sister ran off, they holy-salted the clothes she'd left behind. They chanted, We're the greatest, there's no doubt; heavenly father, we'll sell out.

After midnight in some bar in that winter stillness called the inner city. God's own lonely call. Buy a carnation, sir. Karen welcomed the chance to walk among the lower-downs, the sort of legions of the night. She slipped into semi-trance, detached and martyrish, passing through those bare-looking storefronts, the air jangly with other-mindedness. A number of dug-in drinkers bought a flower or two, men with long flat fingers and pearly nails, awake to the novelty, or hat-wearing men with looks of high scruple, staring hard at the rain-slickered girl. What new harassment they pushing in off the street? An old hoocher told her funny things, a line of sweat sitting on his upper lip. She got the bum's rush fairly often. Don't be so subjective, sir. Then scanned the street for another weary saloon.

Team leader said, Gotta get goin', kids. Pali-pali.

In the van every truth was magnified, everything they said and did separated them from the misery jig going on out there. They looked through the windows and saw the faces of fallen-world people. It totalized their attachment to true father. Pray all night at times, all of them, chanting, shouting out, leaping up from prayer stance, lovely moaning prayers to Master, oh *please*, oh *yes*, huddled in motel room in nowhere part of Denver.

Karen said to them, Which you like to sleep, five hour or four?

FOUR.

She said, Which you like to sleep, four hour or three?

THREE.

She said, Which you like to sleep, three hour or none?

NONE.

In the van every rule counted double, every sister was subject to routine scrutiny in the way she dressed, prayed, brushed her hair, brushed her teeth. They knew there was only one way to leave the van without risking the horror of lifetime drift and guilt. Follow the wrist-slashing fad. Or walk out a high-rise window. It's better to enter gray space than disappoint Master.

Team leader said, Prethink your total day. Then jump it, jump it, jump it.

Oatmeal and water. Bread and jelly. Row row row your boat. Karen said to them, Lose sleep, it is for sins. Lose weight, it is for sins. Lose hair, lose nail off finger, lose whole hand, whole arm, it go on scale to stand against sins.

The man in Indiana who ate the rose she sold him.

Racing through malls at sundown to reach the daily goal. Blitzing the coin laundries and bus terminals. Door to door in police-dog projects, saying the money's for drug centers ma'am. Junette kidnapped by her parents in Skokie, Illinois. Scotch-taping limp flowers to make them halfway salable. Crazy weather on the plains. Falling asleep at meals, heavy-eyed, dozing on the toilet, sneaking some Z's, catching forty winks, nodding off, hitting the hay, crashing where you can, flaked out, dead to the world, sleep like a top, like a log, desperate for some shut-eye, some sack time, anything for beddy-bye, a cat nap, a snooze, a minute with the sandman. Prayer condition helped them jump it to the limit, got the sorry blood pounding. Aware of all the nego media, which multiplied a ton of doubt for less committed sisters. Doing the hokey-pokey. Coldest winter in these parts since they started keeping records. Chanting the monetary goal.

Team leader said, Gotta hurry hurry hurry. Pali-pali, kids.

Rodge sits there in his rumpled sport coat, pockets crammed with traveler's checks, credit cards and subway maps, and he looks through the precision glasses, and looks and looks, and all he sees is repetition and despair. They are chanting again, one word this time, over and over, and he can't tell if it is English or some other known language or some football holler from heaven. No sign of Karen. He puts down the binoculars. People are still taking pictures. He half expects the chanting mass of bodies to rise in the air, all thirteen thousand ascending slowly to the height of the stadium roof, lifted by the picture-taking, the forming of aura, radiant brides clutching their bouquets, grooms showing sunny teeth. A smoke bomb sails out of the bleachers, releasing a trail of Day-Glo fog.

Master leads the chant, *Mansei*, ten thousand years of victory. The blessed couples move their lips in unison, matching the echo of his amplified voice. There is stark awareness in their faces, a near pain of rapt adoration. He is Lord of the Second Advent, the unriddling of many ills. His voice leads them out past love and joy, past the beauty of their mission, out past miracles and surrendered self. There is something in the chant, the fact of chanting, the being-one, that transports them with its power. Their voices grow in intensity. They are carried on the sound, the soar and fall. The chant becomes the boundaries of the world. They see their Master frozen in his whiteness against the patches and shadows, the towering sweep of the stadium. He raises his arms and the chant grows louder and the young arms rise. He leads them out past religion and history, thousands weeping now, all arms high. They are gripped by the force of a longing. They know at once, they feel it, all of them together, a longing deep in time, running in the earthly blood. This is what people have wanted since consciousness became corrupt. The chant brings the End Time closer. The chant is the End Time. They feel the power of the human voice, the power of a single word repeated as it moves them deeper into oneness. They chant for world-shattering rapture, for the truth of prophecies and astonishments. They chant for new life, peace eternal, the end of soul-lonely pain. Someone on the bandstand beats a massive drum. They chant for one language, one word, for the time when names are lost.

Karen, strangely, is daydreaming. It will take some getting used to, a husband named Kim. She has known girls named Kim since she was a squirt in a sunsuit. Quite a few really. Kimberleys and plain Kims. Look at his hair gleaming in the sun. My husband, weird as it sounds. They will pray together, whole-skinned, and memorize every word of Master's teaching.

The thousands stand and chant. Around them in the world, people ride escalators going up and sneak secret glances at the faces coming down. People dangle teabags over hot water in white cups. Cars run silently on the autobahns, streaks of painted light. People sit at desks and stare at office walls. They smell their shirts and drop them in the hamper. People bind themselves into numbered seats and fly across time zones and high cirrus and deep night, knowing there is something they've forgotten to do.

The future belongs to crowds.

PART ONE

I

He walked among the bookstore shelves, hearing Muzak in the air. There were rows of handsome covers, prosperous and assured. He felt a fine excitement, hefting a new book, fitting hand over sleek spine, seeing lines of type jitter past his thumb as he let the pages fall. He was a young man, shrewd in his fervors, who knew there were books he wanted to read and others he absolutely had to own, the ones that gesture in special ways, that have a rareness or daring, a charge of heat that stains the air around them. He made a point of checking authors' photos, browsing at the south wall. He examined books stacked on tables and set in clusters near the cash terminals. He saw stacks on the floor five feet high, arranged in artful fanning patterns. There were books standing on pedestals and bunched in little gothic snuggeries. Bookstores made him slightly sick at times. He looked at the gleaming best-sellers. People drifted through the store, appearing caught in some unhappy dazzlement. There were books on step terraces and Lucite wall-shelves, books in pyramids and theme displays. He went downstairs to the paperbacks, where he stared at the covers of mass-market books, running his fingertips erotically over the raised lettering. Covers were lacquered and gilded. Books lay cradled in nine-unit counterpacks like experimental babies. He could hear them shrieking *Buy me*. There were posters for book weeks and book fairs. People made their way around shipping cartons, stepping over books scattered on the floor. He went to the section on modern classics and found Bill Gray's two lean novels in their latest trade editions, a matched pair banded in austere umbers and rusts. He liked to check the shelves for Bill.

On his way out of the store he saw a man in a torn jacket come stumbling in, great-maned and filthy, rimed saliva in his beard, old bruises across the forehead gone soft and crumbly. People stood frozen in mid-motion, careful to remain outside the zone of infection. The man looked for someone to address. It was a large bright room full of stilled figures, eyes averted. Traffic pounded in the street. One of the man's trouser legs was mashed into a battered rubber boot; the other dragged on the floor in strips. A security guard approached from the mezzanine and the man lifted thick hands in a gesture of explanation.

"I'm here to sign my books," he said.

Everyone waited as the words traveled across the room, slowly unfolding their meaning.

"Bring me a pen so I can sign my books already."

The guard moved in, not actually looking at the man, who drew back quickly.

"Watch with the hands. There's no right that you should touch my person. Just, that's all, don't put no hands on me."

People saw it was all right to move again. Just another New York moment. The guard followed the man out the revolving door and Scott went out behind them. He was running a little late but wanted to look at the Warhols only a few blocks away. The museum lobby was crowded. He went downstairs, where people moved in nervous searching steps around the paintings. He walked past the electric-chair canvases, the repeated news images of car crashes and movie stars, and he got used to the anxious milling, it seemed entirely right, people eager to be undistracted, ray-gunned by fame and death. Scott had never seen work that was so indifferent to the effect it had on those who came to see it. The walls looked off to heaven in a marvelous flat-eyed gaze. He stood before a silk screen called *Crowd*. The image was irregular, deep streaks marking the canvas, and it seemed to him that the crowd itself, the vast mesh of people, was being riven by some fleeting media catastrophe. He moved along and stood finally in a room filled with images of Chairman Mao. Photocopy Mao, silk-screen Mao, wallpaper Mao, synthetic-polymer Mao. A series of silk screens was installed over a broader surface of wallpaper serigraphs, the Chairman's face a pansy purple here, floating nearly free of its photographic source. Work that was unwitting of history appealed to Scott. He found it liberating. Had he ever realized the deeper meaning of Mao before he saw these pictures? A subway rumbled past in the stony dark nearby. He stood and looked a while longer, feeling a curious calm even with people moving steadily in and out. The surge of bodies made its own soft roar.

Outside, a woman in a padded jacket followed him down the street. He had the impression she was small, with close-cropped hair, carrying some kind of animal in her coat. He picked up the pace but she kept on him, saying, "You're from out of town so I can talk to you."

He almost turned and looked at her but then thought no.

Saying, "Don't be ascared of me, mister, I only want to talk."

He walked faster, looking straight ahead, and she was still there, at his shoulder, saying, "I picked your face out of the air as this is someone I can trust."

He pointed to a blinking traffic-sign, hoping she'd understand he was pressed for time and this was goodbye and no hard feelings please, but she hurried across the street right behind him and moved alongside as they reached the curbstone. That's when she tried to give him the animal. He didn't turn to see what it was. Something dark and sick was his impression. He was almost

running now but she kept up, saying, "Take it, mister, take it."
He would listen to her but would not reply and would not let
her touch him or give him anything she had touched. He thought
of the wrecked man in the bookstore who recoiled when the
guard reached for him. Neither side wanted to be touched.

Saying, "Take it outside the city, where it's got a chance to
live."

When there is enough out-of-placeness in the world, nothing
is out of place. He rode to the eighth-floor lobby of a midtown
hotel, an atrium palace in the Broadway ruck, with English ivy
hanging off the tiered walkways, with trelliswork and groves of
trees, elevators falling softly through the bared interior, a dream
that once belonged to freeway cities. He saw her at a table near
the bar, an overnight bag and a carrying case on the floor by her
chair. She was in her late forties, he figured, with whitish blond
hair, thick and rigid, shooting out of a sea-bleached face. Her
eyes were light blue, so clear and nearly startling he knew it
would take an effort not to stare.

"You have to be Brita Nilsson."

"Why?"

"It's the look. I don't know, professional, accomplished, world
traveler, slightly apart. Not to mention the camera case. I'm Scott
Martineau."

"My guide to the frontier."

"In fact I got lost several times on my approach to the city and
then got rattled by traffic even though it's only weekend traffic
and I finally got straightened out and even found a place to park
but there were unsettling moments yet to come, psychic intruders,
sort of living shadows, and they speak. I haven't been to New
York in years and wouldn't mind sitting and chatting a while
before we hit the streets. Are you staying here?"

"Don't be crazy. I have a place way downtown but I thought
it would be simpler to meet somewhere central. It's very nice to

have this opportunity. But you talked about conditions without really specifying. I mean how much time do I get to spend with him? And how long can I expect to be gone because I have a schedule that's really quite firm and I haven't, you know, brought days and days of underwear."

"Wait. Are we moving?"

"It's a revolving bar," she said.

"Jesus. Where am I?"

"Isn't it strange? New York has fallen."

He watched Broadway float into the curved window and felt as if blocks of time and space had come loose and drifted. The misplaced heartland hotel. The signs for Mita, Midori, Kirin, Magno, Suntory—words that were part of some synthetic mass language, the esperanto of jet lag. And the tower under construction across the street, webbed and draped against the weather, figures moving fleetly past gaps in the orange sheeting. He saw them clearly now, three or four kids playing on the girders, making the building seem a ruin, an abandonment.

"I also have to tell you I don't understand the drill. I would prefer to get there on my own."

"Get where? You wouldn't know where you were going."

"You could tell me, couldn't you?" she said.

"Bill insists we do it this way."

"A little melodramatic maybe?"

"Bill insists. Besides, we're very hard to find."

"All right. But for the man's own peace of mind, why not choose a neutral site? That way there's no problem over disclosure. His whereabouts remain secret."

"I don't think you'll have very much to disclose. And Bill knows you won't talk anyway."

"How does he know?"

"We saw the piece about you in Aperture. That's how we decided you were the one. And he couldn't meet you somewhere else because he doesn't go anywhere else, except to hide from the book he's doing."

"I do love his books. They really mattered to me. And he hasn't been photographed in what? We must be speaking in the multi decades. So why don't I just relax?"

"Why don't you just relax?" Scott said.

Above the bar area there was a clock rotating in an openwork tower. From the table he could see through the bare trellis and clock framework to the elevators. He thought he could easily sit all afternoon watching the elevators rise and drop, clear pods ringed with pinpoint lighting. They moved soundlessly, clinging to the surface of a vast central cylinder. Everything was moving, everything was slowly turning, there was music coming from somewhere. He watched the people inside the elevators, deftly falling. High up, on the walkways, an occasional figure looking down, head and upper body. He wondered if the thing the woman tried to give him in the street might be a newborn child. The same musical phrase over and over, coming from somewhere.

"You photograph only writers now."

"Only writers. I frankly have a disease called writers. It took me a long time to find out what I wanted to photograph. I came to this country it's fifteen years. To this city actually. And I roamed the streets first day, taking pictures of city faces, eyes of city people, slashed men, prostitutes, emergency rooms, forget it. I did this for years. Many times I used a wide-angle lens and pressed the shutter release with the camera hanging at my chest from a neck strap so I wouldn't attract the wrong kind of attention, thank you very much. I followed derelicts practically to their graves. And I used to go to night court just to look at faces. I mean New York, please, this is my official state religion. But after years of this I began to think it was somehow, strangely— not valid. No matter what I shot, how much horror, reality, misery, ruined bodies, bloody faces, it was all so fucking pretty in the end. Do you know? And so I had to work out for myself certain complicated things that are probably very simple. You reach a certain age, isn't that the way it works? Then you know what you want to do at last."

She was eating roasted nuts from her loosely clenched fist, popping one at a time and drinking peppered vodka.

"But isn't it restful here?" he said. "I'm mesmerized by the elevators. It might be a new addiction."

"Give me a break," she said, and her slight accent and the worn-out catch phrase and the formal way she offered it, without crunching the first two words together, made him very happy.

"Only writers."

"Only writers," she said.

"And you're making a record, a kind of census in still pictures."

"I will just keep on photographing writers, every one I can reach, novelists, poets, playwrights. I am on the prowl, so to speak. I never stop traveling and taking pictures. This is what I do now. Writers."

"Every face."

"Every man and woman who is out there and who is reachable. If someone's not well known, so much the better. Given a choice, I prefer to search out writers who remain obscure. I get tips all the time, I get names and books from editors and other writers who understand what I'm doing or at least they say they do to make me feel better. A planetary record. For me, it's a form of knowledge and memory. I'm furnishing my own kind of witness. I try to do it systematically, country by country, but there are always problems. Finding some writers is a problem. And there are many writers in prison. This is always a problem. In some cases I've received permission to photograph writers under house arrest. People are starting to know me and this helps sometimes."

"With authorities."

"Yes, and writers. They're willing to see me because they know

I'm simply doing a record. A species count, one writer said. I eliminate technique and personal style to the degree that this is possible. Secretly I know I'm doing certain things to get certain effects. But we ignore this, you and I. I'm four years on this project, which by its nature of course there is no end."

"The question is, what happens to Bill's pictures?"

"This is completely up to you. I make some pictures available to publishers or the media but only if the writer gives consent. This is how I support the project, along with several grants. I have a travel grant I absolutely depend on. Magazines would do anything to run a photo essay on Bill Gray. But I don't want to do pictures that make a revelation, that say here he is after all these years. A simple study piece is better. I want to do pictures that are unobtrusive, shy actually. Like a work-in-progress. Not so permanent and finished. Then you look at the contacts and decide what you want me to do with them."

"These are the answers we were hoping to get."

"Good. So life goes on."

"And what happens ultimately to your pictures of writers as a collection?"

"Ultimately I don't know. People say some kind of gallery installation. Conceptual art. Thousands of passport-size photos. But I don't see the point myself. I think this is a basic reference work. It's just for storing. Put the pictures in the basement of some library. If people want to look, they come and ask. I mean what's the importance of a photograph if you know the writer's work? I don't know. But people still want the image, don't they? The writer's face is the surface of the work. It's a clue to the mystery inside. Or is the mystery in the face? Sometimes I think about faces. We all try to read faces. Some faces are better than some books. Or put the pictures in a space capsule, that would be fantastic. Send them into space. Greetings. We are writers of Earth."

The elevators climb and fall, the clock rotates, the bar slowly turns, the signs appear once more, the traffic lights change, the yellow taxis come and go. Magno, Minolta, Kirin, Sony, Suntory. What does Bill say? The city is a device for measuring time.

"There are kids up there. See them? Around the twentieth floor. Can you believe it?"

"It's safer than the streets. Leave them alone," she said.

"The streets. I guess I'm ready now."

"Then we'll go."

They found the car and Scott drove north along the Hudson and across the bridge at Beacon into dusk and secondary roads, connecting briefly with the thruway and then dropping into networks of two-lane blacktops, hours into night, the landscape reduced to what appears in headlights, to curves and grades and the signs for these, and there were dirt roads and gravel roads and old logging trails, there were steep hills and the sleet-spray of pebbles firing up at the car, there were pine stands lit by the moon. Two near strangers in night confinement inside the laboring drone of the small car, coming out of long silences to speak abruptly, out of long thoughts and memory chains and waking dreams and every kind of mindlife, the narrative that races just behind the eyes, their words sounding clean and shaped in the empty night.

"I feel as if I'm being taken to see some terrorist chief at his secret retreat in the mountains."

"Tell Bill. He'll love that," Scott said.

2

The room was dark and the man stood at the window waiting for headlights to appear at the top of the hill and weave across the field, across the tree stumps and bent stalks and rock debris. It was not eager or needful waiting but only a sense that the thing was about to happen and if he stood here a moment longer he would see the car turn into the rutted lane, a wobbly shadow set behind the lights, and come down the hill toward the house, taking on dimension. He resolved to count to ten and if the lights did not appear he would go to the desk and turn on the lamp and do some work, going over what he'd written during the day, the scant drip, the ooze of speckled matter, the blood sneeze, the daily pale secretion, the bits of human tissue sticking to the page. He counted to ten and when no lights showed he began to count to ten once more, slower now, standing in the dark, making an agreement with himself that this time he would really go to the desk and turn on the lamp if the car did not appear at the top of the hill by the time he reached ten, the mud-spattered compact, and settle down to work because it was only children who thought they could make things happen by counting, and he went to ten one more time and then one more time and then just stood watching until the headlights finally showed, splashy white, the car dipping off the rim of the hill and the lights sweeping briefly across the scrub, and strange children at that, the squinters and crappers, the ones who ball up their fists when they cry.

The car moved into the glow of the porch light. Mud stains on its lower flanks, layers of dust settled at the edges of the windshield outside the overlapping arcs of the wipers. When they got out and walked to the porch steps he went to the door of his workroom and listened to them stamp their feet on the mat and come in downstairs, mingled voices, the ruffle of people entering a house, shaking off coats, making all the incidental noises of transition, the sigh of the full body, homeyness and deep relief, the way it seemed a danger and a lie.

He closed the door and stood in the dark room, moving his hand across the desktop to find his cigarettes.

Glad to be indoors after a long journey on a chill night, nowhere. Goulash soup and black bread. Glad to be reminded that kitchens are places for long talks, the late hour, the wood stove and musty wine. Brita had shared a thousand odd dialogues with strangers on planes, intense and shallow, whispery with *Existenz*. Totally fake really. She could not talk seriously in cars. The car was serial travel, a sprocketed motion that shot her attention span to pieces. Even when the car generated a dull flat landscape she found it hard to unravel herself from the stutter reality of the broken white line and the picture in the window and the Kleenex in the box and break into real talk. She talked in kitchens. She was always following people into kitchens when they cooked meals or got ice for drinks and she talked into their faces or their backs, it didn't matter, making them forget what they were doing.

Scott sat across the table, lean and bushy-haired, something of a monochrome, with a beach glow in his pale brows. She thought he was happy to have company, a full-tilt voice from the breathless cities, pieces of experience, and he leaned toward her as if she were whispering, telling him rare and private things. But all she did was push out words, eat and talk, working the human burble. And he gazed, he stared at her, examined with uncalculating interest. If women her age were creatures who went mainly unseen and if she was a slightly weathered Scandian in jeans and sweatshirt who crushes cigarettes in dinner plates, then maybe he wondered what arresting things they might possibly have in common. He was in his absurdly early thirties, faintly unsure.

"I'll tell you the truth. I have no idea where we are. Not a bloody clue. And I suppose when I leave we do it by night so I don't see landmarks."

"There are no landmarks," he said. "But we do it after dark, yes."

"Now that I'm here it's hard to talk for very long about anything but him. I feel there's something at my shoulder and I can't help thinking I should refer to it now and then. Many people have tried to find him, I'm sure."

"Nobody's gotten this far. There have been media forays that we've heard about, intrepid teams with telephoto lenses. And his publisher forwards mail from people who are setting out to find him, who send word of their progress, who think they know where he is, who've heard rumors, who simply want to meet him and tell him what his books have meant to them and ask the usual questions, fairly ordinary people actually who just want to look at his face."

"Where is he?" she said.

"Upstairs hiding. But don't worry. Tomorrow you get your pictures."

"It's an important shoot for me."

"Maybe it will ease the pressure on Bill. Getting some pictures out. He's felt lately that they're moving in, getting closer all the time."

"All those fairly ordinary people."

"Someone sent him a severed finger in the mail. But that was in the sixties."

Scott showed her a room off the kitchen where some of Bill's papers were kept. Seven metal cabinets stood against the walls. He opened a number of drawers and itemized the contents, which included publishing correspondence, contracts and royalty statements, notebooks, old mail from readers—hundreds of sepia-edged envelopes bound in twine. He narrated matter-of-factly. There were old handwritten manuscripts, printer's typescripts, master galleys. There were reviews of Bill's novels, interviews with former colleagues and acquaintances. There were stacks of magazines and journals containing articles about Bill's work and about his disappearance, his concealment, his retirement, his alleged change of identity, his rumored suicide, his return to work, his work-in-progress, his death, his rumored return. Scott read excerpts from some of these pieces. Then they carried their wineglasses out along the hall where there were shelves filled with booklength studies of Bill's work and of work about his work. Scott pointed out special issues of a number of quarterlies, devoted solely to Bill. They went into another small room and here were Bill's two books in every domestic and foreign edition, hardcover and soft, and Brita went along the shelves studying cover designs, looking at texts in obscure languages, moving softly, not inclined to speak. They went to the basement, where Bill's work-in-progress was stored in hard black binders, each marked with a code number and a date for fairly easy retrieval and all set on freestanding shelves against the concrete walls, maybe two hundred thick binders representing drafts, corrected drafts, notes, fragments, recorrections, throwaways, updates, tentative revisions, final revisions. The slit windows high on the walls were shaded with dark material and there were two large dehumidifiers, one at each end of the room. She waited for Scott to call this room the bunker. He never did. And no hint of ironic inflection anywhere in his comments. But she sensed his pride of stewardship easily enough, the satisfaction he took in being part of this epic preservation, the neatly amassed evidence of driven art. This was the holy place, the inner book, long rows of typewriter bond buried in a cellar in the bleak hills.

There was a back stairway from the kitchen to the second-storey hall and they took Brita's jacket and bag and equipment case and went up that way. She glimpsed pantry shelves set into the wall and more of Bill's reader mail, thick boxed files labeled by month and year. She followed Scott through the door and across the hall. This was Brita's room.

In the bedroom downstairs Karen sat up watching TV. Scott came in and began undressing.

"Long day," she said.

"Let me tell you."

"All that driving, you must be really."

He put on pajamas and got into bed and she reached over and turned off the lamp. Then she picked up the remote control and lowered the volume on the TV, touch touch touch, until it was totally off. Scott's head was flat in the pillow and he was already halfway gone. She was watching the world news of the day. On any given day it was mainly the film footage she wanted to see and she didn't mind watching without sound. It was interesting how you could make up the news as you went along by sticking to picture only.

She sees men and boys at first, a swarming maleness, a thickness of pressed-together bodies. Then a crowd, thousands, filling the screen. It looks like slow motion but she knows it isn't. It is real time with bodies pressed and heaving, like bodies rolling in a sea swell, several arms raised above the crowd. They show bodies at odd angles. They show men standing off to the side somewhere, watching sort of half interested. She sees a great straining knot of people pressed to a fence, forced massively forward. They show the metal fence and bodies crushed against it, arms upflung. They show the terrible slow straining and heaving. What is it called, writhing? The camera is just outside the fence shooting straight in through the heavy-gauge steel wire. She sees men far back actually climbing on top of the mass of bodies, two men crawling on all the heads and shoulders. She sees the crowd pushed toward the fence and people at the fence pressed together and terribly twisted. It is an agony of raised and twisted arms and suffering faces. They show men calmly watching. They show men in shorts and jerseys, soccer players wearing those high stockings they wear, standing in the grass. There are bodies packed solid, filling the screen, and people barely moving at the fence, pressed and forced into one twisted position. She sees a boy in a white cap with a red peak and he has an expression on his face of what a nice day or here I am on my way home from school and they are dying all around him, they are writhing and twisted with open mouths and bloated tongues showing. Soccer is called football abroad. She sees the fence up close and they stop the film and it is like a religious painting, the scene could be a fresco in a tourist church, it is composed and balanced and filled with people suffering. She sees the faces of a woman and a girl and the large hand of a man behind them, the woman's wet tresses, her arm twisted against the steel strands of the fence, the girl crushed and buckled under someone's elbow, the boy in the white cap with red peak standing in the midst, in the crush, only now he senses, his eyes are shut, he senses he is trapped, his face is reading desperation. She sees people caught in strangleholds of no intent, arms upflung, faces popping out at her, hands trying to reach the fence but only floating in the air, a man's large hand, a long-haired boy in a denim shirt with his back to the fence, the face of the woman with the tresses hidden behind her own twisted arm, nails painted glossy pink, a girl or woman with eyes closed and tongue showing, dying or dead. In people's faces she sees the hopelessness of knowing. They show men calmly looking on. They show the fence from a distance, bodies piling up behind it, smothered, sometimes only fingers moving, and it is like a fresco in an old dark church, a crowded twisted vision of a rush to death as only a master of the age could paint it.

3

Brita unpacked the quartz light and screwed it into the top of the portable stand. She was nervous and kept a soft patter going. Bill stood against the wall waiting. He wore work pants and an old sweater, a thick-bodied man with a battered face and smoky hair combed straight back in wide tracks, going faintly yellow at the fringes. She felt the uneasy force, the strangeness of seeing a man who had lived in her mind for years as words alone—the force of a body in a room. She almost could not look at him. She looked indirectly, trying to conceal her glances in flurries of preparation. She thought he might have settled into an oldness, into ways of gesture and appearance that were deeper than his countable years. He watched her handle the equipment, looking past her into another moment somewhere. Already she sensed he was disappearing from the room.

"I'm going to bounce light off this wall and then you can go stand over there and I'll get my camera and stand over here and that's all there is to it."

"Sounds ominous."

There was a typewriter on a desk and sheets of oversized sketch paper taped to the walls and the lower half of one of the windows. These were charts, master plans evidently, the maps of his work-in-progress, and the sheets were covered with scrawled words, boxes, lines connecting words, tiny writing in the boxes. There were circled numbers, crossed-out names, a cluster of stick-figure drawings, a dozen other cryptic markings. She saw notebooks stacked on the radiator cover. There were drifts of paper on the desk, a mound of crumpled butts in the ashtray.

"There's something about writers. I don't know why but I feel I ought to know the person as well as the work and so ordinarily I try to schedule a walk beforehand, just to chat with the person, talk about books, family, anything at all. But I understand you'd rather not go on and on with this, so we'll work quickly."

"We can talk."

"Are you interested in cameras? This is an eighty-five-millimeter lens."

"I used to take pictures. I don't know why I stopped. One day it just ended forever."

"I guess it's true to say that something else is ending forever."

"You mean the writer comes out of hiding."

"Am I right that it's thirty years since your picture has appeared anywhere?"

"Scott would know."

"And together you decided the time has come."

"Well it's a weariness really, to know that people make so much of this. When a writer doesn't show his face, he becomes a local symptom of God's famous reluctance to appear."

"But this is intriguing to many people."

"It's also taken as an awful sort of arrogance."

"But we're all drawn to the idea of remoteness. A hard-to-reach place is necessarily beautiful, I think. Beautiful and a little sacred maybe. And a person who becomes inaccessible has a grace and a wholeness the rest of us envy."

"The image world is corrupt, here is a man who hides his face."

"Yes," she said.

"People may be intrigued by this figure but they also resent him and mock him and want to dirty him up and watch his face distort in shock and fear when the concealed photographer leaps out of the trees. In a mosque, no images. In our world we sleep and eat the image and pray to it and wear it too. The writer who won't show his face is encroaching on holy turf. He's playing God's own trick."

"Maybe he's just shy, Bill."

Through the viewfinder she watched him smile. He looked clearer in the camera. He had an intentness of gaze, an economy, and his face was handsomely lined and worked, embroidered across the forehead and at the corners of the eyes. So often in her work the human shambles was remade by the energy of her seeing, by the pure will that the camera uncovered in her, the will to see deeply.

"Shall I tell you something?"

"Go ahead."

"I'm afraid to talk to writers about their work. It's so easy to say something stupid. Don't drop your chin. Good, that's better, I like that. There's a secret language I haven't learned to speak. I spend a great deal of time with writers. I love writers. But this gift you have, which for me is total delight, makes me feel that I'm an outsider, not able to converse in the private language, the language that will mean something to you."

"The only private language I know is self-exaggeration. I think I've grown a second self in this room. It's the self-important fool that keeps the writer going. I exaggerate the pain of writing, the pain of solitude, the failure, the rage, the confusion, the help-lessness, the fear, the humiliation. The narrower the boundaries of my life, the more I exaggerate myself. If the pain is real, why do I inflate it? Maybe this is the only pleasure I'm allowed."

"Raise your chin."

"Raise my chin."

"Frankly I didn't expect such speeches."

"I've been saving it up."

"I expected you to stand here a few minutes and then get restless and walk off."

"One of my failings is that I say things to strangers, women passing by, that I've never said to a wife or child, a close friend."

"You talk candidly to Scott."

"I talk to Scott. But it becomes less necessary all the time. He already knows. He's at my brainstem like a surgeon with a bright knife."

She finished the roll and went to her case for another. Bill stood by the desk shaking a cigarette out of the pack. There was mud crust and bent weed stuck to his shoes. He didn't seem to be putting across his own picture, his idea of what he wanted to look like or who he wanted to be for the next hour or two. It was clear he hadn't bothered to think it out. She liked the feel of the room with him in it. It was his room in a way in which this wasn't his house. She asked him to stand near one of the wall charts and when he didn't object she moved the lamp and adjusted focus and started shooting. He smoked and talked. He thought he was suffering like the rest of them. They all thought they were bungling and desolate and tormented but none of them ever wanted to do anything else but write and each believed that the only person who might possibly be worse off was another writer somewhere and when one of them mixed too many brandies and little violet pills or placed the nozzle of a revolver just behind the ear, the others felt both sorry and acknowledged.

"I'll tell you what I don't exaggerate. The doubt. Every minute of every day. It's what I smell in my bed. Loss of faith. That's what this is all about."

Space was closing in the way it did when a session went well. Time and light were narrowed to automatic choices. Bill stood before the odd notations on his chart and she knew she had everything she might want or need. Here was the old, marked and melancholy head, the lost man of letters, and there was the early alphabet on the wall, the plan of his missing book in the form of lopsided boxes and felt-tipped scrawls and sets of directional signs like arrows scratched out by a child with a pencil in his fist. And he was animated, leaning and jabbing as he talked. His hands were blunt and nicked. There was a doggedness to him, a sense of all the limits he'd needed to exceed, getting on top of work that always came hard. She was trying to place him in context, fit the voice and body to the books. The first thing she'd thought, entering the room, was wait a minute, no, this can't be him. She'd expected someone lean and drawn, with eyes like hex signs on an Amish barn. But Bill was slowly beginning to make sense to her, to look reasonably like his work.

"I'm forced to steal one of your cigarettes," she said. "I've been giving up cigarettes for twenty-five years and I've made a lot of progress in that time. Okay? But then I see the little glisten of the package."

"Tell me about New York," he said. "I don't get there anymore. When I think of cities where I lived, I see great cubist paintings."

"I'll tell you what I see."

"That edginess and density and those old brownish tones and how cities age and stain in the mind like Roman walls."

"Where I live, okay, there's a rooftop chaos, a jumble, four, five, six, seven storeys, and it's water tanks, laundry lines, antennas, belfries, pigeon lofts, chimney pots, everything human about the lower island—little crouched gardens, statuary, painted signs. And I wake up to this and love it and depend on it. But it's all being flattened and hauled away so they can build their towers."

"Eventually the towers will seem human and local and quirky. Give them time."

"I'll go and hit my head against the wall. You tell me when to stop."

"You'll wonder what made you mad."

"I already have the World Trade Center."

"And it's already harmless and ageless. Forgotten-looking. And think how much worse."

"What?" she said.

"If there was only one tower instead of two."

"You mean they interact. There is a play of light."

"Wouldn't a single tower be much worse?"

"No, because my big complaint is only partly size. The size is deadly. But having two of them is like a comment, it's like a dialogue, only I don't know what they're saying."

"They're saying, 'Have a nice day.' "

"Someday, go walk those streets," she said. "Sick and dying people with nowhere to live and there are bigger and bigger towers all the time, fantastic buildings with miles of rentable space. All the space is inside. Am I exaggerating?"

"I'm the one who exaggerates."

"This is strange but I feel I know you."

"It is strange, isn't it? We're managing to have a real talk while you bob and weave with a camera and I stand here looking stiff and cloddish."

"I don't usually talk, you see. I ask a question and let the writer talk, let the tension drain out a little."

"Let the fool babble on."

"All right if you put it that way. And I listen only vaguely as a rule because I'm working. I'm detached, I'm working, I'm listening at the edges."

"And you travel all the time. You seek us out."

"You're dropping your chin," she said.

"You cross continents and oceans to take pictures of ordinary faces, to make a record of a thousand faces, ten thousand faces."

"It's crazy. I'm devoting my life to a gesture. Yes, I travel. Which means there is no moment on certain days when I'm not thinking terror. They have us in their power. In boarding areas I never sit near windows in case of flying glass. I carry a Swedish passport so that's okay unless you believe that terrorists killed the prime minister. Then maybe it's not so good. And I use codes in my address book for names and addresses of writers because how can you tell if the name of a certain writer is dangerous to carry, some dissident, some Jew or blasphemer. I'm careful about reading matter. Nothing religious comes with me, no books with religious symbols on the jacket and no pictures of guns or sexy women. That's on the one hand. On the other hand I know in my heart I'm going to die of some dreadful slow disease so you're safe with me on a plane."

She inserted another roll. She was sure she already had what she'd come for but a hundred times in her life she thought she had the cluster of shots she wanted and then found better work deep in the contact sheets. She liked working past the feeling of this is it. Important to keep going, obliterate the sure thing and come upon a moment of stealthy blessing.

"Do you ask your writers how it feels to be painted dummies?"

"What do you mean?"

"You've got me talking, Brita."

"Anything that's animated I love it."

"You don't care what I say."

"Speak Swahili."

"There's a curious knot that binds novelists and terrorists. In the West we become famous effigies as our books lose the power to shape and influence. Do you ask your writers how they feel about this? Years ago I used to think it was possible for a novelist to alter the inner life of the culture. Now bomb-makers and gunmen have taken that territory. They make raids on human consciousness. What writers used to do before we were all incorporated."

"Keep going. I like your anger."

"But you know all this. This is why you travel a million miles photographing writers. Because we're giving way to terror, to news of terror, to tape recorders and cameras, to radios, to bombs stashed in radios. News of disaster is the only narrative people need. The darker the news, the grander the narrative. News is the last addiction before—what? I don't know. But you're smart to trap us in your camera before we disappear."

"I'm the one they're trying to kill. You're sitting in a room making theories."

"Put us in a museum and charge admission."

"Writers will always write. Are you crazy? Writers have long-range influence. You can't talk about these gunmen in the same breath. I have to steal another cigarette. You're no good for me, this is obvious. You have a look on your face, I don't know, like a bad actor doing weariness of the spirit."

"I am a bad actor."

"Not for me or my camera. I see the person, not some idea he wants to make himself into."

"I'm all idea today."

"I definitely don't see it."

"I'm playing the idea of death. Look closely," he said.

She didn't know whether she was supposed to find this funny.

He said, "Something about the occasion makes me think I'm at my own wake. Sitting for a picture is morbid business. A portrait doesn't begin to mean anything until the subject is dead. This is the whole point. We're doing this to create a kind of sentimental past for people in the decades to come. It's their past, their history we're inventing here. And it's not how I look now that matters. It's how I'll look in twenty-five years as clothing and faces change, as photographs change. The deeper I pass into death, the more powerful my picture becomes. Isn't this why picture-taking is so ceremonial? It's like a wake. And I'm the actor made up for the laying-out."

"Close your mouth."

"Remember they used to say, This is the first day of the rest of your life. It struck me just last night these pictures are the announcement of my dying."

"Close your mouth. Good, good, good, good."

She finished the roll, reloaded, reached for her cigarette, took a drag, put it down, then moved toward him and touched a hand to his face, tilting it slightly left.

"Stay now. Don't move. I like that."

"See, anything you want. I do it at once."

"Touching Bill Gray."

"Do you realize what an intimate thing we're doing?"

"It's in my memoirs, guaranteed. And you're not cloddish by the way."

"We're alone in a room involved in this mysterious exchange. What am I giving up to you? And what are you investing me with, or stealing from me? How are you changing me? I can feel the change like some current just under the skin. Are you making me up as you go along? Am I mimicking myself? And when did women start photographing men in the first place?"

"I'll look it up when I get home."

"We're getting on extremely well."

"Now that we've changed the subject."

"I'm losing a morning's work without remorse."

"That's not the only thing you're losing. Don't forget, from the moment your picture appears you'll be expected to look just like it. And if you meet people somewhere, they will absolutely question your right to look different from your picture."

"I've become someone's material. Yours, Brita. There's the life and there's the consumer event. Everything around us tends to channel our lives toward some final reality in print or on film. Two lovers quarrel in the back of a taxi and a question becomes implicit in the event. Who will write the book and who will play the lovers in the movie? Everything seeks its own heightened version. Or put it this way. Nothing happens until it's consumed. Or put it this way. Nature has given way to aura. A man cuts himself shaving and someone is signed up to write the biography of the cut. All the material in every life is channeled into the glow. Here I am in your lens. Already I see myself differently. Twice over or once removed."

"And you may think of yourself differently as well. It's interesting how deep a picture takes you. You may see something you thought you'd kept hidden. Or some aspect of your mother or father or children. There it is. You pick up a snapshot and there's your face in half shadow but it's really your father looking back at you."

"You're preparing the body all right."

"Chemicals and paper, that's all it is."

"Rouging my cheeks. Waxing my hands and lips. But when I'm really dead, they'll think of me as living in your picture."

"I was in Chile last year and I met an editor who'd been sent to prison after his magazine did caricatures of General Pinochet. The charge was assassinating the image of the general."

"Sounds perfectly reasonable."

"Are you losing interest? Because I sometimes don't realize the way a session becomes mine. I get very possessive at a certain point. I'm easy and agreeable on the edges of the operation. But at the heart, in the frame, it's mine."

"I think I need these pictures more than you do. To break down the monolith I've built. I'm afraid to go anywhere, even the seedy diner in the nearest little crossroads town. I'm convinced the serious trackers are moving in with their mobile phones and zoom lenses. Once you choose this life, you understand what it's like to exist in a state of constant religious observance. There are no halfway measures. All the movements we make are ritual movements. Everything we do that isn't directly centered on work revolves around concealment, seclusion, ways of evasion. Scott works out the routes of simple trips I occasionally make, like doctor's visits. There are procedures for people coming to the house. Repairmen, deliverymen. It's an irrational way of life that has a powerful inner logic. The way religion takes over a life. The way disease takes over a life. There's a force that's totally independent of my conscious choices. And it's an angry grudging force. Maybe I don't want to feel the things other people feel. I have my own cosmology of pain. Leave me alone with it. Don't stare at me, don't ask me to sign copies of my books, don't point me out on the street, don't creep up on me with a tape recorder clipped to your belt. Most of all don't take my picture. I've paid a terrible price for this wretched hiding. And I'm sick of it finally."

He spoke quietly, looking away from her. He gave the impression he was learning these things for the first time, hearing them at last. How strange they sounded. He couldn't understand how any of it had happened, how a young man, inexperienced, wary of the machinery of gloss and distortion, protective of his work and very shy and slightly self-romanticizing, could find himself all these years later trapped in his own massive stillness.

"Are you fading at all?"

"No."

"I forget how weary all this concentrated effort can make a person. I have no conscience when it comes to work. I expect the subject to be as single-minded as I am."

"This isn't work for me."

"We make pictures together after all."

"Work is what I do to feel bad."

"Why should anyone feel good?"

"Exactly. When I was a kid I used to announce ballgames to myself. I sat in a room and made up the games and described the play-by-play out loud. I was the players, the announcer, the crowd, the listening audience and the radio. There hasn't been a moment since those days when I've felt nearly so good."

He had a smoker's laugh, cracked and graveled.

"I remember the names of all those players, the positions they played, their spots in the batting order. I do batting orders in my head all the time. And I've been trying to write toward that kind of innocence ever since. The pure game of making up. You sit there suspended in a perfect clarity of invention. There's no separation between you and the players and the room and the field. Everything is seamless and transparent. And it's completely spontaneous. It's the lost game of self, without doubt or fear."

"I don't know, Bill."

"I don't know, either."

"It sounds like mental illness to me."

He laughed again. She took pictures of him laughing until the roll was finished. Then she loaded the camera and moved him away from the quartz lamp and started shooting again, using window light now.

"Incidentally. I bring a message from Charles Everson."

Bill hitched up his pants. He seemed to look past her, frisking himself for signs of cigarettes.

"I ran into him at a publishing dinner somewhere. He asked how my work was going. I told him I'd probably be seeing you."

"No reason you shouldn't mention it."

"I hope it's all right."

"The pictures will be out one day."

"Actually the only message I bring is that Charles wants to talk to you. He wouldn't tell me what it's all about. I told him to write you a letter. He said you don't read your mail."

"Scott reads my mail."

"He said that what he had to tell you couldn't be seen or heard by anyone else. Far too delicate. He also said he used to be your editor and good, good friend. And he said it was distressing not to be able to get in touch with you directly."

Bill looked for matches now, clearing papers off the desktop.

"How's old Charlie then?"

"The same. Soft, pink and happy."

"Always new writers, you see. They sit in their corner offices and never have to worry about surviving the failed books because there's always a new one coming along, a hot new excitement. They live, we die. A perfectly balanced state."

"He told me you'd say something like that."

"And you waited to tell me about him. Didn't want to spring it on me prematurely."

"I wanted my pictures first. I didn't know how you'd react to news from out there."

He struck the match and then forgot it.

"Do you know what they like to do best? Run those black-border ads for dead writers. It makes them feel they're part of an august tradition."

"He simply wants you to call him. He says it's a matter of some importance."

He swiveled his head until the cigarette at the corner of his mouth came into contact with the flame.

"The more books they publish, the weaker we become. The secret force that drives the industry is the compulsion to make writers harmless."

"You like being a little bit fanatical. I know the feeling, believe me. But what is more harmless than the pure game of making up? You want to do baseball in your room. Maybe it's just a metaphor, an innocence, but isn't this what makes your books popular? You call it a lost game that you've been trying to recover as a writer. Maybe it's not so lost. What you say you're writing toward, isn't this what people see in your work?"

"I only know what I see. Or what I don't see."

"Tell me what that means."

He dropped the match in an ashtray on the desk.

"Every sentence has a truth waiting at the end of it and the writer learns how to know it when he finally gets there. On one level this truth is the swing of the sentence, the beat and poise, but down deeper it's the integrity of the writer as he matches with the language. I've always seen myself in sentences. I begin to recognize myself, word by word, as I work through a sentence. The language of my books has shaped me as a man. There's a moral force in a sentence when it comes out right. It speaks the writer's will to live. The deeper I become entangled in the process of getting a sentence right in its syllables and rhythms, the more I learn about myself. I've worked the sentences of this book long and hard but not long and hard enough because I no longer see myself in the language. The running picture is gone, the code of being that pushed me on and made me trust the world. This book and these years have worn me down. I've forgotten what it means to write. Forgotten my own first rule. Keep it simple, Bill. I've lacked courage and perseverance. Exhausted. Sick of struggling. I've let good enough be good enough. This is someone else's book. It feels all forced and wrong. I've tricked myself into going on, into believing. Can you understand how that can happen? I'm sitting on a book that's dead."

"Does Scott know you feel this way?"

"Scott. Scott's way ahead of me. Scott doesn't want me to publish."

"But this is completely crazy."

"No, it's not. There's something to be said."

"When will you finish?"

"Finish. I'm finished. The book's been done for two years. But I rewrite pages and then revise in detail. I write to survive now, to keep my heart beating."

"Show someone else."

"Scott is smart and totally honest."

"He's only one opinion."

"Any judgment based strictly on merit is going to sound like his. And how it hurts when you know the verdict is true. And how you try to evade it, twist it, disfigure it. And word could get out. And once that happens."

"You finish, you publish and you take what comes."

"I will publish."

"It's simple, Bill."

"It's just a question of making up my mind and going ahead and doing it."

"And you'll stop redoing pages. The book is finished. I don't want to make a fetish of things are simple. But it's done, so you stop."

She watched him surrender his crisp gaze to a softening, a bright-eyed fear that seemed to tunnel out of childhood. It had the starkness of a last prayer. She worked to get at it. His face was drained and slack, coming into flatness, into black and white, cracked lips and flaring brows, age lines that hinge the chin, old bafflements and regrets. She moved in closer and refocused, she shot and shot, and he stood there looking into the lens, soft eyes shining.

4

S cott told her a story at lunch about his days of wandering,
ten years ago, sick and broke in Athens and trying to cadge
yankee dollars from tourists so he could get on one of those
amphetamine buses that take you to the Himalayas in about a
hundred hours of nonstop terror, through wars and mountain
passes, but he was getting nowhere. He walked into the main
square and saw some people gathered on the steps of a nice-
looking old hotel with a European name he couldn't recall.

"Grande Bretagne."

Right. There was a film crew and some men who looked like
government officials and fifty or sixty people just passing by and
Scott went over there and saw a man on the top step who wore
a khaki field jacket and checkered headscarf, a short guy with a
scratchy beard, and it was Yasir Arafat and he was waving at the
people on the sidewalk. When a hotel guest came out the door,
Arafat smiled and nodded and people in the crowd smiled in
response. Then Arafat said something to an official and the man
laughed and everyone on the sidewalk smiled some more. Scott
realized he was smiling broadly. He could feel the smile stretching
across his face and he looked at the people around him and they
looked back smiling and it was clearly agreed they all felt good
together. And Arafat smiled again, talking to officials, overges-
turing for the camera, pointing toward the entrance and then

moving that way. Everyone applauded now. Someone shook Arafat's hand and there was more applause. He lets a stranger shake his hand. Scott smiled and applauded, he saw the men on the steps applaud. When Arafat went inside, the people on the sidewalk smiled and clapped one last time. They wanted to make him happy.

"Did you get to the Himalayas?"

"I got to Minneapolis. I went back to school for a year but then I dropped out again and fell into another spiral of drugs and nonbeing. There was nothing very special about it, even to me. I was a salesperson for a while in a heavily carpeted shoestore. Somebody gave me Bill's first novel to read and I said, Whoa what's this? That book was about me somehow. I had to read slowly to keep from jumping out of my skin. I saw myself. It was my book. Something about the way I think and feel. He caught the back-and-forthness. The way things fit almost anywhere and nothing gets completely forgotten."

"Yes. Sentences with built-in memories."

"When I read Bill I think of photographs of tract houses at the edge of the desert. There's an incidental menace. That great Winogrand photo of a small child at the head of a driveway and the fallen tricycle and the storm shadow on the bare hills."

"It's a beautiful picture."

"Finish eating. I'll show you the attic."

"Why don't you want him to publish?"

"It's his call. He does what he wants. But he'll tell you himself the book falls short. Woefully short. Bill has been working on and off for twenty-three years on this book. He quits it, then returns. He rewrites it, then puts it aside. He starts something new, then comes back to it. He takes a trip, he returns, he resumes work, goes away, comes back, works every single day for three years, he puts it aside, picks it up, smells it, weighs it, rewrites it, puts it aside, starts something new, goes away, comes back."

"Sounds like total."

"It is. The work has burnt him out. He's burnt out. Bill has always had to struggle for every word. Bill walks five feet from his desk and doubt hits him like a hammer in the back. He has to go back to his desk and find a passage he knows will reassure him. He reads it and he's reassured. An hour later, sitting in the car, he feels it again, the page is wrong, the chapter is wrong, and he can't shake the doubt until he gets back to his desk and finds a passage he knows will reassure him. He reads it and he's reassured. He's been doing this all his life and now he's run out of reassuring passages."

"How long have you been with him?"

"Eight years. The last few have been tough on him. He's gone back to drinking although not so heavily as before. He takes medications for ailments unknown to science. He rarely sleeps past five a.m. Wakes and stares. When the sun comes up, he shuffles to his desk."

"To me, publication is exactly what he needs. You have to show people what you've done. How else do you resolve anything?"

"Bill is at the height of his fame. Ask me why. Because he hasn't published in years and years and years. When his books first came out, and people forget this or never knew it, they made a slight sort of curio impression. I've seen the reviews. Bric-a-brac, like what's this little oddity. It's the years since that made him big. Bill gained celebrity by doing nothing. The world caught up. Reprint after reprint. We make a nice steady income, most of which goes to his two ex-wives and three ex-children. We could make a king's whatever, multimillions, with the new book. But it would be the end of Bill as a myth, a force. Bill gets bigger as his distance from the scene deepens."

"Then why do you want these photographs?"

"I don't want. He wants."

"I see."

"I've said again and again. Craziness. I've harangued the poor man. Don't do it. Madness. Self-destructive."

"I didn't realize from your manner."

"Because I do my job. He makes the decisions, I follow through. If he decides to publish, I'll work with him day and night on the galleys, the page proofs, everything. He knows that. But for Bill, the only thing worse than writing is publishing. When the book comes out. When people buy it and read it. He feels totally and horribly exposed. They are taking the book home and turning the pages. They are reading the actual words."

In the attic there were file cabinets containing research material. Scott recited subject headings and showed her dozens of color-coded folders. His desk and typewriter were here. There were cardboard boxes filled with loose manuscript pages. There was a large photocopy machine and shelves lined with reference books, style manuals and stacks of periodicals. He handed Brita a pale-gray manuscript box, unmarked, and gestured to six identical boxes on the desk and said this was the final version, the typed and corrected and proofread copy of Bill's new novel.

But Bill was still working, making changes. They heard him typing when they went down the stairs.

He had coffee and a sandwich at his desk. Then tapped on the keys, hearing an old watery moan deep in the body. How the day's first words set off physical alarms, a pule and fret, the resistance of living systems to racking work. Calls for a cigarette, don't you think? He heard them come down the stairs and pictured them making an effort not to creak, setting their feet down softly, shoulders hunched. Let's not disturb the family fool in the locked room. He didn't know whether she was leaving right away. He thought it would be awkward to see her again.

There was nothing to say, was there? They'd shared a closeness that felt sorry and cheap the minute she walked out of the room. He couldn't clearly recall what he'd said to her but knew it was all wrong, an effusion, a presumption, all the worse for being mainly true. Who was she anyway? Something strong in her face, the rigor of life choice, of what it takes to make your way, a stripped-down force, a settledness, bare but not unwary. He could easily get up from the desk and go to New York and live with her forever in a terrace apartment overlooking the park or the river or both. Staring past the keys. Used to be that time rushed down on him when he started a book, time fell and pressed, then lifted when he finished. Now it wasn't lifting. But then he wasn't finished. Live in a large bright apartment with gray sheets on the bed, reading perfumed magazines. There is the epic and bendable space-time of the theoretical physicist, time detached from human experience, the pure curve of nature, and there is the haunted time of the novelist, intimate, pressing, stale and sad. His teeth felt soft today. He needed to sneak to the bedroom and mix up some pink-and-yellow fluoride multivitamins and in the meantime let's concentrate on the page, tap a letter, then another. He wanted to fuck her loudly on a hard bed with rain beating on the windows. Please Jesus let me work. Every book is a bug-eyed race, let's face it. Must finish. Can't die yet. He struck enough keys to make a sentence and thought about going down to say goodbye to her but it would only embarrass them both. Got what she came for, didn't she? I'm a picture now, flat as birdshit on a Buick. He saw he'd inverted two letters, which he's been doing a lot of lately, one of many signs there's something growing on his brain, and he elevated the page and whited out the mistake, then had to wait while the liquid dried. How he punished himself for repeated errors at the machine, eternal mis-fingerings, how typing mistakes became despair, meaningless flubs bringing a craze to his eyes, and he stared at the white fluid drying and would not resume work until it faded into the page, which was both the punishment and the escape. Her hand on his face, how surprised he'd been to feel so affected by the gesture, the entireness of simple touch. Want to live like other people, eating tricolor pasta in trattorias near the park. Always whiting out and typing in. He looked at the sentence, six disconsolate words, and saw the entire book as it took occasional shape in his mind, a neutered near-human dragging through the house, humpbacked, hydrocephalic, with puckered lips and soft skin, dribbling brain fluid from its mouth. Took him all these years to realize this book was his hated adversary. Locked together in the forbidden room, had him in a chokehold. He examined the immense complexity of changing the ribbon. So many pros and cons, alters and egos. He felt it coming and then sneezed onto the page, nicely, noting blood-spotted matter but thin and sparse. He would not dignify it by calling it snot. She likes my anger. Live at the center of the cubist city, Sunday papers spread every-where and glossy bagels on a plate. I'm between novels, he used to say, so I don't mind dying. The problem with his second wife. But never mind. Live near the museums and galleries, stand on movie lines, uncork the wines, redo the rooms, sleep in the gray sheets, loving her, ordering out, let's order out tonight, walk the dogs, speak the words, hear the doormen whistle down the cabs, rain beating on the windows.

Brita was packed and ready anytime. She went downstairs and poured a cup of coffee. She sat at the table and looked around the kitchen. A young woman walked in and softly said Hi. She leaned on the table, using a hand to balance, her left foot raised vaguely off the floor. She had long straight hair, light brown, and a slightly jutting mouth that made her look remorseless.

"How many pictures did you take?"

"We talked and worked a while and then I shot some more rolls when we ran out of conversation and then some more after that."

"Would you call this an average day or going into the realm of horrid excess?"

"What's your name?"

"Karen."

"And you live here."

"Scott and I."

"I'll tell you the truth, Karen. I'm not interested in photography. I'm interested in writers."

"Then why don't you stay home and read?"

She reached for a box of muffins on the countertop and put it down near Brita's coffee. Then she curled into a chair and played with a stray spoon. She wore a limp blouse over blue jeans and had the body lines of a teenager, the crooks and skews and smeariness, and a way of merging with furniture, a kind of draped indecision.

Brita said, "I read at home, I read in hotels, I take a book with me on a twenty-minute trip to the dentist. Then I read in the waiting room."

"Did you always know you wanted to be a photographer?"

"I read on planes, I read in laundromats. How old are you?"

"Twenty-four."

"And you help out here."

"Scott does most of it. He manages the expenses, the cash flow, he does taxes, he deals with the utilities, he answers all Bill's mail except the mentals, which we haughtily ignore lest they get encouraged. We share the cooking and shopping except he probably does more than I do. He does all the filing, the organizing of papers. I clean like a little scrub lady, which I don't half mind. I make believe I'm fat and walk with a waddle. We do the typing about fifty-fifty, with Scott doing the last spotless copy, and then we proofread together, which is probably our favorite time."

"And you think it's a mistake, these pictures."

"We love Bill, that's all."

"And you hate me for leaving here with all that film."

"It's just a feeling of there's something wrong. We have a life here that's carefully balanced. There's a lot of planning and thinking behind the way Bill lives and now there's a crack all of a sudden. What's it called, a fissure."

The car pulled up, door opened, then closed. Karen tapped the bowl end of the spoon with her index finger, over and over, making the handle go up and down.

"What do you think of marriage for a professional woman?" she said.

"I'm divorced many years. He lives in Belgium. We don't talk at all."

"Do you have children that are still torn up over the divorce so that everybody's tense around each other and you can see the resentment lurking far back in their eyes even after all this time?"

"Sorry, no."

"I haven't known many people with careers. It sounds so important. Having a career. Do you keep a bottle of vodka handy in your freezer?"

"Yes, I do."

"Do people tell you they like your work? They come up to you at parties in New York and say, 'I just wanted to tell you.' Or, 'You don't know me but I just wanted.' Or, 'I really have to tell you this and I hope you'll forgive the intrusion.' Then you look at them and smile like shyly."

Scott came in with groceries. He poured a cup of coffee and told the story of his journey out of nonbeing. How he started writing letters to Bill care of his publisher. He wrote nine or ten letters, ambitious and self-searching, filled with things a luckless boy wants to say to a writer whose work has moved him. He hadn't known he could summon these deep feelings or express them with reckless style and delight, certain cosmic words typed in caps and others spelled oddly to reveal second and third meanings. The letters released something, maybe a sense that he was not alone, that the world was a place where travelers in language could know the same things. How he finally got one letter back, two lines, handwritten in a hurry, saying there is never time to respond properly but thanks for writing. How Scott took this as encouragement and wrote five more letters, intense and sweeping, the last of them saying that he was setting out to find Bill, that he needed to see and meet and talk to Bill, that the urge to make a journey in search of the man who wrote these books could no longer be contained. How Bill did not reply. And how Scott took this as encouragement because Bill could have written and said, Forget it, stay away, do not even remotely approach. He had the envelope Bill's note had come in, postmarked New York City, but Scott happened to know from reading a magazine piece about Lost Writers that Bill concealed his whereabouts by sending letters to his publisher for remailing.

"And so you hitchhiked."

Yes. He set out thumbing rides at the edges of ripping interstates and the venture was so chancy it made him feel weightless, standing in the wind of rolling diesel rigs. He wore mirrored glasses and carried a timeless Eastern text and he told drivers he was setting out to find a famous writer. Some of them talked about famous people they wished they could meet and it was interesting how very few of these people were alive today. All the famous were either dead or used up. A pickup he was riding in caught fire just west of Fort Wayne and it seemed all right, it seemed appropriate, things were too vivid not to enter deeper states. He was elated, worked to a sensory howl, flying past the low stink of day-to-day. A driver had chest pains outside Toledo and Scott drove him to a hospital, feeling talkative, telling the man the plot of a movie he'd seen last week. The car handled well and he gained in being as he drove, cornering sweetly. I'm glad we had this chance to talk, he said, jogging alongside the gurney as attendants hustled the man into white light. Three days later he had a job in the mailroom at the house that published Bill Gray's books.

How he made friends. How he learned that the letters Bill sent in to be remailed came in a nine-by-twelve manila envelope addressed to the head of the mailroom, a friendly sleepy former IRA man named Joe Doheny, who opened the envelope and processed the letters in the normal way. Scott waited, living at the Y, eating his meals standing up at narrow counters set along streetside windows so he could watch the march of faces and pathologies, people going by in trance states and dancing manias, the crosstown stream of race and shape and ruin, and in these hard streets even the healthy and well-dressed looked afflicted. Because they were sliding deeper into their own lives. Because they knew the future would not take them. Because they refused to give themselves the necessary narrow structure, the secret destiny. After some weeks he spotted a manila envelope addressed to Joe Doheny in Bill's close-woven hand. There was no return address of course but Scott looked at the postmark and then went to the library and lugged an atlas to a table and found that the town in question—he did not reveal its name to Brita—was about two hundred miles outside the gates of the medieval city. He was not necessarily relieved to learn that Bill was only hours from New York. It would be just as easy to go to Chad or Borneo or the Himalayas, with perhaps a greater gain in being.

He took a bus part of the way and then hitchhiked on secondary roads, carrying a sleeping bag and other basics. He walked around town and watched the market and the post office, five weekends of vain surveillance. Not that he minded. He had a life now and that's what mattered. He was in Bill's material mesh, drawing the same air, seeing things Bill saw. He did not ask people if they knew who Bill was or where he lived. He was a backpacker on the amble, determined to go unnoticed. After weekend five he quit his job and lived in campgrounds in the area and saw a man who had to be Bill getting out of a car in front of the hardware store, only eight days after he'd left the city for good.

"Why did it have to be Bill?"

"Had to be. Not the slightest doubt. How can a photographer ask a question like that? Doesn't his work, his life show on his face? Are there other people in that one small rural area who might possibly look as though they'd written those books? No, had to be him. Stocky, running his hand through his hair. Walking toward me. Making his way down the street. Becoming more familiar with every step. Had to be Bill and he was coming right at me and I seemed to need oxygen. Important parts of my body were closing down."

How he stepped up to Bill and told him who he was, the persistent letter-writer, and made an effort to speak slowly and clearly in complete sentences, feeling his mouth dry out and hearing the words come bouncing hollow off his tongue. Hearing the heart noise, a deep staccato in the chest that he'd heard only once before, climbing for hours in mountain country in extreme heat, the sound of blood driving through the aorta and jarring the heart. How he managed to say as Bill's eyes narrowed to rifleman's slits that he wondered if the writer had ever thought an assistant might be helpful, someone to handle the mail (he had experience), a quiet individual who would type and file, even prepare meals if there was no one doing this, a person who would try to ease the writer's beleaguerment (he drew a trace of grim amusement here). And then on instinct simply stopped and let Bill absorb the offer while he stood there looking earnest and dependable. Watching Bill's face begin to change. How the jaw muscles slackened and the eyes grew calm. A great man's face shows the beauty of his work.

5

Karen was in the bedroom looking at the gift Scott had brought back from the city. It was a reproduction of a pencil drawing called *Mao II*. She unrolled it on the bed and used objects in reach to hold down the corners. She studied the picture to see what was interesting about it or why Scott thought she might like it. The face of Mao Zedong. She liked that name all right. It was strange how a few lines with a pencil and there he is, some shading in, a scribbled neck and brows. It was by a famous painter whose name she could never remember but he was famous, he was dead, he had a white mask of a face and glowing white hair. Or maybe he was just supposed to be dead. Scott said he didn't seem dead because he never seemed real. Andy. That was it.

Scott was washing coffee cups.

Bill came in and said, "What are you doing?"

Scott looked into the basin, running a sponge around the inside of a cup.

"We could walk up to the mill. It's a nice enough day."

"You have to work," Scott said.

"I've worked."

"It's early yet. Go back and work some more."

63

"I've put in some good time today."

"Bullshit. You were having your picture taken."

"But I caught up. Come on. We'll get the women and hike to the mill."

"Go back up."

"I don't want to go back up."

"Don't start. I'm not in the mood."

"We'll get the women," Bill said.

"It's early. You ruined your morning with picture-taking. Go back up and do your work."

Scott held the sponge under warm water, rinsing out the soap.

"We have three hours of light. Ample time to get there and back."

"I'm telling you for your own good. It's your idea to write this book forever. I'm only saying what I'm supposed to say."

"You know what you are?"

"Yeah yeah yeah yeah."

"Yeah yeah," Bill said.

"I don't think you did ten good minutes."

"Yeah yeah yeah."

"So go back up and sit down and do your work."

"We're wasting all this light."

"It's really very simple."

"It isn't simple. It's everything in the world that isn't simple wrapped up in one small bundle."

Scott was finished at the sink but stayed there looking into the basin.

"It's simple all right. It really is. You just go back up and sit down and do your work."

"The women would enjoy it."

"I'm only saying what we both know I'm supposed to say."

"I could go back up and just sit there. How would you know I was working?"

"I wouldn't, Bill."

"I could sit there tearing stamps from a twenty-five-dollar roll of stamps with the fucking flag on every stamp."

"As long as you're in the room. I want you in the room, seated."

"I'll tell you what you are," Bill said.

Scott reached for a towel and dried his hands but didn't turn around. He hung the towel on the plastic hook and waited.

Brita stood outside Bill's workroom, in the open doorway, looking in. After a moment she reached in and knocked softly on the door even though it was clear the room was empty. She stood motionless and waited. Then she took one step in, looking carefully at the ordinary things inside as if compelled to memorize the details of whatever had escaped the camera—the placement of objects and titles of reference works, the number of pencils in the marmalade jar. Gazing for history's sake, for the obsessive record of what is on the desk and who is in the snapshots, the oddments that seem so precious to our understanding of the man.

But all she wanted was a cigarette. She spotted the pack, crossed the room quickly and took one out. There were footsteps on the stairs. She found matches and lit up and when Bill appeared in the doorway she gestured with the cigarette and told him thanks.

"I thought you were probably gone," he said.

"Don't you know the rules? We wait for dark. Then we go on side roads and no roads to avoid route signs that might tell me where we are."

"Scott spent weeks on this."

"It takes twice the time, his way."

"I think you're supposed to appreciate the maze aspects."

"I'll try harder. But right now I'm keeping you from your work so we'll meet at early dinner if this is the plan."

Bill moved some papers from a bench near the window and

then seemed to forget that he meant to sit there and stood holding the sheaf chest-high.

"I said things, didn't I?"

"About your work mostly."

"Hard up for sympathy. And I want to say things now but totally fail. I've forgotten how to talk in ordinary ways except to mumble at meals for the salt."

"They shouldn't give it to you."

"I'm sixty-three and it hurts."

"I'll never make it to sixty. I see something coming and I see it complete. Slow, wasting, horrible, deep in the body. It's something I've known for years."

"Fear has its own ego, hasn't it?"

"Do I sound awful?" she said.

"A little boastful maybe."

"What is it you want to say but can't?"

"I want to ask you to come back some time. Or tell me where you live. Or stay and talk."

"I have no trouble talking. But in this house it's not so easy. I think there's an intensity that makes certain subjects a little dangerous. And we don't have the camera between us. This changes everything, doesn't it? Scott said six-thirty."

"Then it must be true."

"He told me how he found you."

"I nearly stove in his head the first thirty seconds. He took over fast. Taught himself many wiles and skills. We talk and argue all the time. He gives me perspectives."

"And Karen."

"Scott says I invented her. But he's the one who snatched her out of the air. She scares me sometimes. She can scare me and delight me in the space of five words. She's smart about people. Looks right through us. Watches TV and knows what people are going to say next. Not only gets it right but does their voices."

"She came here how long after Scott?"

"Maybe five years after. She does their voices with a trueness that's startling. That's our Karen."

Brita lay nearly flat in the long tub, hearing someone chopping wood just below the window. Steam rose up around her. First the crack of the ax, then the soft topple of split logs. She felt a small dim misery stealing through her and wasn't sure what it meant. If there was any day in her recent working life that might be called special, this was it. Not that she thought any longer of building a career. She had no career, only writers hunched in chairs from here to China. There was little income and only passing public mention of the scheme. Pictures of most of the writers would appear exactly nowhere, others in obscure journals and directories. She was the person who traveled compulsively to photograph the unknown, the untranslated, the inaccessible, the politically suspect, the hunted, the silenced. So it was a form of validation, a rosy endorsement, when a writer like Bill offered to pose for her. Then why this strange off-balance mood? She ran more hot water. She knew it was him down there, breathing hard, chanting with the effort. First the crack, then the soft topple. Keep a distance. He is on some rocking edge. The temperature of the bath was perfect now, almost too hot to bear. She felt sweat break out on her face and she moved more deeply in. Isn't this why picture-taking is so ceremonial? Steam hung in the room. The heat was profound, deep-going and dulling and close to stopping the heart. She knew he was strong, saw it in his hands and girth, that dockworker's density of body. She reached for a towel and wiped her face and after a while she stepped out of the tub and went to the window, using the towel to rub vapor off the glass at face level. How could she keep a distance if she'd already taken his picture? This was the partnership, the little misery. Bill was tossing split logs toward the corded wood set under a sagging canopy at the side of the house. The announcement of my dying. She had to rub away vapor several times, standing by the window looking down.

Bill raised his glass.

"This place feels like home tonight. There's a wholeness, isn't there? A sense of extension and completion. And we all know why. Here's to guests and what they mean to civilization."

He drank and coughed.

He said, "It's interesting how 'guest' and 'host' are words that intertwine. The etymologies are curious. Converging, mixing, reciprocating. Like the human groupings marked by the words. Guests bring ideas from outside."

Scott sat facing Brita and spoke to her even when his remarks were meant for Bill.

"I don't think she considers herself a guest in the true sense. She came to work."

"Damn strange work. Quixotic as hell. But I think I admire her."

"You admire her for doing work that often goes unseen. Work that describes a kind of mission, a dedication. Exactly what I've been urging you to do. Keep this book out of sight. Build on it. Use it to define an idea, a principle."

"What principle?" Brita said.

"That the withheld work of art is the only eloquence left."

"This lamb is very nice," Bill said.

Karen came back from the kitchen with bread on a cutting board.

Scott looked at Brita.

"Art floats by all the time, part of the common bloat. But if he withholds the book. If he keeps the book in typescript and lets it take on heat and light. This is how he renews his claim to wide attention. Book and writer are now inseparable."

"Excuse me but it stinks," Brita said.

"He knows I'm right. What puts him on edge is not when I argue with him but when I agree with him. When I bring his little wishes dancing to the surface."

Bill kept a bottle of Irish whiskey flush against the right rear leg of his chair and he reached down for it now and refilled his wineglass.

He said, "We want to have a dinner with a theme. We're four of us tonight. Four is the first square. Foursquare. But we also have a roundness, a rounding-out. Three plus one. And it happens that we're halfway through April, or month number four."

"We were almost five," Scott said. "A woman tried to give me a baby yesterday. She took it out of her coat. A little thing only hours old."

He was staring at Brita.

"Why didn't you take it?" Karen said.

"Because I was on my way to meet Brita at a hotel where babies are not allowed. They have baby detectors at every door. They escort babies to the street."

"We could have found a place for it even if we didn't keep it ourselves. You should have taken it. How could you not take it?"

"People have always given away their babies. It's old stuff. I more or less suspect that I was given away. It explains so much," Scott said.

"My mother used to talk about God's compensation," Brita said. "When her heart began to fail, her rheumatism seemed to ease up. This was her idea of some almighty balance. I wonder about God's compensation for babies that are given away in the street or left in the garbage or thrown out the window."

Karen was talking to Scott about a road sign she'd seen on a walk that morning.

"Because I feel someone owes me something every time this happens," Brita said, "but who can it be if there is no God?"

Scott said, "Karen believes. Bill says he believes but we're not convinced."

"Our theme is four," Bill said. "In many ancient languages, God's name has four letters."

Brita poured more wine for herself and Scott.

"I don't like not believing. I'm not at peace with it. I take comfort when others believe."

"Karen thinks God is here. Like walkin' and talkin'."

"I want others to believe, you see. Many believers everywhere. I feel the enormous importance of this. When I was in Catania and saw hundreds of running men pulling a saint on a float through the streets, absolutely running. When I saw people crawl for miles on their knees in Mexico City on the Day of the Virgin, leaving blood on the basilica steps and then joining the crowd inside, the crush, so many people that there was no air. Always blood. The Day of Blood in Teheran. I need these people to believe for me. I cling to believers. Many, everywhere. Without them, the planet goes cold."

Bill spoke into his plate.

"Did I say how much I like this lamb?"

"Then eat it," Scott said.

"You're not eating it," Karen said.

"I thought I was supposed to look at it. You mean actually eat. As in the dictionary definition."

The dining room was small, with unmatched chairs around an oblong table, and there was a fire going in the old brick chimney corner.

"Do you want me to cut it for you?" Karen said.

Scott was still looking at Brita.

"If it's believers you want, Karen is your person. Unconditional belief. The messiah is here on earth."

"He's here on earth, I'm up there in the sky," Brita said. "Accumulating mileage."

Bill said, "Have you ever flown over Greenland with the rising sun? Four seasons, four major compass headings."

He took his whiskey up off the floor.

Brita said, "I've heard about a man and woman who are walking the length of the Great Wall of China, approaching each other from opposite directions. Every time I think of them, I see them from above, with the Wall twisting and winding through the landscape and two tiny human figures moving toward each other from remote provinces, step by step. I think this is a story of reverence for the planet, of trying to understand how we belong to the planet in a new way. And it's strange how I construct an aerial view so naturally."

"Hikers in shaggy boots," Karen said.

"No, artists. And the Great Wall is supposedly the only man-made structure visible from space, so we see it as part of the total planet. And this man and woman walk and walk. They're artists. I don't know what nationality. But it's an art piece. It's not Nixon and Mao shaking hands. It's not nationality, not politics."

"Yak-hair boots," Scott said.

"Those shaggy boots they wear in the land of the blue snow or whatever."

"When I think of China, what do I think of?"

"People," Karen said.

"Crowds," Scott said. "People trudging along wide streets, pushing carts or riding bikes, crowd after crowd in the long lens of the camera so they seem even closer together than they really are, totally jampacked, and I think of how they merge with the future, how the future makes room for the nonachiever, the nonaggressor, the trudger, the nonindividual. Totally calm in the long lens, crowd on top of crowd, pedaling, trudging, faceless, sort of surviving nicely."

Karen reached across the table and cut Bill's lamb into neat pieces for him.

"I was telling Scott," she said. "What was I saying?"

"They have a security detail trained in babies," Scott said. "A nationwide chain of baby-proof hotels."

"I was saying about this official orange sign of the state."

Brita gave a delayed laugh, scanning the table for cigarettes.

"I believe in the God of the stumblebum," Bill said. "The waitress with a throbbing tooth."

Scott laughed because Brita was laughing.

He cut some bread.

He said, "The book is finished but will remain in typescript. Then Brita's photos appear in a prominent place. Timed just right. We don't need the book. We have the author."

"I am in pain," Brita said. "Pour more wine."

She laughed, turning in her chair to scan the room for cigarettes.

Scott laughed.

Bill looked at his food, seeming to know it was changed somehow.

"Or maybe not a prominent place," Scott said. "Maybe a little journal in the corn belt."

"No, no, no, no," Karen said. "Let's imagine Bill on TV. He is on the sofa talking."

"We have the pictures, let's use them to advantage. The book disappears into the image of the writer."

"No, wait, he is sitting in a chair facing a host in a chair, leaning real close, a bespectacled host with his chin in his fist."

"Did you actually see the baby?" Brita said.

Scott laughed and this made Brita laugh.

Bill said, "Our theme is four. Earth, air, fire and water."

"What's the Day of Blood?" Karen said. "Not that I couldn't easily guess."

Scott didn't take his eyes off Brita.

"Bill has the idea that writers are being consumed by the emergence of news as an apocalyptic force."

"He told me, more or less."

"The novel used to feed our search for meaning. Quoting Bill. It was the great secular transcendence. The Latin mass of language, character, occasional new truth. But our desperation has led us toward something larger and darker. So we turn to the news, which provides an unremitting mood of catastrophe. This is where we find emotional experience not available elsewhere. We don't need the novel. Quoting Bill. We don't even need catastrophes, necessarily. We only need the reports and predictions and warnings."

Karen watched Bill touch his fork to a piece of meat.

He said, "I know the road sign you mean. The one for the deaf child."

"And it's not homemade. It's official orange and black and they put it there for one child who can't hear a car or truck bearing down on her. When I saw that I thought DEAF CHILD. I thought the state that erects a sign for one child can't be so awful and unfeeling."

"Yes, it's a nice sign. It's nice to think about a child with her own sign. But this wholly ridiculous contention I've been hearing. Disappear the book. Define a principle. Do I have the words right? Are those the words?"

He lifted the bottle and held the glass in his lap and poured while talking.

"Keep the book. Hide the book. Make the writer the book. I totally fail."

"Why are you still writing if you know the book is finished and we all know the book is finished and we all know you're still writing?"

"Books are never finished."

"Plays are never finished. Books are finished."

"I'll tell you when a book is finished. When the writer keels over with a great big thump."

Karen said, "I'm enlivened by the road sign every time I see it."

"As many books as a writer has published, those are the books he keeps on writing plus the one in his typewriter. Old books haunt the blood."

Brita poured more wine.

"I'm driving, thank you," Scott said.

He drank.

Bill drank and coughed.

Brita waited for him to take out his cigarettes.

"You can't let the book be seen," Scott said. "It's all over if you do. The book is a grossity. We have to invent words to describe the corpulence, the top-heaviness, the lack of discernment, pace and energy."

"Kid thinks he owns my soul."

"He knows. It's a master collapse. It's a failure so deep it places suspicion on the great early work. People will look at the great early work in a new way, searching for signs of weakness and muddle."

"The book appears. I'm going to do it. Sooner than anyone thinks."

Scott was looking at Brita.

"He knows I'm right. He just hates it when we agree. His words in my mouth. It drives him crazy. But I'm only trying to secure his rightful place."

Bill was looking for something to knock over, a thing, a suitable object he might swat off the table and break into pieces.

"I think we need a pet in this household," Karen said.

Scott wiped bread crumbs off the edge of the table into his hand.

"I'm only saying what he deep down wants me to say."

Karen looked at Brita.

They changed seats and Karen sat close to Bill, pushing her chair against his.

"Now do we want a dog or a cat?" she said in someone else's voice.

Bill went for the butter dish, backhanding it across the table.

The lid hit Scott in the face.

This made Bill angrier and he tried to get up and start smashing in earnest.

"I don't think we want to do this," Karen said.

She kept him in the chair.

Scott held his left hand to his face. He still had bread crumbs in the other hand.

"Pets are famously therapeutic," he said.

"Nobody's hurt, so shut the fuck up."

"For the old, the lonely, the stark and the raving."

"Four out of four. Our theme is four."

Karen put her hand over Bill's eyes to keep him from seeing anything that might get him madder.

Brita said, "I want someone to tell me this is a rare occurrence."

A gesture, a look, almost anything might get Bill going uncontrollably.

Scott wiped his hands and face with a napkin and stood behind Brita's chair, taking her by the arm as she got up and leading her from the room.

Karen took her hands from Bill's eyes.

"People who love each other, it's the old dumb story, Bill, which we all know a thousand times over."

They sat at the table for some minutes.

Then Bill went upstairs to his workroom, where he closed the door and stood by the window in the dark.

■ ■ ■

Scott wanted Brita to see one last thing before they left. They went out the back door and walked a few yards to a low shed built into an angle of the house. She followed him in, hunched over, and he switched on a light and they stood just inside the door looking at the shelves and compartments Scott had built himself—all filled with photocopies of the final draft, carbons of earlier drafts, carbons of notes and fragments, letters from Bill's friends and acquaintances, more galleys, more reader mail in boxed and labeled files, more cardboard boxes stuffed with manuscripts and papers.

The shed was insulated and waterproofed. Brita stood bent and silent and looked at the thick binders filled with words and she thought of all the words on all the pages stacked and filed in other parts of the house and she wanted to get out of here, run down the dark road away from this killing work and the grimness of the lives behind it.

They went around to the front of the house and she waited near the porch steps while Scott went in to get her things. She expected to feel the bystander's separation from a painful scene, the safety and complacence, but it wasn't working that way. She felt guilty of something, implicated in something, and could not face saying goodbye to Bill.

Scott came out and they walked to the car.

"If you glance back over your left shoulder, you'll see him watching from his window."

She looked without thinking but the window was dark and she turned quickly to the front. The night air had force, damp and spiky. When they were in the car and veering off the hard rutted mud onto packed gravel, she looked back again and thought she saw the faintest trace of silhouette centered in the window, man-shaped and dead still, and she kept on looking until the house slipped into distance, lost in trees and shifting perspective, in the spacious power of night.

6

Scott peered into the dark and told his third story of the day, working the wipers periodically to part the soft mist.

They talk about people driving erratically. He found Karen walking erratically down the main street of a northeastern Kansas town called White Cloud, population maybe two hundred ten, and he trailed her in the car. She stopped outside a red brick building with boarded windows under a low mean sky. He put the car in a slot, parking head-on, and watched her try to thumb-nail a candy out of a sticky package. A farm vehicle rolled on past, steered by a bare-chested kid with a knotted hanky on his head. The street was broad and sandy gray with weeds coming out of the curbstone and old tin canopies leaning off the café and the auto-and-bike repair. She stood there and dislodged the candy but then couldn't get it unstuck from the individual wrap. A sign jutted from the front of the general store with a mysterious word on it.

Scott wondered a while what there was about this scene that felt familiar. He was driving back east after seeing his sister, who lived nearby with a doctor husband and a baby flown in from Peru. He was glad to shake free of Bill for two weeks because the man had just remembered whiskey and was doing many mumbling riffs deep in the night.

He got out of the car and leaned on the fender, watching her deal with the candy melt in her hand. It was hard candy in theory and in name but would not separate from the wrap, attaching to it in webby strands as she pulled the paper outward.

Is it the heat wave, you think, or second-rate manufacturing methods that can't compete with the overseas challenge?

She paid no attention.

You think they'd know how to do gumdrops by now.

He took his sunglasses from his breast pocket and worked a fistful of shirtfront out of his pants to clean the glasses with, just to give himself some business in the empty hanging time.

She said, Are you here to deprogram me?

Then he knew what was familiar here. It was like something out of Bill Gray and he should have seen it earlier. The funny girl on the tumbledown street with an undecidable threat in the air, stormlit skies or just some alienating word that opens up a sentence to baleful influence.

If that's why you're here, you better forget it real fast, she said, because they tried it and got nowheres with an s at the end.

Soon they were driving through the top end of Missouri, getting acquainted, and in the same car, headed downstate now, he told Brita how she spoke in streaky lines of recollection about her time as a Moonie, although she didn't use that word herself and wouldn't let anyone else use it in her presence, ever.

In the van all clothing was the same, dumped in a pile and washed together, then given out so many items per person, never mind original owner or previous wearer. This was the truth of the body common. But it sure gives you a strange feeling, wearing someone else's socks and another person's underwear. Gives you the jumps, the cold creeps. Makes you want to walk along a little shriveled inward so you don't touch the clothes you're in.

And she was selling peanuts on the street, which she couldn't help feeling was a personal comedown after flowers. A guilty and dangerous thought. And her peanut team was made up of fairly purposeless sisters, roaming the land without the rooted point of view that their unison prayers affected the lives of every single person on the planet.

And she often thought of her husband, Kim, who was attached to a mission in England, the husband she didn't know. The separation would end in six months but only if each of them brought three new members into the church.

She believed deeply in Master and still thought of herself as a seeker, ready to receive what was vast and true. But she missed simple things, parents' birthdays, a rug underfoot, nights when she didn't have to sleep in a zipped bag. She began to think she was inadequate to the strict plain shapes of churchly faith. Head pains hit her at the end of the day. They came with a shining, an electrochemical sheen, light from out of nowhere, brain-made, the eerie gleam of who you are.

Scott took her to a motel and listened to her talk for much of the night. She peed with the door open and he thought, How fantastic. No sex however just yet. She talked in ten-minute spasms. She could not sleep or was afraid to. He kept going to the machine in the corridor to get her soft drinks and came back expecting to find her gone, a curtain blowing through the open window, except the curtains were too heavy to blow and the windows didn't open anyway.

Then action, bodies moving through the night. Because just as she was beginning to doubt and fear and mind-wander, she stepped out of the van on a cloud-banded evening and three men detached themselves from a playground wall and approached, two strangers and her tank-top cousin Rick, a football player with a clean-shaven head except for one wavy lock right on top, dyed y'know like parrot-green. The other guys wore suits and showed a certain weary expertise. Frankly it's hard to know what to say to people who come off a wall in a nameless town and your own bulging cousin has a look that's unreadable.

They stuffed her in a car and took her to a motel room, where her father sat waiting in a fire-retardant chair, oddly in his stocking feet. There was a lot of emotional talk, tabloid-type reassurances about love and mother and home, and she listened craftily, moved and bored more or less together, and Daddy cried a little and kissed her and put on his shoes and then left with Rick, who'd put his hand in her panties when they were ten, a memory that hung between them like the musky scent of a sniffed finger, and here was Scott in his own motel marveling at the underwear theme that coursed through this young woman's life.

Brita sat with her head back on the padded rest and her eyes closed, hearing his voice go louder when he turned her way.

The two men deprogrammed her eighteen hours a day for eight days. They cited case histories. They repeated key phrases. They played tapes and showed movies on the wall. The shades were drawn all the time and the door stayed locked. No clocks or watches anywhere. They left when she slept or tried to sleep and a local churchwoman arrived and sat in a chair with a headset on, listening to songs of the humpbacked whales.

In these quiet moments of near sleep she sometimes loved her parents and was stirred by the drama of abduction.

You were brainwashed.

You were programmed.

You have the transfixed gaze.

Other times she hated everyone involved and thought it was the logical brutal extension of parent-child, locked in a room and forced to listen to rote harangues. Of course this is what they said the church had been doing to her all along.

Her mother called and they had a normal practical chat about getting enough to eat and we are sending clothes.

The head pains came more often and there were nightmares now. She began to develop a sense that she was only passing through. She couldn't figure out exactly who it was that lived in this body. Her name had broken down to units of sound and it struck her as totally strange. She wanted to get back to her sisters and leaders. Everything outside the church was Satan-made. What does the church teach? Be children again. If you have theories, put them away. If you have knowledge, abandon it for the open heart of the child.

Programmed.

Brainwashed.

Indoctrinated.

When she tried a good-natured escape, sort of ambling dumbly out the door, they slammed her against the wall. Their hands were all over her and she thought they would tear her clothes away just to enjoy the noise of ripped Korean acrylic and so Scott moved closer in the darkened room, showing gentle concern, the tender recompense of the other side of the male equation, but no sympathetic sex just yet, bud.

They rode in silence for a while.

Brita said, "I didn't quite get that business about a husband. If I ever met anyone who didn't seem married."

"Mass-married. Married in a public ceremony involving thousands of others. Bill calls it millennial hysteria. By compressing a million moments of love and touch and courtship into one accelerated mass, you're saying that life must become more anxious, more surreal, more image-bound, more prone to hurrying its own transformation, or what's the point? You take marriage, the faith of the species, the means of continuation, and you turn it into catastrophe, a total implosion of the future. Quoting Bill. But I think he's all wrong."

They drove across Iowa and Illinois and Scott looked at the doubled landscape of his original journey in search of Bill and his return with a character out of Bill's fiction. They saw a horse galloping on the highway, empty-saddled. Karen had her blood pressure taken at a mobile clinic because she liked to feel the puffy tension of the cuff tightening on her arm.

You have the transfixed gaze.

But if being deprogrammed meant getting back home to a quiet room and a bed and regular meals, then maybe for the time being, because her parents loved her and she didn't want to do another winter in the van, she might just let them bend her mind a little.

They brought in Junette, a former sister, carried off by parents, deprogrammed, turned against the church, now used to soften others to the message. She wore the great stain of experience. Karen watched her rush into the room pretending to show deep empathy is the word but actually feeling superior and aloof. They went on with it anyway, falling into their scripted roles of sisterly and intimate, with three weepy embraces. The men waited outside, their shadows mingled on the drawn curtain. Junette tore down Master's teaching. She read letters from disaffected members in the important voice of the dead. Karen saw her teeth needed work, the spaces plugged with yellowish deposits. The famous tartar problem, of tartar and plaque. She was sitting craftily inside her own head, looking out at buttery Junette.

Maybe you know the feeling of being deeply, as they say, conflicted, like you wanna stay but you wanna go, and they bring in a person you'd like to stab in the neck with something jagged.

They stopped at a motel in mid-Ohio and the mood turned uneasy. They were tired and untalkative. Scott knew she was wondering why she was here at all, traveling with a stranger, some suspiciously helpful fellow, who is he anyway, and sitting in a room that was identical to the brown box where they tried to turn her mind inside out like a paper favor at a party. The same room repeats itself in a crosscountry chain and he's going to make me stop at every one.

So he told her about Bill, everything he knew, the man, the work, the murk, his own deep involvement. She didn't say anything but seemed to be trying to listen, to recall another world, the place of language and solitude and wet sedge meadows.

They went out for a real dinner in a restaurant with tasseled menus and a footbridge to the main room. She looked at him for the first time. In other words took him in retroactively, absorbing the accidental wonder of the past day and a half as it registered on his face. They went back to the room. The time was still not right for the sex of compassionate rescue, the sex of self-effacement, and he wondered if he was doing something wrong. She talked and slept and then woke him up to talk some more.

They told her, The trouble with postcult is that you lose your link to the fate of mankind.

They said, We know you're a good person who's just going through a rough adjustment while your parents are waiting and praying and writing a steady stream of checks for your emotional rescue.

They forced her to agree that the church had made a drone of her. She chanted, Made me a drone, made me a drone. That night she got out of bed in a glow of tingling light and tried to say something to the woman with the headset but could not speak and found herself some time later on her hands and knees on the toilet floor, vomiting foods of many nations.

They told her, Okay you are going to a deprogramming center where the lost and wan and wounded of many sects and movements are gathered for humane counseling.

Rick arrived with clothes and spending money and a box of specialty foods packed in impressive crinkly straw and they all drove to the airport. Karen found a cancer coloring book in the door pocket and leafed through. When they got out of the car she saw a policeman and decided to stroll over and tell him she'd been kidnapped. She pointed to the perpetrators, who looked—what is the word that sounds like it means calm and assured but actually means you are baffled? They looked nonplussed. Also guilty, which they were, including the cousin with the slash of green hair. So a multivoice discussion starts on the sidewalk outside the terminal with the normal airport scramble all around. One of the men tried to tell the officer about state conservatorship laws, which entitled them—and Karen was running, gone, through the terminal, down some stairs, feeling light and swift and young, hand-paddling through the crowds, then out a lower-level door and into a taxi, softly saying, *Downtown*.

She didn't know what city the downtown area belonged to but when she got there she put fifty dollars aside and spent the rest on a Greyhound ticket—ridin' the dog—and got off three hours later in White Cloud, a name in the sky, where Scott found her walking zigzag on a nearly empty street.

Brita said, "I have an Eve Arnold photograph of White Cloud, Kansas. It shows the main street, I'm fairly certain, and a structure that could be the brick building where Karen was standing when you approached her and there is definitely a tractor or combine or some other high-wheeled farm machine in the picture."

"But we're not there, she and I."

"And there's the small sign you mentioned on one of the stores with the funny word on it, the Indian word or whatever, and in a way the whole picture, the wide sky and wide street, everything so lonely and eloquent and commonplace at the same time, it all flows into the strange word on that sign."

"I remember now. Ha-Hush-Kah. A Bill Gray touch. It's a Bill Gray place. It really is."

They drove on these same roads finally, going the other way of course, and she asked questions about Bill. Scott realized this was the first time she'd said more than ten words about anything outside herself. He didn't know whether Bill would let her stay.

It turned out the subject never came up in so many words. They walked in and talked to Bill about the trip and he seemed to take to Karen. His eyes showed a detached amusement that meant there are some things that just have to happen before we know how smart or dumb they are.

After she read Bill's novels she moved from the old sofa into Scott's bed and it felt to him as though she'd been there always.

Bill lay smoking in bed, the ashtray resting on his chest. Every time he did this he thought of old rummies in single-residence brownstones expiring in the slow smoke of mattress fires.

Karen came in wearing her briefs and an oversized T-shirt.

"Feeling any better, Mr. Bill?"

She climbed on the bed, straddling Bill near the midsection, her upper body vertical, hands on her thighs.

Light folding in from the hallway.

"Want to put the cigarette away and smoke some of Scott's marijuana? Might help you sleep if you're still upset."

"I don't think I'm ready to sleep just yet."

"I never took to dope for some strange finicky whatever reason."

"It gives me heart-attack dreams."

"Scott uses it mainly to settle him down when he works late on manuscripts or files."

"The operational direction right now is up, not down."

She bounced a little, making him groan, then sat back on her haunches.

"He says you are familiar with a number of substances that alter the biochemistry."

"These are regulated medications. A doctor writes a prescription. All perfectly statutory."

"I definitely feel a stirring under the covers."

"Did I ever tell you what my first wife?"

"Don't think so. What?"

"She used to say I was all dick. I spent so much time locked up and was so tight-lipped about my work and eventually about everything else that there was nothing left but raw sex. And we didn't talk about that either."

"Just did it."

"She didn't like writers. I realized this, stupidly, way too late."

"If you were stupid, what was she? Marrying a writer."

"She expected us to adapt to each other. Women have faith in the mechanics of adjustment. A woman knows how to want something. She'll take chances to secure the future."

"I never think about the future."

"You come from the future," he said quietly.

She took his cigarette and stubbed it out and then put the ashtray on the floor, sliding it toward the foot of the bed.

"What's a heart-attack dream?"

"Panic. Rapid heartbeat. Then I wake up and I'm not sure if the heartbeat was dreamed or real. Not that dreamed isn't real."

"Everything is real."

She shook easily out of the T-shirt, arms unfolding full-length above her head, and Bill almost turned away. Every time she did this, breasts and hair swinging, he felt the shock of seeing something full-measure, almost lost in the force of it. He advanced the action in time to give it stillness and coherence, make it a memory of shape and grace caught unaware. She wouldn't ever know how deep-reaching that painted moment was when her elbows scissored out and she slipped free of the furled shirt and stretched to a figured yawn, making him forget where he was.

"I know it's bad form to ask."

"But what?" she said.

"Does Scott know you come up here?"

They were working him out of his pajama top, one arm at a time, then had to stop while he had a coughing fit.

"Is there anything in this house Scott doesn't know?"

"That's what I thought," he said.

"The mice are his friends. He knows which window gets the best moonlight on any given night on the lunar calendar."

She changed position to lower the bedcovers and undo the drawstring on his pants.

"And it's okay with him," Bill said.

"I don't see what choice. I mean he hasn't shot us yet."

"No, he hasn't."

"And he wouldn't."

"No, he wouldn't, would he?"

"And anyway and anyway and anyway. Didn't he bring me here for you?"

Bill could find no cheery features in this thought. He wanted to believe she'd just found the words tumbling on her tongue, which was how she hit upon much of what she said. But maybe she thought it was true and maybe it was and how interesting for Bill to imagine that he was betraying Scott all along by the other man's design.

His cock was dancing in her hand.

"I think we ought to have our intercourse now."

"Yes, dear," said Bill.

She went to the chest across the room and took a small package out of the middle drawer. She removed a condom and came back to the bed, straddling Bill's thighs, and began to outfit him with the device.

"Who are you protecting, you or me?"

"It's just the norm today."

He saw how absorbed she was in the task, dainty-fingered and determined to be expert, like a solemn child dressing a doll.

. . .

Scott stood looking around the loft apartment. Columns extended
the length of the room. There was a broad plastic sheet slung
under the leaky skylight. Brita walked around switching on lights.
A small kitchen and dining area and a half-hidden recess of files
and shelves. He followed along behind her, turning two lights
off. A sofa and some chairs in a cluster. Then a darkroom and
printing room with black curtains over the doors. Out the south
windows the Trade towers stood cut against the night, intensely
massed and near. This is the word "loomed" in all its prolonged
and impending force.

"I will make tea for the travelers."

"Now I finally feel I've seen New York inside and out, just
standing here in this space and looking through the window."

"When it rains out, it also rains in."

"Brita, despite whatever inconvenience."

"It's small as these places go. But I can't afford it anymore.
And I have to look at the million-storey towers."

"One has an antenna."

"The male."

"Tea is perfect, thank you."

In the kitchen she took things out of cabinets and drawers, an
object at a time, feeling as though she'd been away for a month,
six weeks, a sense of home folding over her now. These cups
and spoons made her feel intact again, reclaimed her from the
jet trails, the physics of being in transit. She was so weary she
could hear it, a ringing in the bones, and she had to keep re-
minding herself she'd been gone for less than two days. Scott
stood at a table across the room looking at strewn magazines and
commenting more or less uncontrollably.

The elevator clanked through the building, the old green iron
gate smashing and rattling in the night.

They drank their tea.

"What makes this city different is that nobody expects to be in one place for ten minutes. Everybody moves all the time. Seven nameless men own everything and move us around on a board. People are swept out into the streets because the owners need the space. Then they are swept off the streets because someone owns the air they breathe. Men buy and sell air in the sky and there are bodies heaped together in boxes on the sidewalk. Then they sweep away the boxes."

"You like to overstate."

"I overstate things to stay alive. This is the point of New York. I completely love and trust this city but I know the moment I stop being angry I'm finished forever."

Scott said, "I used to eat alone. It made me ashamed, having no one to eat with. But not only alone—standing up. This is one of the haunting secrets of our time, that we are willing to eat standing up. I used to stand because it's more anonymous, it suited the way I felt about being in the city. Hundreds of thousands of people eating alone. They eat alone, they walk alone, they talk to themselves in the street in profound and troubled monologues like saints in the depths of temptation."

"I'm getting very sleepy," Brita said.

"I don't want to get back in the car right now."

"You're the driver, Scott."

"I don't think I can drive another fifteen feet."

He got up and turned off another light.

Sirens sounding to the east.

Then he sat near her on the sofa. He leaned toward her and touched the back of his hand to her cheek. She watched a mouse run up the face of a window and disappear. She had a theory the sirens drove them mad.

She said, "In some places where you eat standing up you are forced to look directly into a mirror. This is total control of the person's responses, like a consumer prison. And the mirror is literally inches away so you can hardly put the food in your mouth without hitting into it."

"The mirror is for safety, for protection. You use it to hide. You're totally alone in the foreground but you're also part of the swarm, the shifting jelly of heads looming over your little face. Bill doesn't understand how people need to blend in, lose themselves in something larger. The point of mass marriage is to show that we have to survive as a community instead of individuals trying to master every complex force. Mass interracial marriage. The conversion of the white-skinned by the dark. Every revolutionary idea involves danger and reversal. I know all the drawbacks of the Moon system but in theory it is brave and visionary. Think of the future and see how depressed you get. All the news is bad. We can't survive by needing more, wanting more, standing out, grabbing all we can."

"Speaking of the future."

"You can't send me out there."

"I need to sleep, to stop the noise in my head. I feel I've known all three of you for years and it's goddamn tiring actually."

They were seated far from the one dim light floating over the stove.

"We've gone too far into space to insist on our differences. Like those people you talk about on the Great Wall, a man and woman walking toward each other across China. This isn't a story about seeing the planet new. It's about seeing people new. We see them from space, where gender and features don't matter, where names don't matter. We've learned to see ourselves as if from space, as if from satellite cameras, all the time, all the same. As if from the moon, even. We're all Moonies, or should learn to be."

She heard the elevator gate smash shut again. Her eyes were closed. But Scott was the one who fell asleep. When she realized this, she eased off the sofa and got a blanket for him. Then she went to the other end of the loft, past the kitchen, and climbed the ladder to her bed.

She took off her sneakers and lay face up with her clothes on, suddenly wide awake. The cat appeared at her elbow, watching. She heard shouting in the street, the night voices that called all the time now, kids who pissed on sleeping men, the woman who lived in garbage bags, wearing them, sleeping inside them, who carried a large plastic bag everywhere, filled with other plastic bags. Brita heard her talking now, her voice carried on the river wind, a rasp of static in the night.

Soon the road replayed itself in her mind, the raveled passage down the hours. It was strange to lie still in a small corner and feel the power of movement, the gull-rush of air over the hood. A sense memory pulsing in the skin. The cat moved past her hand, a shrug of lunar muscle and fur. She heard car alarms going off in sequence, the panic data that fed into her life. Everything feeds in, everything is coded, there is everything and its hidden meaning. Which crisis do I trust? She felt she needed her own hidden meanings to get her through the average day. She reached out and snatched the cat, bringing it onto her chest. She thought her body had become defensive, homesick for lost assurances. It wanted to be a refuge against the way things work, against the force of what is out there. To love and touch, the roundness of these moments was crossed with something wistful now. All sex is a form of longing even as it happens. Because it happens against the crush of time. Because the surface of the act is public, a cross-grain of fear and ruin. She wanted her body to remain a secret of the past, untouched by complexity and regret. She was superstitious about talking to doctors in detail. She thought they would take her body over, name all the damaged parts, speak all the awful words. She lay for a long time with her eyes closed, trying to drift into sleep. Then she rubbed the cat's fur and felt her childhood there. It was complete in a touch, everything intact, carried out of old lost houses and fields and summer days into the river of her hand.

She slipped under the quilt, turning on her side and facing the wall to prove she was serious. Slowly now, into that helpless half life of self-commentary, the voice film that runs between light and dark. But the time eventually came when she had to admit she was still awake. She threw off the quilt and lay there on her back. Then she climbed down the ladder and went to a window, seeing steam come heaving out of a vent hole in the street. The telephone rang. Like earthwork art, these vapor columns rising all over the city, white and silent in empty streets. She heard the machine switch on and waited for the caller to speak. A man's voice, sounding completely familiar, sounding enhanced, filling the high room, but she couldn't identify him at first, couldn't quite fix the context of his remarks, and she thought he might be someone she'd known years before, many years and very well, a voice that seemed to wrap itself around her, so strangely and totally near.

"You left without saying goodbye. Although that's not why I'm calling. I'm wide awake and need to talk to someone but that's not why I'm calling either. Do you know how strange it is for me to sit here talking to a machine? I feel like a TV set left on in an empty room. I'm playing to an empty room. This is a new kind of loneliness you're getting me into, Brita. How nice to say your name. The loneliness of knowing I won't be heard for hours or days. I imagine you're always catching up with messages. Accessing your machine from distant sites. There's a lot of violence in that phrase. 'Accessing your machine.' You need a secret code if I'm not mistaken. You enter your code in Brussels and blow up a building in Madrid. This is the dark wish that the accessing industry caters to. I'm sitting in my cane chair looking out the window. The birds are awake and so am I. Another draggy smoked-out dawn with my throat scorched raw but I've had much worse. I stopped drinking when you left last night. And I'm speaking slowly now because there's no sense of a listener, not even the silences a listener creates, a dozen different kinds, dense and expectant and bored and angry, and I feel a little awkward, making a speech to an absent friend. I hope we're friends. But that's not why I'm calling. I keep seeing my book wandering through the halls. There the thing is, creeping feebly, if you can imagine a naked humped creature with filed-down genitals, only worse, because its head bulges at the top and there's a gargoylish tongue jutting at a corner of the mouth and truly terrible feet. It tries to cling to me, to touch and fasten. A cretin, a distort. Water-bloated, slobbering, incontinent. I'm speaking slowly to get it right. It's my book after all, so I'm responsible for getting it right. The loneliness of voices stored on tape. By the time you listen to this, I'll no longer remember what I said. I'll be an old message by then, buried under many new messages. The machine makes everything a message, which narrows the range of discourse and destroys the poetry of nobody home. Home is a failed idea. People are no longer home or not home. They're either picking up or not picking up. The truth is I don't feel awkward. It's probably easier to talk to you this way. But that's not why I'm calling. I'm calling to describe the sunrise. A pale runny light spreading across the hills. There's a partial cloud cover, which makes the light seem to hug the land, quiet light, soft, calm, pale, a landglow more than a light from the sky. I thought you'd want to know these things. I thought this is a woman who wants to know these things more than other things that other people might attempt to tell her. The cloud bank is long and slate-gray and altogether fine. There really isn't any more to say about it. The window is open so I can feel the air. I'm not deeply hung over and so the air does not rebuke me. The air is fine. It's precisely what it is. I'm sitting in my old cane chair with my feet up on a bench and my back to the typewriter. The birds are fine.

I can hear them in the trees nearby and out in the fields, crows in clusters in the fields. The air is sharp and cold and fine and smells altogether as air should smell early on a spring morning when a man is talking to a machine. I thought these are the things this woman wants to hear about. It tries to cling to me, soft-skinned and moist, to fasten its puckery limpet flesh onto mine."

The machine cut him off.

She realized Scott was right behind her. He leaned against her, ardent and sleepy, hands reaching around, hands and thumbs, thumbs sliding into the belt loops of her jeans. She let her head drop back against his shoulder, concentrating, and he pressed in tight. She yawned and then laughed. He put his hands under her sweater, he undid her belt, leaned in to her, put his hands down along her belly, the watchfulness, the startled alert of the body to every touch. He lifted her sweater up onto her shoulders and rubbed the side of his face against her back. She concentrated, she looked like someone listening for sounds in the wall. She felt everything. She was speculative, waiting, her breathing even and careful, and she moved slowly under his hands and felt the sandy buzz of his face on her back.

She knew he would not say a word, not even going up the ladder, not even the faithful little ladder joke, and she welcomed the silence, the tactful boy lean and pale, climbing her body with a groan.

7

Bill opened the door in the middle of traffic, the thick choked blast of yellow metal, and he walked out into it. Scott called after him to wait, stay, watch out. He moved between stalled cabs where drivers sat slumped in the gloom like inmates watching daytime TV. Scott shouted out a place and a time to meet. Bill threw back a wave and then stood at the edge of the one active lane until there was an opening to the sidewalk.

The rush of things, of shuffled sights, the mixed swagger of the avenue, noisy storefronts, jewelry spread across the sidewalk, the deep stream of reflections, heads floating in windows, towers liquefied on taxi doors, bodies shivery and elongate, all of it interesting to Bill in the way it blocked comment, the way it simply rushed at him, massively, like your first day in Jalalabad, rushed and was. Nothing tells you what you're supposed to think of this. Well, it was his first day in New York in many years and there was no street or building he wanted to see again, no old haunt that might rouse a longing or sweet regret.

He found the number and approached an oval desk in the lobby, where two security officers sat behind a bank of telephones, TV monitors and computer displays. He gave his name and waited for the woman to check a visitors' list on the swivel screen. She asked him some questions and then picked up a phone and in a couple of minutes a uniformed man appeared to escort Bill to the proper floor. The woman at the desk gave the man a visitor's badge, an adhesive piece of paper, which he fastened to Bill's lapel.

There was another checkpoint at the elevator bank and they passed without delay and rode an express to the top of the building and when the door came open there was Charlie Everson in a bright tie, waiting. He squeezed Bill's arms at the biceps and looked squarely into his face. Neither man said a word. Then Charlie nodded to the guard and led Bill through a door opposite the reception room. They walked down a long corridor lined with book jackets and went into a large sunny office filled with plant life and polished surfaces.

"Where's your Bushmills?" Bill said. "A bite of the single-malt will do just fine."

"I'm not drinking these days."

"But you keep something in the cabinet for visiting writers."

"Ballygowan. It's water."

Bill looked at him hard. Then he sat down and undid the laces on his shoes, which were new and tight.

"Bill, it's hard to believe."

"I know. So many years, so fast, so strange."

"You look like a writer. You never used to. Took all these years. Do I recognize the jacket?"

"I think it's yours."

"Is it possible? The night Louise Wiegand got drunk and insulted my jacket."

"And you took it off."

"I threw it right down."

"And I said I need a jacket and I did need a jacket and she said or someone said take this one."

"Wasn't me. I liked that jacket."

"It's a nice old tweed."

"Doesn't fit."

"I've worn it maybe four times."

"She gave you my jacket."

"Louise was damn nice that way."

"She's dead, you know."

"Don't start, Charlie."

"What do you hear from Helen?"

"Speaking of dead? Nothing."

"I always liked Helen."

"You should have married her," Bill said. "Would have saved me a ton of trouble."

"She wasn't the trouble. You were the trouble."

"Either way," Bill said.

Charlie's face was broad, with a healthy flush, the windburn that fills the mirror behind the yacht-club bar. Thin pale hair cut short. The custom suit. The traditional loud tie that preserved a link to collegiate fun, that reminded people he was still Charlie E. and this was still supposed to be the book business, not global war through laser technology.

"Those years seem awfully clear to me. And they keep adding on. New things come back all the time. I find myself recalling scraps of dialogue from 1955."

"Be careful, you'll end up writing this stuff down."

"If I live and live and live, boringly into my middle eighties, I wonder how much I'll be able to add to the pleasure of those memories, the intense conversations, all those endless dinners and drinks and arguments we all had. We used to come out of a bar at three a.m. and talk on a street corner because there was so much we still had to say to each other, there were arguments we'd only scratched the surface of. Writing, painting, women, jazz, politics, history, baseball, every damn thing under the sun. I never wanted to go home, Bill. And when I finally got home I couldn't sleep. The talk kept buzzing in my head."

"Eleanor Baumann."

"God yes. Fantastic woman."

"She was smarter than both of us put together."

"Crazier too, unfortunately."

"Strange-smelling breath," Bill said.

"Fantastic letters. She wrote me a hundred amazing letters."

"What did they smell like?"

"For years. I have years of letters from that woman."

Charlie sat parallel to his desk, legs extended, his hands joined behind his neck.

"I was glad to hear from you," he said. "I talked to Brita Nilsson when she got back and she wouldn't tell me anything except that she passed on my message. Took you a while to call."

"I was working."

"And it's going well?"

"We don't talk about that."

"Took you a month. I've always thought I understood precisely why you went into isolation."

"Is that what we're here to talk about?"

"You have a twisted sense of the writer's place in society. You think the writer belongs at the far margin, doing dangerous things. In Central America, writers carry guns. They have to. And this has always been your idea of the way it ought to be. The state should want to kill all writers. Every government, every group that holds power or aspires to power should feel so threatened by writers that they hunt them down, everywhere."

"I've done no dangerous things."

"No. But you've lived out the vision anyway."

"So my life is a kind of simulation."

"Not exactly. There's nothing false about it. You've actually become a hunted man."

"I see."

"And that's what we're here to talk about. There's a young man held hostage in Beirut. He's Swiss, a UN worker who was doing research on health care in the Palestinian camps. He's also a poet. Published maybe fifteen short poems in French-language journals. We know next to nothing about the group that has him. The hostage is the only proof they exist."

"What's your involvement?"

"I'm chairman of a high-minded committee on free expression. We're mainly academics and publishing people and we're just getting started and this is the crazy part of the whole business. This group takes a hostage simply because he's there, he's available, and he apparently tells them he's a poet and what is the first thing they do? They contact *us*. They have a fellow in Athens who calls our London office and says, There's a writer chained to a wall in a bare room in Beirut. If you want him back, maybe we can do a deal."

"Buy me lunch, Charlie. I've come all this way."

"Wait, now listen. I've been talking to the chap in Athens whenever I can reach him. On and off for weeks. Sometimes his phone rings, sometimes I hear an oceanic roar, sometimes he's there and sometimes he's not. We've finally agreed on a plan. We want to have a news conference, small and tightly controlled. Day after tomorrow in London. We talk about the captive writer. We talk about the group that has him. And then I announce that the hostage is being freed at that moment on live television in Beirut."

"Sounds pretty fucking fishy to me."

"I know. An element of mutual interest. But listen."

"Your new group gets press, their new group gets press, the young man is sprung from his basement room, the journalists get a story, so what's the harm."

"Right. And with this one success we can open up everybody's thinking. How do you create a shift in rooted attitudes and hard-line positions if not through public events that show us how to imagine other possibilities? Besides, it's the only way to get this poor guy out of there. Isn't that enough, all by itself? We're obligated to do everything we can to save him and if we learn something about the people who took him, so much the better."

"Where the hell do I fit in?"

"If I hadn't run into Brita that evening, you wouldn't fit in at all. But when she said she was taking your picture, bells went off in my head. If you're willing to be photographed after all these years, why not take it one step further? Do something that will help us show who we are as an organization and how important it is for writers to take a public stand. Frankly I'm hoping to create a happy sensation. I want you to show up in London and briefly read from the poet's work, a selection of five or six poems. That's all."

"Get a Swiss writer. Won't the Swiss feel left out?"

"I can get any writer I want. But I want Bill Gray. Look, I didn't tell anyone you were coming here today. Not even my secretary. Because if I had there'd be a queue outside that door stretching like a conga line into the distance. There's an excitement that attaches to your name and it will help us put a mark on this event, force people to talk about it and think about it long after the speeches fade. I want one missing writer to read the work of another. I want the famous novelist to address the suffering of the unknown poet. I want the English-language writer to read in French and the older man to speak across the night to his young colleague in letters. Don't you see how beautifully balanced?"

Bill said nothing.

"This is the soul's own business, Bill. I think it's something you need to do. Get out of your room, away from your preoccupations. And I make these promises. There will be no advance announcement of your presence. No interviews after your appearance. Still cameras only. The conference will be kept to fifty or sixty people, all inclusive. I want a ripple effect. Word will spread, follow-up stories will appear, curiosity will build. I want our work to have a future. Your French still passable?"

Bill began searching for a cigarette. There was a silence, a period of thoughtful review. The bright badge at Bill's lapel read Visitor Access Only.

Charlie said softly, "We used to argue on street corners at three in the morning."

"It's true, Charlie."

"There were times you made me furious. All those infamous ideas of yours. I felt so sensible and petty. You were almost always wrong but there was no chance I could ever win an argument in any way that really counted."

"I think I'm supposed to be out of here soon."

"Don't you find yourself remembering? Things come flooding back with a force that's overwhelming. Christ, Bill, I'm happy to see you."

"I remember everything. Almost constantly."

"What do you hear from Sara?"

"Are we doing my former wives in chronological order?"

"What do you hear from her?"

"She's okay. She likes to stay in some kind of touch. It means a lot to her that we still talk once in a while."

"Of course I barely knew her. You had some kind of quarantine in effect."

"She was young, that's all."

"Too young. Not ready for the hopeless task of wifing a writer like you."

"They're all like me."

"Not that I was any readier. I was never sure what I was supposed to be guilty of."

"You were guilty of being my editor. A writer has complaints."

"Well, this is surely true."

"You were guilty of being in the vicinity. No matter what you said or did, I had a way of using it to my bleak advantage."

"For many happy years I've listened to writers and their brilliant kvetching. The most successful writers make the biggest complainers. This is so interesting to me. I wonder if the qualities that produce a top writer also account for the ingenuity and size of his complaints. Does writing come out of bitterness and rage or does it produce bitterness and rage?"

"Or both," Bill said.

"Everyone complains about the loneliness. The solitude is killing. The nights are sleepless. The days are taut with worry and pain. Bemoan, bemoan. The novelists are doing interviews. The interviewers are writing novels. The money is never enough. The acclaim is falling short. Come on, Bill, what else?"

"It must be hard for you, dealing with these wretches day after day."

"No, it's easy. I take them to a major eatery. I say, Pooh pooh pooh pooh. I say, Drinky drinky drinky. I tell them their books are doing splendidly in the chains. I tell them readers are flocking to the malls. I say, Coochy coochy coo. I recommend the roast monkfish with savoy cabbage. I tell them the reprint bidders are howling in the commodity pits. There is miniseries interest, there is audiocassette interest, the White House wants a copy for the den. I say, The publicity people are setting up tours. The Italians love the book completely. The Germans are groping for new levels of rapture. Oh my oh my oh my."

"And yourself, Charlie."

"I'm adjusting to the new style."

"How long have you been here?"

"Two years."

"Who owns this company?"

"You don't want to know."

"Give me the whole big story in one quick burst."

"It's all about limousines."

Bill leaned down to lace his shoes.

"All right. Who else is dead that I should know about?"

"Do we really want to do this?"

"Probably not."

"We're next," Charlie said.

"I'm next, you bastard."

"I want the new book, Bill."

"I'm still working."

"Whatever relationship you maintain with the old dusty lovable skinflint house."

"I'm in the final pages."

"Whatever crumbling remnants of a contract, there are ways around it."

"I'm polishing. That's what I'm doing."

"I want this book, you bastard."

They stirred in their chairs. Charlie flexed his right knee, grimacing. They got to their feet at the same time and stretched, working their shoulder muscles. Bill looked out the east window into a sky mural of bridge spans and ship cranes, factory smoke over Queens.

"You're not the hermit, the woodsman-writer, you're not the crank with a native vision. You're the hunted man. You don't write political novels or books steeped in history but you still feel the clamor at your back. This is the conflict, Bill."

"I think I got rooked on these shoes."

"You'll call me about London at home tonight. Here's my number. Or tomorrow at the absolute latest, right here, by noon if possible. I'm taking a night flight. It's something I think you need to do. Remember. One less writer in the hands of killers."

The guard was waiting in the reception area. Bill asked him where the men's room was. The guard had a key and stood by the drying machine as Bill went through his pockets looking for the tin with his mixed medications. He took precut segments of three brands of amphetamine tablets out of the tin. The colors were a blue, a white and a pink. He placed them on his tongue but when he realized the tap would not deliver water unless he kept his hand on the valve he took the pill fragments out of his mouth so he could ask the guard to turn on the cold water for him. The guard was willing to do this. Bill put the pieces back on his tongue, cupped his hands under the spout and brought the water to his mouth and drank, throwing back his head when he swallowed. The guard looked at him as if to ask whether everything had gone as planned. Bill nodded and they went out to the elevator and rode to the lobby together.

Bill stood near the entranceway, about fifty feet from the oval desk and directly in front of the register that listed the building's occupants. He could see Scott waiting just outside, standing at the far end of a shop window that jutted at an angle from the recessed entranceway, forming a border extending to the sidewalk. He carried a small package, books probably, and had his back to the shop window. Bill stepped away from the glass doors and smoked a cigarette. He stood in thought, his arms folded and his head cocked slightly left. His gaze seemed to end at the tip of the cigarette dangling from his right hand. When he peered out again, Scott was nearer the entranceway but had turned to look in the shop window. Bill walked across the front of the lobby past two sets of revolving doors. He exited by the last single door, peeling the visitor's badge from his lapel and moving out onto the sidewalk, where he joined the surge of the noontime crowd.

PART TWO

8

The boy took off the prisoner's hood when he came to feed him. The boy also wore a hood, a crude cloth piece with ragged slashes at the eyes.

Time became peculiar, the original thing that is always there. It seeped into his fever and delirium, into the question of who he was. When he spat up blood he watched the pink thing slug into the drain and it carried time quivering in it.

It made the prisoner anxious, not knowing why the boy needed to be concealed.

They drove him here in a car with a missing door. He saw an old man with no shirt who was stuck to a coil of military wire in a sewage meadow somewhere.

Be alert and note the details said the conscientious tape running in his head, the voice that whispers you are smarter than your captors.

The prisoner felt the boy come close to pull away his hood and stuff his face with food and he looked into the eyeholes of the boy's own hood.

Time permeated the air and food. The black ant crawling up his leg carried time's enormity, the old slow all-knowing pace.

Poor old guy probably lost at night wanders dizzy into the wire, senile, shirtless, pinned, still living.

He waited for the moment when he could count the launched

rockets flashing. When he heard the rockets he also saw the flash although he wore a hood that had no eyeholes.

He was new at this and eager to succeed. All the time he chewed his food he estimated meters wall to wall. Measure the walls, then the bricks in the walls, then the mortar between the bricks, then the hairline cracks in the mortar. See it as a test. Show them how advanced you are.

He saw laundry lines going through shell holes in gray masonry, looking through the missing door.

The boy pulled away the hood and fed him by hand, always too fast, pushing food into his mouth before he was finished chewing the previous handful.

He conceded the fact of his confinement. He admitted to the presence of the plastic wire they'd used to fasten his wrist to the water-supply pipe. He conceded the hood. His head was covered with a hood.

The prisoner was full of plans. With time and tools he would learn Arabic and impress his captors and greet them in their language and have basic conversations, once they gave him the tools to teach himself.

The boy tortured him sometimes. Knocked him down, told him to stand. Knocked him down, told him to stand. The boy tried to pull his teeth out of his mouth with his bare hands. The pain extended long past the boy's departure from the room. This was part of the structure of time, how time and pain became inseparable.

And there were authorities to impress as well. At his release they would take him to a secret place and recite their questions in the same voice he heard on the instruction tape and he would impress the authorities with his recall of detail and his analysis of facets and aspects and they would quickly determine the location of the building and the identity of the group that held him.

He knew it was evening by the war noise. In the early weeks it began at sundown. First the machine-gun clatter, then car horns blowing. It's interesting to think of traffic jams caused by war. Everything is normal in a way. All the usual cursing complaints.

The boy had him lie on his back with legs bent up and he beat the bottoms of the prisoner's feet with a reinforcing rod. The pain made it hard for him to sleep and this stretched and deepened time, gave it a consciousness, a quality of ingenious and pervasive presence.

He thought of the no-shirt man caught on the wire. His memories didn't extend past the moment of abduction. Time started there except for small dim snatches, summer flashes, compact moments in a house somewhere.

But even with authorities, what do authorities know, did he really expect authorities to learn important things from the length and width of a brick even if there were bricks to count and measure and there weren't, or meaningful sounds that barely petered through the walls.

There was no sequence or narrative or one day that leads to another. He saw a bowl and spoon at the edge of his foam mattress but the boy continued to feed him by hand. Sometimes the boy forgot to replace the hood after mealtime. This made the prisoner anxious.

The mortars came next, a sound of dust in the heavy crumple of the shells, slow-motion dust, dust specks colliding by the millions.

It was hard to think about women except desperately and incompletely. If they could send him a woman, just once, for half a second, so he could set eyes on her.

The only meaningful sound he heard was the VCR on the floor above. They were looking at videos of the war in the streets. They wanted to see themselves in their scuffed khakis, the vivid streetwise troop, that's us, firing nervous bursts at the militia down the block.

The ants and baby spiders transported time in its vastness and discontent and when he felt something crawling on the back of his hand he wanted to speak to it, explain his situation. He wanted to tell it who he was because this was now a matter of some confusion. Cut off from people whose voices were the ravel of his being, growing scant and pale because there was no one to see him and give him back his body.

The boy forgot to replace the hood after meals, he forgot the meals, the boy was the bearer of randomness. The last sense-making thing, the times for meals and beatings, was in danger of collapse.

If they could send a woman wearing stockings who might whisper the word "stockings." This would help him live another week.

Then what he was waiting for, the sound-flash of the big Grad rockets sliding off multibarreled launchers, twenty thirty maybe forty at a time in the incandescent dusk of a major duel across the Green Line.

He wanted paper and something to write with, some way to sustain a thought, place it in the world.

He refused to exercise or count bricks or make up bricks that he might measure and count. He talked aloud to his father early in the morning, after the war died down. He told his father where he was, how positioned, how tied to a pipe, where in present pain, how in spirit, but with assurances that he was hopeful of rescue as they say on the instruction tape of Western man.

He tried to make them up, women in nets and straps, but could only manage drifting images, half finished.

There was something about the sound of launched rockets that induced a cortical flash, the brainlight under the hood that meant the Christians and the Muslims, that meant the sky was glowing, the city banded in rhapsodies of light and fire all the way to morning, when men came out of stifling shelters in their underwear to sweep away the rubble and buy bread.

There was no one to remind him who he was. The days were not connected. The prisoner sensed the vanish of the simplest givens. He began to identify with the boy. As all his voices fled he thought he might be somewhere in the boy.

He tried to repeat the old stories, sex with a shadowy woman on a passenger jet crossing the ocean at night (and it has to be night and it has to be water) or encounters in unexpected places with women in tight things, crisscrossed with black straps, sealed for his unsealing, but he couldn't seem to do it, braced and cinctured, women stuck fast in the middle of a thought.

No one came to interrogate him.

He looked through the missing door and there were kids playing in the rubble and a gun at the side of his neck and he kept telling himself I am riding in a car with a missing door.

The old stories tried and true. Sex with a shadowy woman on a stairway in an empty building on a rainy day. The more banal, the more commonplace, the more predictable, the triter, the staler, the dumber, the better. The only thing he didn't have time for was originality. He wanted the same junior fantasies the boy had, sucking on the images that would trail them into middle age, into the final ruin, those sad little picture-stories so dependable and true.

The food was usually takeout, coming in a bag with Arabic letters and a logo of three red chickens standing in a row.

No, he didn't hate the boy, who had scrappy hands and chewed-up fingers and was not the author of his lonely terror. But he did hate him, didn't he, or did he, or not?

Soon, though, he felt these talks with his father were a form of exercise, of self-improvement, and he stopped talking, he let this last voice flee, he said okay and fell to mumbling.

He thought of the no-shirt man on the razor wire and saw him turning neon in the gorgeous dawn of the war.

In the beginning, what?

In the beginning there were people in many cities who had his name on their breath. He knew they were out there, the intelligence network, the diplomatic back-channel, technicians, military men. He had tumbled into the new culture, the system of world terror, and they'd given him a second self, an immortality, the spirit of Jean-Claude Julien. He was a digital mosaic in the processing grid, lines of ghostly type on microfilm. They were putting him together, storing his data in starfish satellites, bouncing his image off the moon. He saw himself floating to the far shores of space, past his own death and back again. But he sensed they'd forgotten his body by now. He was lost in the wavebands, one more code for the computer mesh, for the memory of crimes too pointless to be solved.

Who knew him now?

There was no one who knew him but the boy. First his government abandoned him, then his employer, then his family. And now the men who'd abducted him and kept him sealed in a basement room had also forgotten he was here. It was hard to say whose neglect troubled him most.

Bill sat in a small apartment above a laundromat about a mile east of Harvard Square. He wore a sweater over his pajamas and an old terry-cloth robe over the sweater.

His daughter Liz made dinner and talked to him through a serving hatch stacked with magazines and play scripts.

"It's impossible to save a nickel so I don't even think about moving out of here. I'm at the point where I feel lucky to at least be doing something I like."

"And never mind the little miseries."

"But watch out for the big ones."

"Last time I was here."

"Right."

"You look a lot better, kid."

"Last time was a crisis. Which I see you found your robe and pajamas. Always leaving things, Daddy."

"I take after you."

He was barefoot, reading a newspaper.

"And let someone know you're coming for God's sake. I could have met you at the airport."

"Spur of the moment. I figured you were working."

"Monday's off."

"I'll bet you're good at your job."

"Tell *them*. I'm going to be like thirty any minute and I'm still trying to lose the word 'assistant.' "

"Now, look, about the inconvenience. I'm out of here tomorrow."

"The sofa's yours as long as you want it. Stay a while. I'd like you to."

"You know me."

"We're all going to Atlanta for Memorial Day. I'll be able to report on the rare visit of the Mythical Father."

"You'll ruin their weekend."

"Why don't you ask me how they're doing?"

"I don't give a damn."

"Thank you."

"I've reached a long-distance agreement with those two about the value of not giving a damn. ESP. We're in perfect unspoken communication."

He put down one section of the paper and started on another.

"They're interested in what you're doing," she said.

"What am I doing? I'm doing what I always do. How could anyone be interested in that?"

"You're still a popular subject. Except with Mother of course. She doesn't want to hear about it."

"Neither do I, Lizzie."

"But it comes up. We're like little brown doggies gnawing and pulling at the same spitty rag."

"Report that my drinking is completely under control."

"What about your remoteness?"

"What about it?" he said.

"Your anger. The airspace we weren't allowed to enter when you were brooding. What about your vanishing act?"

"Look, why even bother with me if you really believe I was all that difficult?"

"I don't know. Maybe I'm a coward. I can't bear the thought that bad feelings might harden between us and I'll grow old always regretting. And maybe it's because there are no kids in my future. I don't have to live my life as a history lesson in how not to be like my father. There won't be anyone I can fuck up the way you did the job on Sheila and Jeff."

She put her head into the opening between the rooms, showing a sly smile.

"*We* don't think your behavior had anything to do with writing. *We* think the Mythical Father used writing as an excuse for just about everything. That's how *we* analyze the matter, Daddy. *We* think writing was never the burden and the sorrow you made it out to be but as a matter of fact was your convenient crutch and your convenient alibi for every possible failure to be decent."

"What does a stage manager do anyway?"

Her smile widened and she looked at him as if he'd made the one remark that might prove he loved her.

"I remind the actors where they're supposed to fall in the death scene."

Gail came out of the bedroom and got a jacket from the closet.

Bill said, "Am I chasing you out of here? Stay around and

referee. An Old Testament sandstorm is falling on my head."

"I have my hypnotist tonight. He's my last hope of taking off pounds."

"I tell her try not eating," Liz said.

"She says it like it's common sense. I have an outside range of maybe eight days' strict diet and then something comes on automatic and I know I'm cleared of blame and guilt."

"Talk to my father. Writers have discipline."

"I know. I envy that. I could never do it. Sit down day after day."

"Army ants have discipline," Bill said. "Don't ask me what writers have."

Gail went out and the two of them sat down to dinner. He had his daughter figured for the senior dyke in this tandem, the decision-maker and stancher of wounds. He tried being impressed. He poured the wine he'd bought after he left the taxi and went wandering in the area looking for familiar streets and houses because he realized he had no idea what the name of her street was and couldn't find her address or phone number in his wallet and wondered how the hell he expected to get into the apartment even if he knew where she lived and finally spotted a phone and called information and she was not only listed but home.

"Now, look, I'm trying to remember what else I might have left behind last time."

"Gail wears your robe."

"Hypnosis. It could be the answer to everything."

"You left a billfold with traveler's checks and passport. Look surprised, Daddy."

"I've been wondering where the hell."

"You knew where it was. That's why you're here, isn't it?"

"I'm here to see you, kid."

"I know."

"Christ, I can't make a move."

"It's all right. I don't spend my time obsessing over Daddy's motives."

"Only his negligence."

"Well there's that of course."

"Actually I wasn't even around when you were born. Ever hear about that?"

"Only just recently."

"I was at Yaddo."

"What's that?"

"It's a retreat, a place where writers go for some ordinary fucking peace and quiet. In fact this is the institution's motto, engraved on a frieze over the entranceway. The *u* in 'fucking' comes out as a *v*, in accordance with classical precedent."

He looked up from his food to see if she was smiling. She seemed to be thinking about it. He helped her clean up and then called Charles Everson in New York.

Charlie said, "Your man Scott showed up not long after you left. I was in the boardroom for a luncheon meeting. He apparently raised something of a ruckus in the lobby. Tried to get up to our offices. Security finally called up and asked me to speak to him. He wanted to know where you were. Of course I couldn't tell him because I didn't know."

"You still don't."

"This is true, Bill."

"You didn't say anything about our London chat."

"London is the last thing I'd tell anyone. But he's not an easy fellow to pacify. I finally had to go down there and talk to him. First I convinced security to produce the guard who accompanies special guests. Then the guard convinced Scott that he took you up and he took you down and you weren't lying dead in the elevator. Eternally riding. A warning to us all."

They talked about arrangements.

Then Bill said, "He'll call you. He'll keep calling. Not a word."

"I haven't revealed a thing about you to a single soul in twenty-five years, Bill. I keep the faith."

When Gail came back they played rummy for a while. The women wanted to go to sleep and Bill tried to keep them going with card tricks. The wine was gone. He read for an hour and made up the sofa, recalling how cramped it was. Then he found a scratch pad and a pencil and made notes for some revisions on his novel.

Scott came out of the bathroom with toothpaste on a brush. He looked at Karen, who was sitting up in bed watching TV. He stared, waiting for her to see him. There were times she became lost in the dusty light, observing some survivor of a national news disaster, there's the lonely fuselage smoking in a field, and she was able to study the face and shade into it at the same time, even sneak a half second ahead, inferring the strange dazed grin or gesturing hand, which made her seem involved not just in the coverage but in the terror that came blowing through the fog.

He stared until she turned and saw him.

"Then where is he?" she said.

"I'll figure it out. It's been a long time since he was a step ahead of me. Bastard."

"But where could he go?"

"Somewhere that makes sense only to him. But if it makes sense to him, I'll eventually figure it out."

"But how can you be sure he's not sick or hurt?"

"I went in the building and talked to them. We had an actual scuffle, some bumping and pushing. They have security at the level of war is imminent. Anyway it's clear to me he just walked out the door."

"Well then I think he's with Brita."

Scott stood with the toothbrush held level across his chest.

"He's not with Brita. Why is he with Brita?"

"Because why else would he stay in New York?"

"We don't know he stayed there. We don't even know for sure why he went there. He told me it was just a visit with Charles Everson. Everson told me they talked about the new book. No, he hasn't been in touch with Brita or I'd know it. The phone bill came the other day. The calls would be itemized."

"Maybe she called him."

"No, he's got something deeper. He's down deeper somewhere."

"He's running away from his book again."

"The book is finished."

"Not to him."

"He never left without telling me where he was going. No, he's down deeper this time."

He went in and brushed his teeth. When he came out he stared at her until she realized he was looking.

"We need to do lists," he said.

"But if he's not here."

"All the more reason. We need to give his workroom a good going-over."

"He doesn't like us in there."

"He doesn't like me in there," Scott said. "I believe there are times in the night when he definitely consents to your presence. In the night or in the late afternoon when I'm out buying the onions for the stew."

"Or the cucumbers for the salad."

"The workroom needs to be cleaned and organized. So when he gets back he can find things for a change."

"He'll call us in a day or two and we can ask him if it's okay."

"He won't call."

"I'm hopeful he'll call."

"If there was something he wanted to call us about, he'd still be here, living amongst us."

He got into bed, turning up the collar of his pajama shirt.

"Let's give him a chance to call," she said. "That's all I'm saying."

"He's got some deep and dire plan and it doesn't include us."

"He loves us, Scott."

She watched the set at the foot of the bed. There was a woman on an exercise bike and she wore a gleaming skintight suit and talked into the camera as she pedaled and there was a second woman inserted in a corner of the screen, thumb-sized, relaying the first woman's monologue in sign language. Karen studied them both, her eyes sweeping the screen. She was thin-boundaried. She took it all in, she believed it all, pain, ecstasy, dog food, all the seraphic matter, the baby bliss that falls from the air. Scott stared at her and waited. She carried the virus of the future. Quoting Bill.

9

B ill reminded himself to read the pavement signs before he crossed the street. It was so perfectly damn sensible they ought to make it the law in every city, long-lettered words in white paint that tell you which way to look if you want to live.

He wasn't interested in seeing London. He'd seen it before. A glimpse of Trafalgar Square from a taxi, three routine seconds of memory, aura, repetition, the place unchanged despite construction fences and plastic sheeting—a dream locus, a doubleness that famous places share, making them seem remote and unreceptive but at the same time intimately familiar, an experience you've been carrying forever. The pavement signs were the only things he paid attention to. Look left. Look right. They seemed to speak to the whole vexed question of existence.

He hated these shoes. His ribs felt soft today. There was a slight seizing in his throat.

He wanted to get back to the hotel and sleep a while. He wasn't staying at the place in Mayfair that Charlie had mentioned. He was in a middling gray relic and already beginning to grouse to himself about reimbursement.

In his room he took off his shirt and blew on the inside of the collar, getting rid of lint and hair, drying the light sweat. He had Lizzie's overnight bag with his robe and pajamas and there were some socks, underwear and toilet articles he'd bought in Boston.

He didn't know if he wanted to do this thing. It didn't feel so right anymore. He had a foreboding, the little clinging tightness in the throat that he knew so well from his work, the times he was afraid and hemmed in by doubt, knowing there was something up ahead he didn't want to face, a character, a life he thought he could not handle.

He called Charlie's hotel.

"Where are you, Bill?"

"I can see a hospital from my window."

"And you find this encouraging."

"I look for one thing in a hotel. Proximity to the essential services."

"You're supposed to be at the Chesterfield."

"The very name is incompatible with my price structure. It smells of figured velvet."

"You're not paying. We're paying."

"I understood about the plane fare."

"And the hotel. It goes without saying. And the incidentals. Do you want me to see if the room's still available?"

"I'm settled in here."

"What's the name of the place?"

"It'll come to me in a minute. In the meantime tell me if we're set for this evening."

"We're working on a change of site. We had a wonderful venue all set up, thanks to a well-connected colleague of mine. The library chamber at Saint Paul's Cathedral. Precisely the dignified setting I was hoping to find. Oak and stone carving, thousands of books. At noon today they began receiving phone calls. Anonymous."

"Threats."

"Bomb threats. We're trying to keep it absolutely quiet. But the librarian did ask if we wouldn't like to conduct our meeting elsewhere. We think we've got a secure site just about pinned down and we're arranging a very discreet police presence. But it hurts, Bill. We had a gallery and vaulted ceiling. We had wood-block floors."

"People who make phone calls don't set off bombs. The real terrorists make their calls after the damage is done. If at all."

"I know," Charlie said, "but we still want to take every possible precaution. We're cutting the number of press people invited. And we're not revealing the location to anyone until the last possible moment. People will gather at a decoy location, then be driven to the real site in a chartered bus."

"Remember literature, Charlie? It involved getting drunk and getting laid."

"Come to the Chesterfield at seven. You'll have some time to look at the poems you're going to read. Then we'll go off together. And when it's over, a late dinner, just the two of us. I want to talk about your book."

Bill felt better about the reading now that he knew someone was paying his hotel bill. He put a menu card on the coffee table and got his medication tin from his jacket pocket. He emptied the contents onto the card, a total of four uncut tablets. The rest of his supply sat in prescription vials of lovely amber plastic in a bureau drawer in his bedroom at home. Depressants, anti-depressants, sleep-inducers, speed-makers, diuretics, antibiotics, heart-starters, muscle relaxants. In front of him now were three kinds of sedatives and a single pink cortical steroid for intractable skin itches. Pathetic. But of course he hadn't known he'd be doing Boston and London. And the meager sampling would not diminish the surgical pleasure of slicing and dividing, the happy sacrament of color mixing. He bent over the low table, wrapped in the calm that fell upon him when he was cutting up his pills. He liked the sense of soldierly preparation, the diligence and rigor that helped him pretend he knew what he was doing. It was the sweetest play of hand and eye, slicing the pills, choosing elements to take in combination. It was right there on the card, nicely and brightly pebbled, a way to manage the confusion, to search out a state of being, actually shop among the colors for some altering force that might get him past a momentary panic or some mischance of the body or take him safely through the long evening tides, the western end of the day, a wash of desperation coming over him.

He regretted not having his illustrated guides with their cautions and warnings and side effects and interactions and lovely color charts. But he hadn't known he'd be doing an ocean.

He concentrated deeply, sectioning the tablets with his old scarred stag-handle folding knife, undetected by security at three airports.

The taxi swung onto Southwark Bridge. Bill had the poems in his lap and occasionally raised a page to his face, muttering lines. A soft warm rain made shaded patterns on the river, bands of wind-brushed shimmer.

Charlie said, "About this fellow."

"Who?"

"The fellow in Athens who initiated the whole business. I'd like to get your sense of the man."

"Is he Lebanese?"

"Yes. A political scientist. He says he's only an intermediary, with imperfect knowledge of the group in Beirut. Claims they're eager to release the hostage."

"Are they a new fundamentalist element?"

"They're a new communist element."

"Are we surprised?" Bill said.

"There's a Lebanese Communist Party. There are leftist elements, I understand, aligned with Syria. The PLO has always had a Marxist component and they're active again in Lebanon."

"So we're not surprised."

"We're not unduly surprised."

"I depend on you to tell me when we're surprised."

Two detectives met them in a deserted street not far from Saint Saviours Dock. There was renovation in progress in the area but the buildings here were still intact, mainly red brick structures with hoists and loading bays. They approached an old grain-warehouse leased to a plumbing-supply firm that had just gone out of business. The police had arranged entry and there was still a working telephone.

The four men went inside. They checked the open space being used for the conference. A rostrum, folding chairs, auxiliary lighting. Then they went into the main office and Charlie telephoned his colleagues and told them to load the bus and come ahead. Bill looked around for a toilet. Seconds after Charlie hung up, the phone rang. One of the detectives answered and all of them could hear the voice at the other end shouting, "Bomb, bomb, bomb," and the man's accent made it sound like boom boom boom. This seemed pretty funny to Bill, who had to take a leak and saw no reason to do it in the street.

The call annoyed the detectives. One of them anyway. The other just gazed across the office at a bookshelf filled with specification manuals. Bill found a toilet and was the last one out. One detective took up a position near the front door and the second man moved their car about fifty yards up the street and then called headquarters.

Charlie said, "I wish I understood the point."

He and Bill went across the street and waited for the bomb unit to arrive and search the building.

"The point is control," Bill said. "They want to believe they have the power to move us out of a building and into the street. In their minds they see a hundred people trooping down the fire stairs. I told you, Charlie. Some people make bombs, some people make phone calls."

Soon they were talking about something else. The rain stopped. Charlie crossed the street, said something to the detective and came back shrugging. They talked about a book Charlie was doing. They talked about the day Charlie's divorce became final, six years earlier. He recalled the weather, the high clear sky, distanceless, flags whipping on Fifth Avenue and a movie actress getting out of a taxi. Bill reached for his handkerchief. The blast made him jerk half around but he didn't leave his feet or go back against the wall. He felt the sound in his chest and arms. He jerked and ducked, shielding his head with his forearm, windows blowing out. Charlie said goddamn or go down. He turned his back to the blast wave, bracing himself against the wall with his elbows, hands clasped behind his head, and Bill knew he would have to remember to be impressed. He also knew it was over, nothing worse coming, and he straightened up slowly, looking toward the building but reaching out to touch Charlie's arm, make sure he was still there, standing and able to move. The detective across the street was in a deep crouch, fumbling with the radio on his belt. The street was filled with glass, snowblinking. The second detective remained in the car a moment, calling in, and then walked toward his partner. They looked over at Charlie and Bill. Dust hung at the second-storey level of the warehouse. The four men met in the middle of the street, glass crunching under their shoes. Charlie brushed off his lapels.

The bomb experts arrived and then the press bus and some publishing people, more detectives, and Bill sat in the back of the unmarked police car while Charlie huddled with different groups making new plans.

About an hour later the two men sat under the vaulted skylight in a dining room at the Chesterfield, eating the sole.

"It means a day's delay. Two at the most," Charlie said. "You definitely ought to change hotels so we can move quickly once we're set."

"You showed presence of mind, taking that protective stance."

"Actually that's the recommended air-crash position. Except you don't do it standing up. I knew I was supposed to lower my head and lock my hands behind my neck but I couldn't place the maneuver in context. I thought I was on a plane going down."

"Your people will find another site."

"We have to. We can't stop now. Even if we go to the bare minimum. Fifteen people in five rowboats on a secluded lake somewhere."

"Anybody have a theory?"

"I talk to an antiterrorist expert tomorrow. Want to come along?"

"Nope."

"Where are you staying?"

"I'll be in touch, Charlie."

"Rowboats are not the answer, come to think of it. Isn't that where they got Mountbatten?"

"Fishing boat."

"Close enough."

Bill knew someone was looking at him, a man sitting alone at a table across the room. It was interesting how the man's curiosity carried so much information, that he knew who Bill was, that they'd never met, that he was making up his mind whether or not to approach. Bill even knew who the man was, although he could not have said how he knew. It was as if the man had fitted himself to a predetermined space, to an idea of something that was waiting to happen. Bill never looked at the man directly. Everything was a shape, a fate, information flowing.

"I want to talk about your book," Charlie said.

"It's not done yet. When it's done."

"You don't have to talk about it. I'll talk about it. And when it's done, we can both talk about it."

"We were nearly killed a little while ago. Let's talk about that."

"I know how to publish your work. Nobody in this business knows you better than I do. I know what you need."

"What's that?"

"You need a major house that also has a memory. That's why they hired me. They want to take a closer look at tradition. I represent something to those people. I represent books. I want to establish a solid responsible thoughtful list and give it the launching power of our mass-market capabilities. We have enormous resources. If you spend years writing a book, don't you want to see it fly?"

"How's your sex life, Charlie?"

"I can get this book out there in numbers that will astound."

"Got a girlfriend?"

"I had some prostate trouble. They had to reroute my semen."

"Where did they send it?"

"I don't know. But it doesn't come out the usual place."

"You still perform the act."

"Enthusiastically."

"But you don't ejaculate."

"Nothing comes out."

"And you don't know what happens to it."

"I didn't ask them what happens to it. It goes back inside. That's as much as I want to know."

"It's a beautiful story, Charlie. Not a word too long."

They looked at dessert menus.

"When will the book be done?"

"I'm fixing the punctuation."

"Punctuation's interesting. I make it a point to observe how a writer uses commas."

"And you figure two days tops and we're out of here," Bill said.

"This is what we're hoping. We're hoping it doesn't continue. The bomb was the culmination. They made their point even if we don't know exactly what it is."

"I may need to buy a shirt."

"Buy a shirt. And let me check you in here. Under the circumstances I think we ought to be able to find each other as expeditiously as possible."

"I'll think about it over coffee."

"We use acid-free paper," Charlie said.

"I'd just as soon have my books rot when I do. Why should they outlive me? They're the reason I'm dying before my time."

The man stood by the table waiting for them to finish the exchange. Bill looked off into space and waited for Charlie to realize the man was standing there. The table was large enough to accommodate another person and Charlie handled introductions while the waiter brought a chair. The man was George Haddad and when Charlie called him a spokesman for the group in Beirut the man made a gesture of self-deprecation, leaning away from the words, both hands raised. He clearly felt he hadn't earned the title.

"I'm a great admirer," he said to Bill. "And when Mr. Everson suggested you might join us at the press conference I was surprised and deeply pleased. Knowing of course how you shun public appearances."

He was clean-shaven, a tall man in his mid-forties, hair gone sparse at the front of his head. He had moist eyes and appeared sad and slightly hulking in a drab gray suit and a plastic watch he might have borrowed from a child.

"What's your connection?" Bill said.

"With Beirut? Let's say I sympathize with their aims if not their methods. This unit that took the poet is one element in a movement. Barely a movement actually. It's just an underground current at this stage, an assertion that not every weapon in Lebanon has to be marked Muslim, Christian or Zionist."

"Let's use first names," Charlie said.

Coffee came. Bill felt a stinging pinpoint heat, a shaped pain in his left hand, bright and slivered.

Charlie said, "Who wants to stop this meeting from taking place?"

"Maybe the war in the streets is simply spreading. I don't know. Maybe there's an organization that objects in principle to the release of any hostage, even a hostage they themselves are not holding. Certainly they understand that this man's release depends completely on the coverage. His freedom is tied to the public announcement of his freedom. You can't have the first without the second. This is one of many things Beirut has learned from the West. Beirut is tragic but still breathing. London is the true rubble. I've studied here and taught here and every time I return I see the damage more clearly."

Charlie said, "What do we have to do in your estimation to conduct this meeting safely?"

"It may not be possible here. The police will advise you to cancel. The next time I don't think there will be a phone call. I'll tell you what I think there will be." And he leaned over the table. "A very large explosion in a crowded room."

Bill picked a fragment of glass out of his hand. The others watched. He understood why the pain felt familiar. It was a summer wound, a play wound, one of the burns and knee-scrapes and splinters of half a century ago, one of the bee stings, the daily bloody cuts. You slid into a base and got a raspberry. You had a fight and got a shiner.

He said, "We have an innocent man locked in a cellar."

"Of course he's innocent. That's why they took him. It's such a simple idea. Terrorize the innocent. The more heartless they are, the better we see their rage. And isn't it the novelist, Bill, above all people, above all writers, who understands this rage, who knows in his soul what the terrorist thinks and feels? Through history it's the novelist who has felt affinity for the violent man who lives in the dark. Where are your sympathies? With the colonial police, the occupier, the rich landlord, the corrupt government, the militaristic state? Or with the terrorist? And I don't abjure that word even if it has a hundred meanings. It's the only honest word to use."

Bill's napkin was bunched on the table in front of him. The two men watched him place the glass fragment in a furrow in the cloth. It glinted like sand, the pebbly greenish swamp sand that belongs to childhood, to the bruises and welts, the fingers nicked by foul tips. He felt very tired. He listened to Charlie talk with the other man. He felt the deadweight of travel, the apathy and vagueness of being in a place that didn't matter to him, being invisible to himself, sleeping in a room he wouldn't recognize if he had a picture of it in front of him.

George was saying, "The first incident was unimportant because it was only a series of phone calls. The second incident was unimportant because nobody was killed. For you and Bill, pure trauma. Otherwise strictly routine. A few years ago a neo-Nazi group in Germany devised the slogan 'The worse the better.' This is also the slogan of Western media. You are nonpersons for the moment, victims without an audience. Get killed and maybe they will notice you."

In the morning Bill had breakfast in a pub near his hotel. He found he was able to order a pint of ale with his ham and eggs even though it was just past seven because night workers from the meat market were on their meal shift now. Extremely progressive licensing policy. White-coated doctors from Saint Bartholomew's sat at the next table. He looked at the cut on his hand. Seemed to be doing nicely but it's good to know the medics are near if you need advice or assistance. Old hospitals with saints' names are the ones you want to go to if you have cuts and abrasions. They haven't forgotten how to treat the classic Crusader wounds.

He took out a notepad and entered the breakfast bill and last night's taxi fare. The sound of the blast was still an echo in his skin.

Later in the day he met Charlie by prearrangement in front of the Chesterfield. They walked through Mayfair in a lazy dazzle of warm light. Charlie wore a blazer, gray flannels and bone-and-blue saddle oxfords.

"I talked to a Colonel Martinson or Martindale. Got it written down. One of those hard sharp technocrats whose religion is being smart. He knows all the phrases, he's got the jargon down pat. If you've got the language of being smart, you'll never catch a cold or get a parking ticket or die."

"Was he in uniform?" Bill said.

"Too smart for that. He said there wouldn't be a news con-ference today. Not enough time to secure a site. He said our friend George is an interesting sort of academic. His name appears in an address book found in an apartment raided by police some-where in France—a bomb factory. And he has been photographed in the company of known terrorist leaders."

"Every killer has a spokesman."

"You're almost as smart as the colonel. He talked about you in fact. He said you ought to get on a plane and go back home. He will make arrangements."

"How does he know I'm here, or why I'm here, or who I am?"

"After the first series of threatening calls," Charlie said.

"I thought I was the unannounced presence. But you told George I was here. And now this colonel with a brush mustache."

"I had to report the names of all the people invited to the conference. Because of the phone calls. The police needed a list.

And I told George actually the day before because I thought it would help. Anything that helps."

"Why does the colonel want me to go home?"

"He says he has information that you may be in danger. He hinted that you would be worth a great deal more to the group in Beirut than the hostage they're now holding. The feeling is he's too obscure."

Bill laughed.

"The whole thing is so hard to believe I almost don't believe it."

"But of course we do believe it. We have to. It doesn't break any laws of logic or nature. It's unbelievable only in the shallowest sense. Only shallow people insist on disbelief. You and I know better. We understand how reality is invented. A person sits in a room and thinks a thought and it bleeds out into the world. Every thought is permitted. And there's no longer a moral or spatial distinction between thinking and acting."

"Poor bastard, you're beginning to sound like me."

They walked in silence. Then Charlie said something about the loveliness of the day. They chose their topics carefully, showing a deft indirectness. They needed some space in which to let the subject cool.

Then Bill said, "How do they plan to get me into a hostage situation?"

"Oh I don't know. Lure you eastward somehow. The colonel was vague here."

"We don't blame him, do we?"

"Not a bit. He said the explosive was Semtex H. A controlled amount. They could have brought down the building if they'd wanted to."

"The colonel must have enjoyed dropping that name."

"The material comes from Czechoslovakia."

"Did you know that?"

"No, I didn't."

"See how stupid we are."

"Where are you staying, Bill? We really have to know."

"I'm sure the colonel knows. Just go ahead and arrange the conference. I came here to read some poems and that's what I'm going to do."

"Nobody wants to be intimidated. But the fact is," Charlie said.

"I'm going back to my hotel. I'll call you at noon tomorrow. Get a new location and let's do what we came here to do."

"I think we ought to have dinner, the two of us. We'll talk about something else completely."

"I wonder what that might be."

"I want this book, you bastard."

People stood gathered in a rambling white space set on several levels under ducts and sprinklers and track lights, chatting over silver cocktails. The walls were hung with works of living Russians, mainly large color-brave canvases, supernation paintings, ambitious and statement-making.

Brita moved through the crowd, edging sideways, drink held high, and she felt the interplay of glances, the way eyes consume their food, taking in faces, asses, tapestry jackets, raw-silk shirts, the way bodies slant involuntarily toward a well-known figure in the room, the way people carry on one dialogue and listen to another, the way every energy is directed somewhere else, some brightness nearby, the whole shape and state and history of this little hour of truth. There seemed to be some imaginary point of major interest, a shifting middle cluster of conversation, although every person in the room retained an awareness of the street beyond the plate-glass windows. They were here, in a way, for the people in the street. They knew exactly how they appeared to those who were walking or driving by, to standees on crammed buses. They appeared to float outside the world. They were only art browsers but they appeared privileged and inviolate, transcendent souls lighted against the falling night. They shared a stillness, a way of looking sharply etched. This gave the incidental scene a claim to permanence, as if they believed they might still be here a thousand nights from now, weightless and unperspiring, stirring the small awe of passersby.

It took her a while to reach the picture that had attracted her. A silk screen on canvas measuring roughly five feet by six feet. It was called *Gorby I* and showed the Soviet President's head and boxed-off shoulders set against a background of Byzantine gold, patchy strokes, expressive and age-textured. His skin was the ruddy flush of TV makeup and he had an overlay of blond hair, red lipstick and turquoise eye shadow. His suit and tie were deep black. Brita wondered if this piece might be even more Warholish than it was supposed to be, beyond parody, homage, comment and appropriation. There were six thousand Warhol experts living within a few square miles of this gallery and all the things had been said and all the arguments made but she thought that possibly in this one picture she could detect a maximum statement about the dissolvability of the artist and the exaltation of the public figure, about how it is possible to fuse images, Mikhail Gorbachev's and Marilyn Monroe's, and to steal auras, Gold Marilyn's and Dead-White Andy's, and maybe six other things as well. Anyway it wasn't funny. She'd taken the trouble to cross the room and look closely at this funny painted layered photo-icon and it wasn't funny at all. Maybe because of the undertaker's suit that Gorby wore. And the sense that these were play-death cosmetics, the caked face-powder and lemon-yellow hair color. And the very echo of Marilyn and all the death glamour that ran through Andy's work. Brita had photographed him years ago and now one of her pictures hung in a show a few blocks down Madison Avenue. Andy's image on canvas, Masonite, velvet, paper-and-acetate, Andy in metallic paint, silk-screen ink, pencil, polymer, gold leaf, Andy in wood, metal, vinyl, cotton-and-polyester, painted bronze, Andy on postcards and paper bags, in photomosaics, multiple exposures, dye transfers, Polaroid prints. Andy's shooting scar, Andy's factory, Andy tourist-posing in Beijing before the giant portrait of Mao in the main square. He'd said to her, "The secret of being me is that I'm only half here." He was all here now, reprocessed through painted chains of being, peering out over the crowd from a pair of burnished Russian eyes.

Brita heard someone say her name. She turned and saw a young woman in a denim jacket slow-mouthing the word Hi.

"I heard the message on your machine about how you might be here around seven or eight or so."

"That was meant for my dinner date."

"Remember me?"

"Karen, isn't it?"

"What am I doing here, right?"

"I think I'm afraid to ask."

"I'm here to look for Bill," she said.

He lay in bed open-eyed in the dark. There were intestinal moans from his left side, where gas makes a hairpin turn at the splenic flexure. He felt a mass of phlegm wobbling in his throat but he didn't want to get out of bed to expel it, so he swallowed the whole nasty business, a slick syrupy glop. This was the texture of his life. If someone ever writes his true biography, it will be a chronicle of gas pains and skipped heartbeats, grinding teeth and dizzy spells and smothered breath, with detailed descriptions of Bill leaving his desk to walk to the bathroom and spit up mucus, and we see photographs of ellipsoid clots of cells, water, organic slimes, mineral salts and spotty nicotine. Or descriptions just as long and detailed of Bill staying where he is and swallowing. These were his choices, his days and nights. In the solitary life there was a tendency to collect moments that might otherwise blur into the rough jostle, the swing of a body through busy streets and rooms. He lived deeply in these cosmic-odd pauses. They clung to him. He was a sitting industry of farts and belches. This is what he did for a living, sit and hawk, mucus and flatus. He saw himself staring at the hair buried in his typewriter. He leaned above his oval tablets, hearing the grainy cut of the blade. In his sleeplessness he went down the batting order of the 1938 Cleveland Indians. This was the true man, awake with phantoms. He saw them take the field in all the roomy optimism of those old uniforms, the sun-bleached dinky mitts. The names of those ballplayers were his night prayer, his reverent petition to God, with wording that remained eternally the same. He walked down the hall to piss or spit. He stood by the window dreaming. This was the man he saw as himself. The biographer who didn't examine these things (not that there would ever be a biographer) couldn't begin to know the catchments, the odd-corner deeps of Bill's true life.

His book, smelling faintly of baby drool, was just outside the door. He heard it moan solemnly, the same grave sound that welled in his gut.

In the morning there was a knock at the door. Bill was sitting in a chair, dressed except for shoes and socks, cutting his sepia toenails. The visitor was George Haddad. Bill was only slightly surprised. He went back to the chair and resumed trimming. George stood in a bare corner with his arms folded.

"I thought we might talk," he said. "I felt we were slightly inhibited with Mr. Everson in attendance. Besides, it's difficult to have a productive dialogue with bombs going off. And one can't talk in London anyway. It's the latest language hole in the Western world."

"What do we want to talk about?"

"This young man can't be saved. I'm not even saying released. He can't be saved, his life is at risk unless we're able to work without organizational pressures and without a constant police presence."

"You said his freedom is tied to the media. Do we work without them?"

"London has failed. Everyone has a script he brings along. No one talks about ideas. I think we have to reduce the scale of this operation."

"The bomb has done that."

"Reduce it radically. You and I need to trust each other enough to start over, just the two of us, somewhere else. I live in Athens now. I'm conducting a seminar at the Hellenic-American Institute. It's very possible, although I can't actually promise, but it's possible I can arrange for you to meet the one man who can literally open the basement door and let the hostage go."

Bill said nothing. A moment passed. George sat in the chair near the window.

"There's something I wanted to ask the other evening at dinner."

"What's that?"

"Do you use a word processor?"

Bill had his right foot bent into his left hand and was working the curved blade of the scissors under an inward twist in the hard thick nail of the big toe and he paused briefly, pursing his lips and shaking his head no.

"Because I find I couldn't conceivably operate without one. Move words, paragraphs, move a hundred pages, plus instant corrections. When I prepare material for lectures, I find the machine helps me organize my thoughts, gives me a text susceptible to revision. I would think for a man who clearly reworks and refines as much as you do, a word processor would be a major blessing."

Bill shook his head no.

"Of course I've asked myself what you have to gain by traveling to Athens under circumstances that might be called—what do we want to call these circumstances, Bill?"

"Shadowy."

"I've asked myself, Why would he say yes? What does he have to gain?"

"And what's your answer?"

"You have nothing to gain. There is no guarantee of accomplishing the slightest thing. There is only risk. Any adviser would stress the possibility of personal danger."

"I'd have to buy a shirt," Bill said.

"It's possible to talk in Athens. Beneath the frantic pace there is something I find conducive to reason and calm, to a settlement of differences. Not that I think you and I have deep disagreements at the level of ideas. Just the opposite in fact. We'll have a dialogue, Bill. Unfettered. No one coming round to set guidelines or issue ultimatums. I have a terrace with a sweeping view."

Bill had breakfast with the doctors. Just before noon he packed his bag and then paused by the open door and looked back into the room to make sure he'd left nothing behind. He went down to the lobby, checked out and walked a couple of blocks to a taxi rank. Look left. Look right. He imagined Charlie standing before a mirror knotting a brilliant necktie and waiting for the phone to ring. A cab came around a corner and headed toward him, the dark surface worked to a high shine. He got in, rolled down the window and sat back. For the first time he thought about the hostage.

10

Scott was still doing lists, moving toward late May now, making lists of things that needed doing, doing the things, going along project by project, room by room. Of course the lists of things were also things. An item on a list might generate a whole new list. He knew if he wasn't careful he'd get mired in a theory of lists and lose sight of the things that needed doing. There was pleasure in lists, taut and clean. Making the list, crossing off the items as you complete the tasks. It was a small whole contentment, a way of working toward a new reality.

He knew where Karen was but not a word from son of a bitch Bill.

He went through the house, noting things that needed doing, determined to do them, bills, mail, some minor caulking and scraping, all the rearranging of papers. The point of these lists and tasks seemed to be that when you performed each task and crossed off the corresponding item on the list and when you crumpled and discarded all the lists and stood finally and self-reliantly in a list-free environment, sealed from worldly contact, you were proving to yourself that you could go on alone.

He sat at the desk in the workroom now, cleaning the typewriter. He blew on the keys, using a damp rag to lift dust and hair from the felt pad. He opened the drawer to his left, thinking of the next major item on his list, a plan to reorganize reader mail. The drawer held a couple of old wristwatches and some stamps, rubber bands, erasers and foreign coins.

Bill was not a list-making novelist. He thought sentences lost their heft and edge when they were stretched too far and he didn't seem to find the slightest primal joy in world-naming or enumerating, in penetrating the relatedness of things or words, those breathy sentences that beat with new exuberance.

Scott stood and looked at the wall charts, the blueprints of Bill's long book. In over eight years here, he'd never had so close a look. Large foxed sheets filled with mystical graffiti. Even the tape that fixed the paper to the wall was sun-stained and coming loose. These were interesting things to study, all the arrows and scribbles and pictographs, the lines that connected dissimilar elements. Something primitive and brave-natured here. At least that's how it looked to Scott, examining each sheet. Themes and characters attempting to draw together, linked in squiggles and dash trails, an obsessive need to meet and maintain. Bill's long-suffering book. And Bill's own scratchy voice in one of his clear-souled semidrunks of some years ago, saying, "Stories have no point if they don't absorb our terror."

Charles Everson was not returning calls. Not that he knew where Bill was and not that he would tell Scott even if he knew. No one knew. This was the essence of Bill's disappearance as Scott understood it. Scott understood it as a kind of simulated death.

He sat at the desk again, putting his face to the keys and blowing hard.

Bill had his picture taken not because he wanted to come out of hiding but because he wanted to hide more deeply, he wanted to revise the terms of his seclusion, he needed the crisis of exposure to give him a powerful reason to intensify his concealment. Years ago there were stories that Bill was dead, Bill was in Manitoba, Bill was living under another name, Bill would never write another word. These were the world's oldest stories and they were not about Bill so much as people's need to make mysteries and legends. Now Bill was devising his own cycle of death and resurgence. It made Scott think of great leaders who regenerate their power by dropping out of sight and then staging messianic returns. Mao Zedong of course. Mao was pronounced dead many times in the press—dead or senile or too sick to run a revolution. Scott had recently come across a photograph of Mao taken in the course of his famous nine-mile swim at the age of seventy-two, following a long disappearance. Mao's old pelt head sticking out of the Yangtze, godlike and comic.

He opened the drawer to his right and found some more foreign coins, some binder clips and lapsed driver's licenses. He knew where Karen was, blank-faced in Manhattan, all receptors working. The next major item was reader mail, how to take it out of chronological order and structure it geographically, country by country, state by state.

He put his face to the keys and blew.

He raised the front end of the typewriter and rubbed the damp cloth over the pad, lifting dust and hair.

Mao used photographs to announce his return and demonstrate his vitality, to reinspire the revolution. Bill's picture was a death notice. His image hadn't become public yet and he was already gone. This was the crucial turn he needed in order to disappear completely, even from those he'd loved and trusted all these years. He would return in his own way, living somewhere else, more remotely, in one or another kind of disguise. Scott thought the photograph might make him look older. Not older in the picture but older as himself, after the fact of the picture. The picture would be a means of transformation. It would show him how he looked to the world and give him a fixed point from which to depart. Pictures with our likeness make us choose. We travel into or away from our photographs.

He opened the middle drawer and found a narrow black brush, some stamps, some rubber bands and old lead pennies and a bottle of typewriter correction fluid.

Bill would make a return to the book. This was the essence of Bill's return. He would work on the novel with fresh energy, cut it back, gut it, strip it six ways to Sunday. He's a new man now. He has the power of a reconstructed secret. Scott imagined him hunched over a desk, working the old spare territories of the word.

He lifted the typewriter cover and cleaned the hammers with the black brush.

He put his face to the keys and blew.

Karen's life had no center with Bill on the lam. She was all drift and spin. Scott missed her in more ways than he could name. He was left with the memorized body, the ageless shape and cadence and the way she arched and twisted, dull-eyed in the near terror of this approaching thing, then all the noise descending on their last held stroke. It was broken down to matchlight in his brain. He half hated her and badly wanted her back. She was the one love, the routine astonishment, someone you could dream of as your sister and then wake to find next to you in bed, without shame or contradiction. Every time she heard a creak in the floor she thought it was an armed attack. Always on nameless alert. She used to say to him, If people knew what I was thinking they would put me away forever. But they would put us all away, he said. They have put us away. We are put away for our thoughts, one way or another. We have put ourselves away, he said. Pleasure in lists. The old black keys were smudged by years of anxious pawing. He used the damp cloth, rubbing one key at a time. There was happiness in these little fixit missions, the dignity of keeping on.

Everson was tight-lipped in his tower redoubt. Mao aswim in his river. The night before on TV Scott had seen some footage shot by a tourist in rural China and it showed strange things, it showed a Chinese Christian cult in a meeting by a river and they were in the midst of a collective ascension with young men and women walking into the river arms aloft, faltering, swirling, many swept downstream. The footage was shaky and had a quality of delirium, an abnormal subjectivity, the kind of offhand amateur fleetness that was hard to trust, but they used slow motion and stop-action and they circled floating heads and then they ran it all from the start, people dressed mainly in white marching into the river in sets of two and three, arms still flying as the heads disappeared. And Karen not here to see it. A bonanza for our gal Karen. And Karen drifting and spinning. He looked at the wall charts. He could arrange the reader mail geographically or maybe book by book, although there was a great deal of mail that referred to both books or neither book, the philosophical mail, the stories of writerly desire, the verities and nullities. Bill was hiding from his photograph. He'd engineered the whole damn thing the same damn way he developed impressionistic ailments that he could then control with medication.

He put his face to the keys and blew.

He opened the lower righthand drawer, the deep compartment designed for files, and he saw some old passports, old bank books, he saw some postcards from daughter Liz.

Bill's return would not be complete without Scott, of course. When the time was right Bill would contact him. A phone call, a few terse instructions. Scott would deal with the house and furnishings, all the legalities of selling and closing, and he would spend many days packing manuscripts and books and shipping them to Bill and would then work out the final quiet arrangements and do the last little things and drive off in the long night to join Bill and make their new beginning.

There was a packet of letters from Bill's sister. He knew Bill had grown up with an older sister in various places in the Midwest and the Great Plains but the most recent of the letters was eleven years old, so maybe she was dead. He found Bill's army discharge papers and some insurance policies and a document labeled Notification of Birth Registration. This piece of paper advised that there was a record of birth preserved in the state office for the registration of vital statistics, Des Moines, Iowa. Near the bottom of the page was a seal marked Department of Commerce. The date on the document corresponded to Bill's date of birth, which Scott had seen many times on records and forms, and the name of the child was Willard Skansey Jr.

He put his face to the keys and blew.

He moved the typewriter and other objects to the radiator cover and ran the damp cloth over the desktop.

He took a closer look at the army discharge and saw the same name that appeared on the birth registration.

Bill was not an autobiographical novelist. You could not glean the makings of a life-shape by searching his work for clues. His sap and marrow, his soul's sharp argument might be slapped across a random page, sentence by sentence, but nowhere a word of his beginnings or places he has lived or what kind of man his father might have been.

He put the typewriter back on the desk.

A bank robber's name. Or a tough welterweight of the 1930s with his hair parted in the middle. A bank robber lying low between jobs.

He read some of the letters. He read the postcards from Liz, he looked at the photographs in the canceled passports and read the place names stamped on the old pages, thick and web-engraved. He read the rest of the letters from sister Clair, moving the chair nearer the window as dusk fell, ordinary news of weather and children and croup, pale-blue ink on lined paper.

There's so much paper in this house.

Then he turned on the lamp and went to work on his lists until it was time for dinner.

She talked to the woman who lived in a plastic bag half a block from Brita's building. This person knew some things about bundling and tying. Survival means you learn how to narrow the space you take up for fear of arousing antagonistic interest and it also means you hide what you own inside something else so that you may seem to possess one chief thing when it is really many things bundled and tied and placed inside each other, a secret universe of things, unwhisperable, plastic bags inside plastic bags, and the woman is somewhere in there too, bagged with her possessions. Karen talked to her about what she ate, did she have a hot meal ever, was there something she needed that I can get for you. Practical talk. The woman looked out at her, dark-eyed and sooty, barely ever responding, showing the soot that deepens into the face and becomes the texture of the person.

It is hard to find a language for unfortunates. One word out of place and their eyes call up a void.

She saw a man weaving through the subway saying, "I have holes in my sides." Not even asking for money or shaking a plastic cup. Just going car to car in that firm-footed pace you learn to adopt in the subway even if you are broken-bodied. She tried to read the Spanish directions about what to do in an emergency. "I have holes in my sides." There must be something about the tunnels and crypts of the city that makes people think they are Jesus.

Uptown there were schoolboys wearing ties as headbands. They widened the neck part to fit around the forehead with the knot near the right ear and the main part drooping over the shoulder. Shooting with their schoolbags. In other words lifting the schoolbag to the hip Uzi-style and spraying imaginary fire with their lips pushed out. Only Catholic boys wore uniforms back home. She remembered nuns in station wagons and how she walked among them at a football game. They were in black and white, she was in color.

There were water-main breaks and steam-pipe explosions, asbestos flying everywhere, mud propelled from caved-in pavement, and people stood around saying, "It's just like Beirut, it looks like Beirut."

On the bus you have to push a narrow tape to signal for a stop. English on the buses, Spanish on the subways. Bring hurry-up time to all man.

The saxophonist in white sneakers played in a deep crouch, leaning forward on his toes, knees bent high, the low-slung metal nearly scraping the pavement, buses, cars, trucks, there are magazines for sale on the sidewalk, totally old copies of Life and Look, the generosity of those old covers, the way they seem a pity and a consolation, forgiving us the years between, and the saxman shuts his eyes, nodding to the sounds.

In the loft she looked at a photograph of refugees in a camp, the whole picture out to the edges nothing but boys crowded together, most of them waving urgently, pale palms showing, all looking in the same direction, bareheaded boys, black faces, palms that catch the glare, and you know there are thousands more outside the edges of the picture but in the midst of the visible hundreds who are jammed and pushed together waving, this suffocating picture of massed boys, she noticed a single worried adult, one man's head showing at upper right, and he is wearing a knit cap and has his hand near his forehead possibly shielding his eyes from the glare and all the boys are looking in the general direction of the camera and he is standing diagonally and peering over the heads and across the frame and out of the picture. He does not look like an official or a leader. He is part of the mass but lost there, stuck there on the page that is filled with waving boys, and nowhere in the picture is there a glimpse of ground or sky or horizon, it is only heads and hands, and she wondered if the waving was for food, throw the food, all those grimacing boys looking at the camera. Are there truckloads of food on the other side of the camera or is it just the camera they're waving at, the camera that shows them an opening to the food? A person comes with a camera and they think it means food. And the lost-looking man whose mind is not on the food or the camera but on the crowd, how he might escape before they trample him.

Brita said, "And I don't mind your staying for a while. But we both know I have to kick you out one of these days and it's going to be sooner rather than later. And I'm telling you there is no Bill to be found around here."

"I'm not looking for him face by face in the street. I just need this time away from Scott. I'm looking for Bill kind of in my mind, to think where he might be."

"And you and Scott."

"I really love Scott in most of the ways that count. God that sounds awful. Forget I said that. We just stopped talking the way we used to. We actually lacked the strength to talk to each other. We silently agreed we are going to let this get as bad as it can get and then see what happens. It was a question of willfully let it fester. All alone in Bill's house. And these are two people who had a constant daily plan for getting things done. Who used to totally talk."

Brita went away to take pictures of writers and left the keys and some money. She gave Karen oral and written instructions for feeding the cat and working the locks and the alarm system and she left phone numbers and dates—San Francisco, Tokyo and Seoul.

She felt the warning aura in the street, the sense that she was glowing, cars and people glowing, the electric shiver down her arm and then the full truth of the pain, the pain in full surround, streaming from the neurons, a brain trail so deep it might crack the skin. She could not see for a number of seconds, maybe half a minute, or could see only glow, intense white shadow, and she stood dizzily where she was and waited for the street to reappear so she might walk out of the glow and come into objects and surfaces and the words that we attach to them.

She took a taxi back to the building. She began taking taxis here and there, yellow cabs driven by fantastically named men from Haiti, Iran, Sri Lanka, the Yemen—names so wondrous she couldn't always tell whether they were printed last name first or in the normal sequence. Karen talked to them. She was loose in the city of overflowing faces and needed to find ways to tell them apart. One man said he was from the Yemen and she tried to imagine where that might be. She talked to Sikhs and Egyptians, calling through the partition or putting her mouth to the cash slot, asking family questions or what about religious practices, did they pray facing east.

She saw pictures of missing children on shopping bags and milk cartons, on posters stuck to building walls, and then you hear about women who give away babies, leave babies in the trash. She came upon this park, saw it from a cab. She saw the normative life of the planet, businesspeople crossing streets beneath the glass towers, the life of sitting on buses that take you logically to destinations, the unnerved surface of rolling plausibly along. Saw sleeping bodies in the tunnels and ramps, heads hidden, sooty feet, tightly bundled objects clutched to the knees.

Sony, Mita, Kirin, Magno, Midori.

She saw these soot-faced people pushing shopping carts filled with bundled things and she thought they were like holy pilgrims marching on endlessly but possibly thinking more and more about how to get through the next ten minutes, their priorities now revealed to them, and never mind Jerusalem.

She began to form pictures of people falling in the street. She'd see a man just walking and then he had a cut head or whatnot, getting up dazed. Or see a man stepping off the curb and form a picture of a car that's bearing down and then he's in the street all bloodied up.

She came upon this park. It was something you come upon and then stop in your tracks. A tent city. Huts and shacks, she was thinking of the word; lean-tos; blue plastic sheeting covering the lean-tos and the networks of boxes and shipping containers that people lived in. A refugee camp or the rattiest edge of some dusty township. There was a bandshell with bedding on the stage, a few bodies stirring, a lump of inert bedding suddenly wriggling upward and there's a man on his knees coughing up blood. She walked in a kind of straight-legged bobbing way as if to mock her own shy curiosity or conceal her awe. Stringy blood looping from his mouth. There were bodies shrouded on benches, bedding set out to dry on the fence of the children's pool. And the makeshift shelters draped in blue, the box huts, the charcoal stoves and shaving mirrors, smoke rising from fires set in oil drums. It was a world apart but powerfully here, a set of milling images with breath and flesh and a language everywhere that sounded like multilingual English, like English in grabs and swoops, broken up and cooked. People in stages of rag-wearing, some less badly equipped, belongings bundled in milk crates and shopping carts. She saw a man sitting in a collapsed armchair outside his shipping box and he resembled a sketch of an ordinary homeowner on a shady street before the picture is fully drawn. He talked to himself in an everyday voice, a man with some education, with a history of possessions and relations, this was clear to her. Talking intelligently to himself, making sense, and when he saw Karen standing there he shifted his remarks directly to her as if they'd been having this conversation all along. And from the spot where she stood now, a distance from the bandshell, she could see more bodies stirring, hear the coughing, and she realized the whole deep stage was spread with bedding and there were people moving everywhere, a slowly spreading ripple and moan, or not moving, or lying completely still, half forms, beating hearts, faces and names.

She had to walk slowly to accommodate her awe. She went home to feed the cat but returned right away, taking a Jamaican taxi and saying Tompkins Square. It might be ten-plus acres with pigeons walking everywhere but not a single one aloft and even when she tried to kick-scatter several birds they only scurried away at best, not so much as flapping a fitful wing. People in clusters and larger groups, tending toward evening. Somebody cooked meat on a skewer and there was a fight not far away, a man and woman pushing an older man, backing him up, and he slapped at their hands and did a scat step, turning, and fell down hard. The whole thing absorbed into the background. Things fading all the time, hard to retain. A police minicab came by like some Bombay cartoon.

When night came down she was talking to a tall kid wearing a sweatshirt with Coke bottles pictured across the front, row after row. He was selling marijuana at the edge of the park, going, *Grass grass grass grass*. His voice got lower as he went through the chant, ending in a kitty-cat hiss. People walking by said Omar. He had a long face, sloped forehead and shallow chin and his tightly webbed hair was so close to the scalp and so clearly defined and widely parted it had a maplike contrast and precision.

The fallen man was still down, trying to get something out of his back pocket. An old white came by wearing a rag coat and baseball cap and high sneakers and the two men fell into conversation.

Omar said, "But sometimes you get an EDP and the police come with stun guns and blinding lights."

"All the paraphernalia."

"They have a gun that shoots fifty thousand volts. Be surprised how sometimes it only slows the guy down. Shoot him again, gets up again. It's your adrenaline."

"What's an EDP?"

"Motionally disturb person. People taking meth and cocaine is what could do it to you. It's your adrenaline and your temperature both. Call it getting high is the absolute truth."

On the bandshell stage people were still getting up, going to sleep, they were sitting there staring, they were zippering sleeping bags and smoking cigarettes and there was a constant rolling drone, statements and set responses that made Karen think of formal prayers, a protocol of half words, dream cries, bursts and murmurs. One voice answered by another, the gasping stab for breath followed by the curse. Fragments of an American flag were fixed to the blue plastic of a sagging lean-to. A man and woman sat under a beach umbrella. A woman peeled an orange. A man slept face down on a bench, shirtless, with Bill's exact hair color and shoulders and back.

She heard Omar going, *Dime bag dime bag dime bag.*

Someone crawled out of a box and got up shaky and walked after her, begging, rough-tailing, a mean slur in his voice, and she felt for the first time since coming here that they could *see* her, that she wasn't concealed by the desperation of the place. This wasn't a public park but some life-and-death terrain where everything is measured for its worth. She realized they *saw* her. This was a shock. She gave the man a dollar, which he stopped and studied, which he looked at resentfully, talking to himself in the shadows.

She heard a voice beyond the fence, a woman saying clearly, "What a lovely spring night," and it startled Karen, the speaker's animation and delight, the distance traveled in a scatter of simple words.

She wondered what if the man hadn't stopped coming after her when she gave him the dollar. She wondered what if there was no special sum that might have kept him away.

Omar told her, "Once you live in the street, there's nothing but the street. Know what I'm saying. These people have one thing they can talk about or think about and that's the little shithole they live in. The littler the shithole, the more it takes up your life. Know what I'm saying. You live in a fuckin' ass mansion you got to think about it two times a month for like ten seconds total. Live in a shithole, it takes up your day. They cut the shithole in half, you got to go twice as hard to keep it so it's livable. I'm telling you something I observe."

She imagined the encrumpled bodies in the lean-tos and tents, sort of formless as to male or female, asleep in sodden clothes on a strip of cardboard or some dragged-in mattress stained with the waste of the ages.

She looked around for Omar but he was gone.

All the odd belongings bundled in a corner, wrapped and tied, many things concealed as one, things inside other things, some infinite collapsible system of getting through a life. She walked through the park, east to west, hearing the rustle and mutter of dreaming souls.

In the morning she began to forage for redeemable bottles and cans, anything she could find in trash baskets or curbside, in garbage bags massed in restaurant alleyways. Bottles, matchbooks, swayback shoes, whatever usable cultural deposit might be shut away in the dark. She took these things to the park and left them at the openings of lean-tos or stuck them just inside if she was sure no one was there. She slipped into those stinking alleyways and undid the twists on garbage bags and dumped out the garbage and took the bags. It was not a whole lot different from selling sweet williams in the lobby of the Marriott. She stood on garbage cans and went through dumpsters at demolition sites, salvaging plasterboard and nails, strips of plywood. Bottles and cans were her main mission, things that could be turned into money.

A man showed her his mutilated arm and asked for spare change. She found broken umbrellas, bruised fruit that was edible when washed. She washed the fruit and took it to the park. She took everything to the park. She placed things inside the huts. She saw people turning park benches into homes with walls and tilted roofs. Someone vomited loudly against the side of the maintenance building and she saw the parks department man in his khaki trappings walk by with nary a glance. A routine spatter of greensick sliding down a wall. She watched the people in the bandshell struggle out of their bedding, humped and gasping, looking up dazed into the span of light and sky that hung above the blue encampment.

Only those sealed by the messiah will survive.

II

Bill stood outside a shop that sold religious articles. Many
medallion images of sacred figures with shiny disks behind their heads. They've got their game together here,
he thought. Name many saints, get them in the windows, do
not stint on halos, crosses, shields or swords. The priests were
damn impressive too. He saw them everywhere, round-hatted
and intensely bearded, wrapped in floating robes. Sturdy men
every one. Even the elderly were healthy-looking. Bill thought
they were deathless in a way, fixed to national memory, great
black ships of faith and superstition.

In his room he thought about the hostage. He tried to put
himself there, in the heat and pain, outside the nuance of civ-
ilized anxiety. He wanted to imagine what it was like to know
extremes of isolation. Solitude by the gun. He read Jean-Claude's
poems many times. The man remained invisibly Swiss. Bill tried
to see his face, hair, eye color, he saw room color, faded paint
on the walls. He pictured precise objects, he made them briefly
shine with immanence, a bowl for food, a spoon constructed out
of thought, perception, memory, feeling, will and imagination.

Then he went to see George Haddad.

"What are you drinking, Bill?"

"A small quantity of the local brandy poured gently into a short
glass."

"What do we want to talk about today?"

"Semtex H."

"I can tell you I had nothing to do with setting off the explosive in that building."

"But you know who did it."

"I'm one man. I deal in concepts. This business of hostages is rife with factional complexity. Don't assume I know important things. I know very little in fact."

"But you have relationships with people who know a great deal."

"Special Branch would say so."

"And someone thought it might be interesting to look more carefully at the available writers."

George looked up. He wore a wrinkled white shirt with the collar open and the sleeves rolled up, an undershirt visible beneath the sheer material. Bill watched him take a walk around the room and come back to his scotch and soda.

"It was just in the talking stage," he said finally. "One man released in Beirut, another taken in London. Instantaneous worldwide attention. But it was thought the British would be quick to act if they found out where you were being held. Unacceptable danger. For the hostage-takers and for you."

"Don't look so sad," Bill said.

"Your safety was foremost in mind. And your release would have come in a matter of days. These things were discussed at a certain level, hastily. I admit it."

"Then the bomb went off. The more I think about it, the more sense it makes. I didn't expect an explosion. But the second it happened I stood in the blast and it seemed completely logical. It seemed legitimate and well argued. From the beginning there was something in this situation that spoke to me directly. Beyond a poetry reading to lend aid to a fellow writer. When Charlie finished explaining, I felt a recognition. Then again in London.

I knew who you were before we were introduced. I picked that speck of glass out of my hand and I felt it had been there all my life."

"No one knew you would be anywhere near that building."

"Don't look so sad."

"I'm in a very delicate position," George said. "I want it to end here, you see. We gather a few press people, you make a statement supporting the movement, the hostage is freed, we all shake hands. Provided I'm able to convince you that the movement is worth supporting."

"But that's not your major problem, is it?"

"Actually no."

"You're getting pressure from Beirut. They don't want it to end here."

"They may yet come round to my way of thinking. He comes to Athens, meets you, speaks to the press. It appeals to my sense of correspondence, of spiritual kinship. Two underground figures. Men of the same measure in a way."

There was a rattling at the door and George's wife and teenage daughter came in. Bill stood partway up for introductions. There was a moment of nods and shy smiles and then they were gone down the hall.

"He calls himself Abu Rashid. I honestly think you'd be fascinated by the man."

"Isn't it always the case?"

"And I'm still hopeful he'll turn up here."

"But in the meantime."

"We're here to talk."

"To have a dialogue."

"Exactly," George said.

"For some time now I've had the feeling that novelists and terrorists are playing a zero-sum game."

"Interesting. How so?"

"What terrorists gain, novelists lose. The degree to which they influence mass consciousness is the extent of our decline as shapers of sensibility and thought. The danger they represent equals our own failure to be dangerous."

"And the more clearly we see terror, the less impact we feel from art."

"I think the relationship is intimate and precise insofar as such things can be measured."

"Very nice indeed."

"You think so?"

"Completely marvelous."

"Beckett is the last writer to shape the way we think and see. After him, the major work involves midair explosions and crumbled buildings. This is the new tragic narrative."

"And it's difficult when they kill and maim because you see them, honestly now, as the only possible heroes for our time."

"No," Bill said.

"The way they live in the shadows, live willingly with death. The way they hate many of the things you hate. Their discipline and cunning. The coherence of their lives. The way they excite, they *excite* admiration. In societies reduced to blur and glut, terror is the only meaningful act. There's too much everything, more things and messages and meanings than we can use in ten thousand lifetimes. Inertia-hysteria. Is history possible? Is anyone serious? Who do we take seriously? Only the lethal believer, the person who kills and dies for faith. Everything else is absorbed. The artist is absorbed, the madman in the street is absorbed and processed and incorporated. Give him a dollar, put him in a TV commercial. Only the terrorist stands outside. The culture hasn't figured out how to assimilate him. It's confusing when they kill the innocent. But this is precisely the language of being noticed, the only language the West understands. The way they determine how we see them. The way they dominate the rush of endless streaming images. I said in London, Bill. It's the novelist who understands the secret life, the rage that underlies all obscurity and neglect. You're half murderers, most of you."

He found the thought happy and attractive and he smiled through Bill's hand-wagging and the motion of his shaking head.

"No. It's pure myth, the terrorist as solitary outlaw. These groups are backed by repressive governments. They're perfect little totalitarian states. They carry the old wild-eyed vision, total destruction and total order."

"Terror is the force that begins with a handful of people in a back room. Do they stress discipline? Are they implacable in their will? Of course. I think you have to take sides. Don't comfort yourself with safe arguments. Take up the case of the downtrodden, the spat-upon. Do these people feel a yearning for order? Who will give it to them? Think of Chairman Mao. Order is consistent with permanent revolution."

"Think of fifty million Red Guards."

"Children actually, Bill. It was about faith. Luminous, sometimes stupid, sometimes cruel. Look today. Young boys everywhere posing with assault rifles. The young have a cruelty and unyieldingness that's fully formed. I said in London. The more heartless, the more visible."

"And the harder it becomes to defend a thing, the more you relish your position. Another kind of unyielding."

They had another drink, sitting crouched, face to face, with motorcycles going by in the brassy street.

"Is it a little Maoist band you're speaking for, George?"

"It's an idea. It's a picture of Lebanon without the Syrians, Palestinians and Israelis, without the Iranian volunteers, the religious wars. We need a model that transcends all the bitter history. Something enormous and commanding. A figure of absolute being. This is crucial, Bill. In societies struggling to remake themselves, total politics, total authority, total being."

"Even if I could see the need for absolute authority, my work would draw me away. The experience of my own consciousness tells me how autocracy fails, how total control wrecks the spirit, how my characters deny my efforts to own them completely, how I need internal dissent, self-argument, how the world squashes me the minute I think it's mine."

He shook out a match and held it.

"Do you know why I believe in the novel? It's a democratic shout. Anybody can write a great novel, one great novel, almost any amateur off the street. I believe this, George. Some nameless drudge, some desperado with barely a nurtured dream can sit down and find his voice and luck out and do it. Something so angelic it makes your jaw hang open. The spray of talent, the spray of ideas. One thing unlike another, one voice unlike the next. Ambiguities, contradictions, whispers, hints. And this is what you want to destroy."

He found he was angry, unexpectedly.

"And when the novelist loses his talent, he dies democratically, there it is for everyone to see, wide open to the world, the shitpile of hopeless prose."

There was no more medication. Ingested and absorbed. He decided so what, don't need it anymore, and he didn't bother finding out what was available over the counter in the pharmacy near the hotel. He wondered if he could get away with charging hotel and meals to Charlie's conglomerate even though he'd severed connections. It was for the good of mankind after all.

You have to climb hills to get a drink.

He kept an eye out for priests and spent half a minute in an ancient church so small it was wedged between columns of a modern tower, a one-man refuge from the rumble of time, candles burning in the cool gloom.

He was often lost. He got lost in the hotel every time he walked out of his room and turned left to get to the elevator, which was consistently to the right. Once he forgot what city he was in and saw an honor guard of four men marching toward him on the sidewalk, going from their guard duty to their barracks, and they carried rifles with fixed bayonets and wore embroidered tunics, pleated skirts and pompom slippers and he knew he wasn't in Milwaukee.

He climbed a hill to a taverna and ordered by pointing at dishes on three other tables. It wasn't that no one spoke English. He forgot they did or preferred not to speak himself. Maybe he liked the idea of pointing. You could get to depend on pointing as a kind of self-enforced loneliness that helps you advance in moral rigor. And he was near the point where he wanted to eliminate things that no longer mattered, things that still mattered, all excess and all necessity, and why not begin with words.

But he tried to write about the hostage. It was the only way he knew to think deeply in a subject. He missed his typewriter for the first time since leaving home. It was the hand tool of memory and patient thought, the mark-making thing that contained his life experience. He could see the words better in type, construct sentences that entered the character-world at once, free of his own disfiguring hand. He had to settle for pencil and pad, working in his hotel room through the long mornings, slowly building chains of thought, letting the words lead him into that basement room.

Find the places where you converge with him.

Read his poems again.

See his face and hands in words.

The foam mat he lives on is one deep stain, a lifetime's convincing stink. The air is dead and swarms with particles, plaster dust lifted off the walls when the shelling is intense. He tastes the air, he feels it settle in his eyes and ears. They forget to untie his wrist from the water pipe and he can't get to the toilet to urinate. The ache in his kidneys is time-binding, it beats with time, it speaks of the ways in which time contrives to pass ever slower. The person they send to feed him is not allowed to talk.

Who do they send? What does he wear?

The prisoner perceives his own wan image in the world and knows he's been granted the low-status sainthood of people whose suffering makes everyone ashamed.

Keep it simple, Bill.

George cranked open the wooden shutters. Light and noise filled the room and Bill poured another drink. He realized he'd been clear of symptoms ever since he stopped gobbling pills.

"I'm still convinced you ought to get one. Instant corrections," George said. "The text is lightweight, malleable. It doesn't restrict or inhibit. If you're having any trouble with the book you're doing, a word processor can make a vast difference."

"Is your man coming here or not?"

"I'm doing what I can."

"Because I can talk to him there as well as here. Doesn't matter to me."

"Trust me. It matters."

"You put a man in a room and lock the door. There's something serenely pure here. Let's destroy the mind that makes words and sentences."

"I have to remind you. There are different ways in which words are sacred. The precious line of poetry often sits in ignorance of conditions surrounding it. Poor people, young people, anything can be written on them. Mao said this. And he wrote and he wrote. He became the history of China written on the masses. And his words became immortal. Studied, repeated, memorized by an entire nation."

"Incantations. People chanting formulas and slogans."

"In Mao's China a man walking along with a book in his hand was not seeking pleasure or distraction. He was binding himself to all Chinese. What book? Mao's book. The Little Red Book of Quotations. The book was the faith that people carried everywhere. They recited from it, brandished it, they displayed it constantly. People undoubtedly made love with the book in their hands."

"Bad sex. Rote, rote, rote."

"Of course. I'm surprised to hear you offer these trite responses. Of course rote. We memorize works that serve as guides to conducting a struggle. In committing a work to memory we make it safe from decay. It stands untouched. Children memorize parts of stories their parents tell them. They want the same story again and again. Don't change a word or they get terribly upset. This is the unchanged narrative every culture needs in order to survive. In China the narrative belonged to Mao. People memorized it and recited it to assert the destiny of their revolution. So the experience of Mao became uncorruptible by outside forces. It became the living memory of hundreds of millions of people. The cult of Mao was the cult of the book. It was a call to unity, a summoning of crowds where everyone dressed alike and thought alike. Don't you see the beauty in this? Isn't there beauty and power in the repetition of certain words and phrases? You go into a room to read a book. These people came out of their rooms. They became a book-waving crowd. Mao said, 'Our god is none other than the masses of the Chinese people.' And this is what you fear, that history is passing into the hands of the crowd."

"I'm not a great big visionary, George. I'm a sentence-maker, like a donut-maker only slower. Don't talk to me about history."

"Mao was a poet, a classless man dependent on the masses in important ways but also an absolute being. Bill the sentence-maker. I can see you living there actually, wearing the wide cotton trousers, the cotton shirt, riding the bicycle, living in one small room. You could have been a Maoist, Bill. You would have done it better than I. I've read your books carefully and we've spent many hours talking and I can easily see you blending into that great mass of blue-and-white cotton. You would have written what the culture needed in order to see itself. And you would have seen the need for an absolute being, a way out of weakness and confusion. This is what I want to see reborn in the rat warrens of Beirut."

George's wife came in with coffee and sweets on a tray.

"The question you have to ask is, How many dead? How many dead during the Cultural Revolution? How many dead after the Great Leap Forward? And how well did he hide his dead? This is the other question. What do these men do with the millions they kill?"

"The killing is going to happen. Mass killing asserts itself always. Great death, unnumbered dead, this is never more than a question of time and place. The leader only interprets the forces."

"The point of every closed state is now you know how to hide your dead. This is the setup. You predict many dead if your vision of the truth isn't realized. Then you kill them. Then you hide the fact of the killing and the bodies themselves. This is why the closed state was invented. And it begins with a single hostage, doesn't it? The hostage is the miniaturized form. The first tentative rehearsal for mass terror."

"Some coffee," George said.

Bill looked up to thank the woman but she was gone. They heard a series of noises in the distance, small blowy sounds gathered in the wind. George stood and listened carefully. Four more soft thuds. He went out to the balcony for a moment and when he came back he said these were small explosive charges that a local left-wing group attached to the unoccupied cars of diplomats and foreign businessmen. They liked to do ten or twelve cars at a time. It was the music of parked cars.

He sat down and looked closely at Bill.

"Eat something."

"Maybe later. Looks good."

"Why are you still here? Don't you have work to do back home? Don't you miss your work?"

"We don't talk about that."

"Drink your coffee. There's a new model that Panasonic makes and I absolutely swear by it. It's completely liberating. You don't deal with heavy settled artifacts. You transform freely, fling words back and forth."

Bill laughed in a certain way.

"Look. What happens if I go to Beirut and complete this spiritual union you find so interesting? Talk to Rashid. Can I expect him to release the hostage? And what will he want in return?"

"He'll want you to take the other man's place."

"Gain the maximum attention. Then release me at the most advantageous time."

"Gain the maximum attention. Then probably kill you ten minutes later. Then photograph your corpse and keep the picture handy for the time when it can be used most effectively."

"Doesn't he think I'm worth more than my photograph?"

"The Syrians are doing sweeps of the southern suburbs, looking for hostages. Hostages have to be moved all the time. Rashid frankly can't be bothered."

"And what happens if I get on a plane right now and go home?"

"They kill the hostage."

"And photograph *his* corpse."

"It's better than nothing," George said.

■ ■ ■

Brita watched the in-flight movie and listened to some brawling jazz on the earphones. The movie seemed subjective, slightly distracted, the screen suspended in partial darkness and specked and blotched by occasional turbulence and the sound track strictly optional. She thought movies on planes were different for everybody, little floating memories of earth. She had a magazine on her food tray with a soft drink and peanuts and she flipped pages without bothering to look at them. A man across the aisle talked on the telephone, his voice leaking into her brain with the bass line and drums, all America unreeling below.

She was thinking that she'd let Karen stay in her apartment and look after her cat and she didn't even know the girl's last name.

She was thinking that everything that came into her mind lately and developed as a perception seemed at once to enter the culture, to become a painting or photograph or hairstyle or slogan. She saw the dumbest details of her private thoughts on postcards or billboards. She saw the names of writers she was scheduled to photograph, saw them in newspapers and magazines, obscure people climbing into print as if she carried some contagious glow out around the world. In Tokyo she saw a painting reproduced in an art journal and it was called *Skyscraper III*, a paneled canvas showing the World Trade Center at precisely the angle she saw it from her window and in the same dark spirit. These were her towers, standing windowless, two black latex slabs that consumed the available space.

The man on the phone was saying, "One o'clock your time tomorrow."

Interesting. Brita had a one o'clock appointment the next day with a magazine editor who'd been pressing her for a meeting and she suspected that he'd heard about a certain set of pictures.

She was thinking that she would have to develop those rolls of film. But it troubled her, the memory of Bill's face in the last stages of the morning. There was some terrible brightness in the eye. She'd never seen a man lapse so wholly into his own earliest pain. She thought there were lives that constantly fell inward, back to first knowing, back to bewilderment, and this was the reference for every bleakness that passed across the door.

An attendant took her empty cup.

She was thinking that she felt guilty about Scott. It was a case of misdirected sex, wasn't it, and all the time they were together she was the woman naked from the bath looking down at the writer chopping wood. Strange how images come between the physical selves. It made her sad for Scott. She tried to call him once, looking at upstate maps and making an effort to remember road signs and finally calling information in several counties. But there was no Scott Martineau listed or unlisted and Bill Gray did not exist at any level and Karen had no last name.

The face on the screen belonged to an actor who lived in her building. He owed her a hundred and fifty dollars and three bottles of wine and she realized for the first time that she'd never get paid, seeing his face in the half light, with jazz racing in her brain.

She was thinking that one of the writers she'd tried to photograph in Seoul had nine years left in his sentence for subversion, arson and acting like a communist. They wouldn't let her see him and she became angry and cursed the bastards. Shameless artistic ego, all wrong, but she thought it was important to get his face on a strip of film, see his likeness rise to the ruby light in the printing room seven thousand miles from his cell.

She'd entrusted her home, her work, her wine and her cat to a ghost girl.

The child at the end of the row raised the shade and she was thinking that she didn't want to look at the magazine in front of her because she might see something from her life in there. She was strapped in, sealed, five miles aloft, and the world was so intimate that she was everywhere in it.

He stepped off the curbstone and took about seven strides and when he heard the car braking he had time to take one step in reverse and turn his head. He saw worry beads dangling from the rearview mirror of a car coming the other way and then the first car hit him. He walked sideways in a burlesque quickstep, arms pumping, and went down hard, striking his left shoulder and the side of his face. He tried to get up almost at once. People came to help him, a small crowd collecting. Already there was a clamor of blowing horns. He got to his knees, feeling stupid, holding up a hand in reassurance. Someone lifted him under the shoulder and he stood up nodding. He dusted off his clothes, feeling his left hand burn but refusing to look just yet. He smiled tightly at the faces, watching them recede. Then he turned and went back to the sidewalk and looked for a place to sit. People walked around him and the sun beat down. He closed his eyes and faced up into it. Traffic was moving now but in the distance they still leaned on their horns, raising a wail, a lingering midday awe. The sun was a mercy on his face.

There was something at stake in these sentences he wrote about the basement room. They held a pause, an anxious space he began to recognize. There's a danger in a sentence when it comes out right, a sense that these words almost did not make it to the page. He forgot to shave or leave his clothes in the laundry bag for the maid or he left his clothes but did not fill out the itemized slip. He came back to the room and looked at his clothes in the plastic bag and wondered whether they were clean or dirty. He took them out and held them to the light and saw bloodstains here and there and put them back in the bag to await the disposition of the maid. The work had a stunned edge, a kind of whiteness. He put antiseptic cream on his scraped hand and took warm baths to ease the scattered aches. Even if he'd remembered to shave, he could have done only half his face. A crescent stain extended from his left eye to his jaw and it was shiny and ripe and looked impressively living. He smoked and wrote, thinking he might never get it right but feeling something familiar, some-thing fallen into jeopardy, a law of language or nature, and he thought he could trace it line by line, the shattery tension, the thing he'd lost in the sand of his endless novel.

He learned how to pronounce the word Metaxa, with the accent on the last syllable, and the harsh taste of the brandy began to make sense.

In London there were doctors nearby when he ate breakfast. Here he had priests buying apples in the market. He went into a church in the Plaka and saw a curious set of metal emblems strung beneath an icon of some armor-clad saint. The objects depicted body parts mainly but there were soldiers and sailors embossed on some of the badges, there were naked babies and Volkswagens, there were houses, cows and donkeys. Bill decided these things were votive tokens. If you had an ear infection or heart trouble you requested supernatural aid by buying a ready-made emblem with a heart on it or an ear or a breast, they had breasts, Bill saw, if you had cancer, and then you simply placed the thing near the appropriate saint. The idea extended to a thousand conditions or calamities that might strike your loved ones or your possessions and it made good sense in principle, it made your appeal specific and dynamic, it inspired a democracy of icons, but he thought he might like to go into a shop and buy a token for the whole man and hang it near the appropriate saint. They had saints for everything from smallpox to animal attacks but he doubted there was a patron of the whole man, body, soul and self, and he also had a peculiar twinge deep in his right side,

a pang he liked to call it, that he doubted they'd found a saint
for, or designed a medal he might buy in a store.

George said, "We have to see a doctor, don't we?"

"It's all right."

"But your face. Don't we have to see a doctor for this? Let me
call."

"It's healing normally. Gets better every day."

"Did you get the driver's name?"

"I don't want his name."

"He hit you, Bill."

"It wasn't his fault."

"Let me call someone. You should report this. Don't we have
to talk to someone for a thing like this?"

"Get me a drink, George."

They talked into early evening. Then they sat on the terrace
watching the streetlights come on, a thousand cars a minute
racing toward the gulf in tailing red streamers, the mortal sadness
of an ordinary dusk. George's daughter came out and slouched
against the rail, an unhappy girl in jeans.

"I worry about you, Bill."

"Do me a favor. Don't."

"Why have you involved yourself in this?"

"It was your idea."

"But you've come along so readily."

"True enough."

"Let me call someone for your face. Jasmine, get the little
book with the phone numbers."

"It's late. I'll see a doctor in the morning."

"This is a promise," George said.

"Yes."

"And it won't be in Beirut. The airport is closed again due to
heavy fighting. I've been in touch with Rashid. He could arrange
to get out by boat and then fly here from Cyprus but now sea

travel is also very dangerous and I don't think he wants to come here anyway. This is deeply disappointing. I was looking forward to working with you on this."

"And Jean-Claude?"

"Who is that?"

"That's the hostage, George."

"Don't tell me his name."

"You know his name."

"Slipped my mind. Forgotten. Gone forever."

The girl stood behind her father, hands on his shoulders, softly, miserably massaging.

"How will they kill him?"

"Go home, Bill, and do your work. I enjoy these talks but there's no longer any reason for you to be here. And think about what I told you. A word processor. The keyboard action is effortless. I promise you. This is something you dearly need."

He went to his room and tried to get some sleep. There was a line he kept repeating to himself that had the mystery and power he'd felt nowhere else but in the shared past of people who had loved each other, who lived so close they'd memorized each other's warts and cowlicks and addled pauses, so the line was not one voice but several and it spoke a more or less nonsensical theme, it was a line for any occasion or none at all, mainly meant to be funny but useful also in grim times to remind them that words stick even as lives fly apart.

Measure your head before ordering.

It was the line that says everything. All the more appropriate and all the funnier because outsiders did not understand and all the better finally because there was nothing to understand.

At six in the morning he was walking the streets, checked out, hobbling. Every ten paces he looked back for a taxi. He had this one pair of pants he'd been wearing since New York and it was smeared at the knees with blood from his scraped hand and he still had Charlie's tight old tweed jacket and Lizzie's overnight bag and the razor he'd bought in Boston, although he wasn't using it, and the shoes he'd bought the day before the razor, finally broken in.

He was in a residential area now, completely lost. A man in an undershirt dragged three garbage bags across the street. A clean light soaked into the shaggy bark of a eucalyptus and it was a powerful thing to see, the whole tree glowed, it showed electric and intense, the branches ran to soft fire, the tree seemed revealed. The man dumped the bags at the corner and came back across the street and Bill nodded to him and walked on, hearing a garbage truck work up the hill.

He kept looking back for a taxi.

12

S he carried many voices through New York. She talked to people in the park, telling them about a man from far away who had the power to alter history. The networks of inhabited boxes became elaborate. The nights were warm and people were drawn to the park from places all around. They were textured with soot. A woman carried her things in a cluster of plastic bags, the neck of one bag tied to the neck of another and the woman in full trudge dragging the bags behind her with a trusty length of twine. Karen saw how pigeons and squirrels took on ratlike qualities. You saw them go right into tents after food. The pigeons were permanently afoot and the squirrels crouched and bobbed and waited, going boldly into paper bags left standing at the feet of people on the benches. The original rats arrived with night, silent and gliding.

People come out of houses, gather in dusty squares and go together, streams of people calling out a word or name, marching to some central place where they join many others, chanting.

There was Omar in his dope-dealing crouch. A couple of times he helped her carry bottles to the store so she could redeem them. Once they went to an art gallery and stood looking at a large construction that meandered along a wall. She counted metal, burlap, glass, there was clotted paint on the glass, a ledge of weathered wood, there were flashlight batteries and postcards of

Greece. Karen looked at a food-crusted spoon that was stuck to the burlap. She thought she might like to touch it, just to touch, for the sake of putting a hand to something that is one of a kind. So she reached over and touched it, then checked around to see if anyone looked askance. On a further whim she lifted slightly. The spoon came off the burlap with a Velcro swish. She was stunned to learn it was detachable. She looked at Omar with her mouth fixed in that slight protrusion and her eyes large and serious. He did a face of exaggerated awe, walking back and forth. In other words a series of open-mouth antics with a strutting component. She held the spoon in her hand, standing totally frozen. She didn't know when she'd been so scared. The thing came right off the painting. A real spoon with impacted food that was also real. She tried to smell the food, careful not to move the spoon too quickly and cause further horrible dislodgement. Omar strutted toward the door like a trombonist at a funeral, making the actual motions. She didn't think the spoon would restick to the burlap and there was no place nearby to set it down. The room was totally bared down, walls, floor and artworks. She decided to follow Omar with the spoon held openly so someone could spot it and she could then return it with a muttered apology, which she envisioned completely, setting the spoon carefully on the desk near the door. But no one said anything and then she was out on the street and it was still in her hand, complete with crusted food, and she was even more frightened than before. She'd left the premises with part of an artwork in her possession. Omar strutted and gleamed. She watched him gait away down the street past mannequins in black kimonos with elbows jutting.

There were gas-main ruptures and fireballs outside famous restaurants and people kept saying, "Beirut, Beirut, it's just like Beirut."

Near the park she went past the beggar who says, "Spare a

little change, still love you." Every time she passed he was doing his daylong refrain. People went by. Still love you. They went by. Still love you. Spare a little change. They went by. Still love you. She left empty bottles and soda cans at the openings of lean-tos and took other bottles to be redeemed, buying food for the squatters in the park and telling them there was a man from far away. Omar took her into tenements where he did his swift business in figures of speech she never quite caught on to. There were tile floors in the hallway and they had these punctures in the door where they put in locks and took out locks. It was a civilization of locks. A pointing hand painted on an alley wall seemed to lead nowhere.

In the loft she went through many books of photographs, amazed at the suffering she found. Famine, fire, riot, war. These were the never-ceasing subjects, the pictures she couldn't stop looking at. She looked at the pictures, read the captions, looked at the pictures again, rebels with hoods, executed men, prisoners with potato sacks on their heads. She looked at the limbs of Africans starving. The hungry were everywhere, women leading naked children in a dust storm, the way their long robes billowed. She read the caption and then looked at the picture again. The picture was bare without the words, alone in open space. Some nights she came into the loft and went straight to the pictures. Delirious crowds swirling beneath enormous photographs of holy men. She might study the same picture seven times in seven nights, children falling from a burning tenement, and read the caption every time. It was suffering through and through. It was who is dying in the jungle rot. The words helped her locate the pictures. She needed the captions to fill the space. The pictures could overwhelm her without the little lines of type.

She talked to Israelis and Bangladeshis. A man with sparkly eyes turned halfway in his seat, driving breakneck downtown, and she formed a picture of the taxi in a steep career, shooting still-life flames. She talked to all the drivers, asking questions in the cash slot.

They went by. Still love you. Went by. Still love you.

There was a dialect of the eye. She read the signs and sayings near the park. The Polish bars, the Turkish baths, Hebrew on the windows, Russian in the headlines, there were painted names and skulls. Everything she saw was some kind of vernacular, bathtubs in kitchens and old Waterman stoves, the liquor-store shelves enclosed in bulletproof plastic like some see-through museum of bottles. She kept seeing the words Sendero Luminoso on half-demolished walls and boarded storefronts. Sendero Luminoso on the cinder-block windows of abandoned tenements. Beautiful-looking words. They were painted over theater posters and broadsheets on all the peeling brick walls in the area.

"I'm not in too good of a mood," Omar said.

"I'm only asking."

"Don't slime up to me. All I'm saying, okay."

"I'm asking a simple question. Either you know or you don't."

"No time for sex, okay, then you come around, which I don't even know your name."

"I found out how old you are. They told me in the park."

"Hey I make my living. I protect my corner regardless. Know what I'm saying. Be it I'm six or sixty."

"So all right, you're mature and experienced to the sky. But that's the way I feel about it."

"The Shining Path. Sendero Luminoso. Spanish for Shining Path."

"Is it religious?"

"It's guerrillas and whatnot. Making their presence felt."

"Where?"

"Wherever," Omar said.

Bodies stirring in the bandshell, lost children on the milk cartons. She recalled the sign for DEAF CHILD and formed a picture of a Sunday hush on a country road. It's just like Beirut. She talked to certain familiars in the park, telling them how to totalize their lives according to the sayings of a man with the power. In the subways she read the Spanish emergency even if the English was right next to it. She reasoned that in an actual emergency she could switch to the English if needs be and in the meantime she was trying out voices in her head.

In the subways, in many of the streets, in corners of the park at night, contact could be dangerous. Contact was not a word or touch but the air that flashed between strangers. She was learning how to alter the way she walked and sat, how to hide her glances or sort of root them out. She remained in the deep core. She walked within herself, did not cross the boundary into the no-man's-land of a glance, a fleeting ray of recognition. Like I'm a person and you're a person, which gives you the right to kill me. She formed a picture of people running in the streets.

She liked climbing the ladder to Brita's bed with the little TV in hand and the loft all dark and sitting near the ceiling in the glow, watching without sound.

A daylit scene comes on of a million people in a great square and many banners swung aloft with Chinese writing. She sees people sitting with hands calmly folded over knees. She sees in the deep distance a portrait of Mao Zedong.

Then rain comes on. They're marching in the rain, a million Chinese.

Then people riding bicycles past burnt-out vehicles. Bicyclists wearing rain shrouds and holding umbrellas. She sees scorched military trucks with people inspecting closely, awed to be so near, and lampposts in the distance arching over trees.

A group of old men come on stiffly posed in Mao suits.

She sees soldiers in the darkness who come jogging through

the streets. She is mesmerized by rows and rows of jogging troops and those riot guns they carry.

Then people being routed in the dark, great crowds rent and split, the way a crowd folds away, leaving a space that looks confused.

They show high officials in Mao suits.

The soldiers jogging in the streets, entering the vast area of the daylit square although it is night now. There is something about troops jogging out of streets and avenues into a great open space. They are jogging in total drag step almost lazily with those little guns at port arms and the crowd breaking apart.

Then the portrait of Mao in the daylit square with paint spattered on his head.

The troops come jogging in total cadence in that lazy drag step, row after row, and she wants it to keep on going, keep showing the rows of jogging troops with their old-fashioned helmets and toylike guns.

They show a smoldering corpse in the street.

There are dead bodies attached to fallen bicycles, flames shooting in the dark. The bodies are still on the bikes and there are other bicyclists looking on, some wearing sanitary masks. You could actually say a pile of bodies and many of the dead still seated on their bikes.

What is the word, dispersed? The crowd dispersed by jogging troops who move into the great space.

One crowd replaced by another.

It is the preachment of history, whoever takes the great space and can hold it longest. The motley crowd against the crowd where everyone dresses alike.

They show the portrait of Mao up close, a clean new picture, and he has those little mounds of hair that bulge out his head and the great wart below his mouth that she tries to recall if the wart appears on the version Andy drew with a pencil that she has on the wall in the bedroom at home. Mao Zedong. She likes that name all right. But it is funny how a picture. It is funny how a picture what?

She hears a car alarm go off in the street.

She changes channels and a million Chinese come on in the daylit square. She is hoping to catch more shots of jogging troops. They show the bicycle dead, a soldier's body hanging from a girder, the row of old officials in Mao suits.

What does it mean that all these old men are dressed in Mao suits and the people in the square are all in shirtsleeves?

The motley crowd dispersed.

They show the great state portrait in the deep distance and she is pretty certain there is no wart in Andy's drawing.

There is something about troops entering a square, jogging row after row in lazy cadence. She keeps changing channels to see the troops.

They show the bicycle dead.

The daylit square comes on again. It is funny how a picture shows the true person even when it is incomplete.

And in the street when she goes out later there is a taxi that has skidded into a parked car and a third car's alarm is sounding. People stand around eating and watching. The sodium-vapor lamps bend over the incandescent scene and in the vertigo of intermingled places, the great square in Beijing and the wind-smoked downtown street and the space in the squat building where the TV sits, she stands peering at the crushed car, looking for upside-down bodies and blood dashed everywhere.

They went by. Spare a little change. Went by. Still love you. Spare a little change. Went by. Still love you.

She followed a man who looked like Bill but he turned out on further inspection to be not a writer type at all.

She took the gentlest possible care of the food-encrusted spoon from the art gallery. She kept it on a shelf, clearing some of the books so it could sit undisturbed and in open sight but also out of the sun. She was worried about the food. If the food was somehow touched or rubbed by another object or if it was softened by warm air, it might crumble off the spoon and this would be a defacement she didn't think she could bear. The spoon and food were one.

She spoke sincerely to a couple in the park, a man and woman textured in soot. They sat on a mattress inside their box hut. Karen squatted at the opening, her fingertips touching the ground, and there was a plastic bag that was the entrance curtain sort of draped over her shoulder.

Our task is to prepare for the second coming.

The world will be a universal family.

We are the spiritual children of the man I talked about from far away.

We are protected by the total power of our true father.

We are the total children.

All doubt will vanish in the arms of total control.

Omar Neeley was fourteen. She walked with him past the Ukrainian Jesus on the church façade. They walked past the AIDS hotel. She realized she didn't know where he lived or if he had parents or siblings. She used to think siblings were strictly white and middle-class due to something in the nature of the word. They walked past the black cube sculpture that was balanced on a point. It had ten men sleeping beneath it with their shopping bags and shopping carts alongside, with crutches lying beside some of them, some arms and legs in casts. Omar was supposed to help her carry plasterboard left at a demolition site. Take it to the park. But down one of the factory streets two men in undersized hats came up, those little fedora hats and muscle T-shirts. She felt the contact in the air, the streak of meaning that takes the blood out of your face. But all they did was talk. They talked to Omar in figures of speech she couldn't make out. Then they walked along with him and he never looked back, and they walked and he went with them. What about my plasterboard. One of them talked to him with a hand on his arm and he walked along with that jangling gait, big for his age.

People with supermarket carts. When did these things come out of the stores and into the streets? She saw these things everywhere, pushed, dragged, lived in, fought over, unwheeled, bent, rolling haywire, filled with living trivia, the holistic dregs of everything if that is correctly put. She talked to the woman in the plastic bag, offering to get a shopping cart for her, which is something I might be able to do. The woman spoke out at her from inside the bag, spoke in raven song, a throttled squawk that Karen tried to understand. She realized she understood almost no one here, no one spoke in ways she'd ever heard before. The whole rest of her life had been one way of hearing and now she needed to learn another. It was a different language completely, unwritable and interior, the rag-speak of shopping carts and plastic bags, the language of soot, and Karen had to listen carefully to the way the woman dragged a line of words out of her throat like hankies tied together and then she tried to go back and reconstruct.

The woman seemed to be saying, "They have buses in this city that they crouch for wheelchairs. Give us ramps for people living in the street. I want buses that they crouch for us."

She seemed to say, "I want my own blind dog that it's allowed in the movies."

But maybe it was something else completely.

There are people gathering in clusters everywhere, coming out of mud houses and tin-roof shanties and sprawling camps and meeting in some dusty square to march together to a central point, calling out a name, collecting many others on the way, some are running, some in bloodstained shirts, and they reach a vast open space that they fill with their pressed bodies, a word or name, calling out a name under the chalk sky, millions, chanting.

She said, "Let me into vibration" or "Get me annihilation," and when Karen brought her hot food on a pie plate she took it into her bag and disappeared.

Brita came home and they sat eating a meal that Karen carefully prepared. She had cleaned the place and packed her own small belongings in a tote bag she set by the door, to show she was ready to leave anytime the word was given.

Brita was impressive, she was frantically lagged and talkative, charged with a stark energy that had the center drained out and was all restless edges. She looked hollow-boned and beautiful like someone back from glaring tropic solitude.

"Do you like baths or showers?" Karen said.

"I take baths when there's time. I give myself up to my bath. It's the only place where I'm happy in the present moment."

"I'll run you a bath."

"Usually I'm happy only thinking about it later. About five years later. Except for my bath and except for my writers. I'm happy doing writers."

"I don't think I've ever said that before. 'I'll run a bath for you.' It sounds strange coming out."

"And what about Bill, so where is he, does anyone know, that foolish man?"

"There's no news or Scott would have called me."

"There is a tendency of men to disappear. What do you think? Although I guess you've done some disappearing yourself. I could never just disappear into the blue. I would have to make certain announcements. Let the bastards know why I'm leaving and let them know where to find me so they can tell me how sorry they are that I'm gone."

"Did your husband disappear?"

"He went on a business trip."

"When was this?"

"Eighteen years ago."

"It's like what's the name of that myth?"

"Exactly. And he has a series of adventures and performs legendary feats and comes back with a contract for a million spare parts."

"Tell me when you want me to run a bath."

"Did your husband disappear?" Brita said.

"They sent him to England to be a missionary. I don't know where he is now."

"And you were married in this church."

"There is a thing called a matching ceremony. This is before the wedding. They have mate selection."

"Do I really want to hear this?"

"Some members wear actual labels saying Infertile, like, or May Be Gay. Just so the surprises are kept in check."

"Listen, there are going to be surprises. I would be the tattooed lady if I had to list the full particulars."

"Taking Powerful Tranquilizers."

"And who selected your mate?"

"Reverend Moon."

"And how did you feel about this?"

"I thought it was perfectly lovely. I stood up when my name was called. I went to the front of this ballroom-type place. Master was way over at the other end of the stage with many people standing between us, officials and members of the blessing committee and so forth. So then he just pointed to a man in the audience."

"And you looked at him and knew he was the right one."

"I thought I honestly loved him even before he finished rising to his full height. I thought how great he's Korean because many Koreans have been church members for a long time and this would give us a deeper foundation to build on. And I liked the darkness and sleekness of his hair."

"My husband was largely bald."

"But guess what I found out later. The day before the ceremony Master had looked at photographs of members and he actually matched us by photograph. So I thought how great, I have an Instamatic husband."

"Do you know how lucky you are to be out of there?"

"I don't like hearing that expressed, necessarily."

"You are extremely lucky."

"There are more potatoes," Karen said.

"There are always more potatoes. I'm talky by nature. Okay? I make a lot of noise, I see people, I see men, I like to talk to men, I have affairs but I never know I'm happy for five years minimum. Think about Scott."

"I think about him. But I think about Kim too. He was husband-for-eternity. He wore a dark blue suit and maroon tie. They all did. And all the brides wore Simplicity Pattern number eight three nine two with the neckline two inches higher."

"Go back to Scott and stay with him. You people belong together, all three of you. I think it's a strange and sad way to live in many respects but who am I to say that something is strange and anyway you desperately need each other. I don't like thinking of Bill being off alone somewhere."

"How do you know he's alone?"

"Of course he's alone. He wants to be so alone that he can forget how to live. He doesn't want it anymore. He wants to give it all back. I'm completely certain he's alone. I know that man for a hundred years."

"I'll run your bath now," Karen said.

■ ■ ■

Scott was doing reader mail. It was all over the attic, mail arrayed in slanted ranks on the desk and table, on the tops of file cabinets and bookshelves. He was structuring the mail by country. Once that was done he would put each country in chronological order so he might easily locate a letter sent from Belgium, say, in 1972. There was no practical reason why he'd ever want to find such a letter or any other piece of reader mail in particular. The point is that he would have it all in place. The house would make more sense in this alignment. And once he had all the other countries in place, he would do the United States. He would do it state by state, masses of letters through the decades. Most mail made Bill uneasy. It cut into his isolation and made him feel he was responsible for the soul of the sender. Scott laughed at this of course. About the only letters Bill looked at came from jerk-water towns and junctions, wide places in the road. He lingered over postmarks and return addresses. He liked to recite place names that carried the ghost music of remote terrain, hamlets that sat in a summer buzz under the Indian sky. He wanted to believe that only a few shy high-school kids or army recruits or piano teachers in small lost towns might truly see what was important in his work.

That evening Scott reread the letters from Bill's sister. Then he went through the bedroom looking for anything that might tell him where Bill was or when he would call or if he would call. The medications were spread through two upper drawers in the bureau. There were many more than he'd known about and he examined the brand names. They were like science-fiction gods. And he glanced at the manuals and reference works and little paperback pill books. He looked for personal letters and documents. There was a single empty suitcase at the top of the closet and a small old electric fan set on a folded paper bag down among the shoes. He looked for sealed instructions, mocking himself for the thought and the phrase, but still thinking there might be something he was supposed to find eventually.

Willard Skansey. A welterweight fighting outdoors in steaming holiday weather before a crowd of straw hats.

Scott would never reveal the name change to anyone. He would keep absolutely silent. He was happy to keep silent, even now, beginning to feel abandoned. For many years Bill had been able to trust people to keep silent on his behalf. It would sustain and expand Scott, it would bring him closer than ever to Bill, keeping the secret of his name.

He went into the workroom and studied the wall charts again. He read the postcards from Liz. Then he made a list of things to do when he was finished with the mail.

Karen rode in a taxi, she loved these jouncing yellow cabs with their slender Ethiopians at the wheel. They had padded wheels, they had furry covers for their wheels and religious pictures pasted to the dash. She was looking at a wedge-shaped building in Times Square and it had a band of glowing letters running all around it. In other words the news of the day flashing across a moving-message unit. There was something about the funeral of someone famous but she couldn't get a clear look from out the taxi window and the words went fleeting off the edge and continued around the corner and she had this stopped feeling you get when there's something awesome in the news, this stoppage in the body, the cold stilled excitement that prepares you for something vast. She waited for the main news to return but the taxi started up again. She formed a picture of people massing in a square.

A crazy storm broke over the city. Box huts struck and pummeled by slashing hail. She thought, Hailstones the size of hailstones. It was only the lucky construction sheeting that saved the boxes from melting on people's heads.

They used big canvas carts from the postal service for garbage or belongings.

They talked and mumbled to themselves, they nodded and talked, lone figures deep in monologue, they gesture to themselves and nod convincingly.

The messiah is here on earth and he is a chunky man in a business suit from the Republic of Korea.

She stood just looking at the spoon sometimes. She told Brita she didn't want to take it with her when she left. It had a new setting now, detached from the burlap, and she was afraid that moving the spoon again might damage it in some mysterious inner way.

She asked everywhere for Omar but he wasn't to be seen except for one time he was sitting on a fire escape with a Spanish woman and it took Karen a while to get him to come down and talk to her. All he said was he was off the corner now. He would have other things to do that he was setting up. He got somebody pregnant in Coney Island that he would have to deal with and Karen felt a deep pause, something in her chest opening to jealousy and loss. Plus there was a man coming around who lyingly claimed Omar had stolen his handgun. A piece of bent metal with a taped handle. She listened to him and felt the weight of those tiled hallways and punctured doors, the crack alleys where women left their babies wrapped in headlines. He told her he didn't miss the corner. He was full of major plans. There were schemes that he could turn to cash. She listened to him and missed him. His gaze tended to drift and she knew he didn't really see her. It made her feel strange, knowing she was about to disappear forever from sight and mind and memory, and there was someone she would think of often and he'd forget who she was, he was forgetting even as she stood there. But that was the weight of his life, those were the turns of phrase she could never understand.

In the worst noise of the subway there was music playing. Saw musicians under stairways and scattered along passages and they had keyboards and amps and violins, they had hi-hat cymbals and wagging saxophones. Gospel preachers worked the turnstiles, testifying strongly. Men sat in the grime with sand pails at their side waiting for a coin to drop. The musicians kept their odds and ends in shopping carts and played with the trains screaming in and announcements coming in gauzy bursts.

The warning aura came when she was alone in the loft. A mercury glow moved up the shanks of the towers out there. She came away from the window with a feeling in her arm that was like running current. She saw zigzags of silvery light and thought at once of the fleeting text that ran around the building in Times Square. Suddenly she knew who had been buried in the news of the day. She saw the lightning-lit word streams and the name she'd missed when she sat in the taxi and the line about weeping chanting mourners in the millions. She groped to the sofa and sat motionless for fifteen minutes, seeing the words streak across the building and go over the edge and continue on the other side. She was able to see the other side. Then the pain and nausea rolled in. She had no sense of time. The light was metallic and intense. Sendero Luminoso. It was right inside her, gleaming out of the pain mass. The beautiful-sounding Shining Path.

She realized Brita was in the room with her now. It was okay now. She kept saying okay. This is a word they know in numerous countries.

That night they sat together on the sofa with the TV juxtaposed against the conversation. They talked and watched. Then they saw what was on and listened to the voice that spoke behind the images.

It was the death of Khomeini.

It was the body of Ayatollah Ruhollah Khomeini lying in a glass case set on a high platform above crowds that stretched for miles. The camera could not absorb the full breadth of the crowd. The camera kept panning but could not inch all the way out to the edge of the anguished mass. On the screen the crowd had no edge or limit and kept on spreading.

The voice said, Crowds estimated, and the picture showed the crowds of mourners and Karen could go backwards into their lives, see them coming out of their houses and shanties, streams of people, then backwards even further, sleeping in their beds, hearing the morning call to prayer, coming out of their houses and meeting in some dusty square to march out of the slums together.

The voice said, Weeping chanting mourners.

There were mourning banners in the streets. Great photographs of Khomeini hung from building walls and many people in the crowd beat themselves on the head and chest.

The voice said, Rivers of humanity, and Karen realized this was the next day now, the funeral, with crowds estimated at three million and everybody dressed in black, all the streets and highways packed with black-clad mourners, and there were people who ran twenty-five miles to the cemetery, ran in grief and mourning, collapsed, carried, pulled along by others, and the roof of a bus fell in under the weight of people trying to see the body.

The voice said, Frenzied mourning. Beating their hands against their heads in grief.

The body was wrapped in a white burial shroud in a refrigerated van that could not get through the streets. Police fired shots in the air to disperse the crowd and make way for the body and there were pictures of fire hoses spraying tight arcs.

The crowd grew and clamored and the van turned back and the body had to be transported to the cemetery by helicopter.

There were aerial shots of the burial site surrounded by crowds. Karen thought they were like pictures of a thousand years ago, some great city falling clamorously to siege.

Then the helicopter landed and the crowds broke through the barriers. The living were trying to bring the dead man back among them.

Karen's hands were over her mouth.

The living forced their way into the burial site, bloodying their heads and tearing at their hair, choking in the thick dust, and the body of Khomeini rested in a flimsy box, a kind of litter with low sides, and Karen found she could go into the slums of south Teheran, backwards into people's lives, and hear them saying, We have lost our father. All the dispossessed waking to the morning call. Sorrow, sorrow is this day.

The living fell upon the body and knocked it to the ground.

The living do not accept the fact that their father is dead. They want him back among them. He should be the last among them to die. They should be dead, not him.

The voice said, Distraught and chanting mourners.

The living beat themselves and bled. They ripped the funeral shroud and tried to take the dead man into their tide, their living wave, and reverse the course of time so that he lives.

Karen's hands were pressed to her face.

The living touched the body, they pressed the imam's flesh to keep him warm. They had bloody shirts and there were towels around the heads of many men, soaked with blood.

Karen felt she was among them. She saw the shrouded body on the litter surrounded by bearded men, black-clad mourners and revolutionary guards, and they were fighting to touch the imam and take pieces of his shroud.

She could see his thin white legs exposed to the light. They were fighting over the body and beating their own faces.

She thought of the delicate tending of the dead and watched the frenzy of this scene and believed she might pass out. It was an injury to the idea that the dead are protected. His delicate hands and legs were so unfairly exposed. The living paraded the body around the compound and there were soldiers firing shots and men with bloodied heads.

But they were only trying to bring him back among them.

The voice said, Eight people trampled to death and many thousands injured.

But it was the tale of a body now. It was beginning to be the story of a body that the living will not yield to the earth. They were passing out from heat and grief. There were people diving into the grave. She saw them throw themselves rag-bodied into the opening. Their bodies did not matter anymore and were limp and bent with grief. They wanted to occupy the grave to keep the imam out.

Karen went backwards into their lives, into the hovels and unpaved streets, and she watched the pictures on the screen.

Water cannons were turned on and the soldiers fired shots and took back the body at last. They pushed it aboard the helicopter and she could see the litter hanging out of the open door and the body exposed on the litter as the rotors turned and the craft began to lift.

But the living swarmed over the helicopter and dragged it back down.

It was possible to believe that she was the only one seeing this and everyone else tuned to this channel was watching sober-sided news analysis delivered by three men in a studio with makeup and hidden mikes. Her hands were pressed against her temples.

She watched the body sticking out of the door and dust kicking up and that mass of black-clad mourners hanging off the skids and dragging the craft down to the ground.

It was the delicate tending of the dead that was forgotten here.

The troops drove the crowd back and the helicopter climbed once more. This time it swept the living away. They fell back from the wind-blast of the rotors and beat their heads and chests.

The voice said, Six hours later, and Karen saw a whole new barrier set up around the site. Cargo containers and double-decker buses. There was a sound track with amplified warnings carrying over the plain that stretched beyond the burial site and there were crowds to the horizon, crowds out to the edge of the long-distance lens.

The helicopter landed with the body in a metal casket, which revolutionary guards carried on their shoulders a short distance to the grave. But then the crowd surged again, weeping men in bloody headbands, and they scaled the barriers and overran the gravesite.

The voice said, Wailing chanting mourners. It said, Throwing themselves into the hole.

Karen could not imagine who else was watching this. It could not be real if others watched. If other people watched, if millions watched, if these millions matched the number on the Iranian plain, doesn't it mean we share something with the mourners, know an anguish, feel something pass between us, hear the sigh of some historic grief? She turned and saw Brita leaning back on the far arm of the sofa, calmly smoking. This is the woman who talked about needing people to believe for her, seeing people bleed for their faith, and she is calmly sitting in this frenzy of a nation and a race. If others saw these pictures, why is nothing changed, where are the local crowds, why do we still have names and addresses and car keys?

Here they come, black-clad, pushing toward the grave. Helicopters flew in low over the plain. They dipped at perilous angles over the heads of the living and enveloped them in dust and noise. People beat themselves unconscious and were passed limply hand to hand over the heads of the crowd to recovery areas nearby.

Sorrow, sorrow is this day.

It was ten meters to the grave but it took the guards at least ten frenzied minutes to reach the spot and put the casket in the earth. It was the story of a body that the living did not want to yield.

Once the body was buried they put concrete blocks on top of it. The helicopters kicked up dust and many mourners wept and fell. When evening came the guards moved a black cargo container on a flatbed truck and placed it over the gravesite. The living climbed the sides of the container and spread flowers across the top and there were photographs of Ayatollah Ruhollah Khomeini fixed to the metal surface.

The voice said, The black turban, the white beard, the familiar deep-set eyes.

Black-veiled women, the women in full-length veils, Karen tried to think of the word, chadors, women wrapped in chadors came forth and moved in close and there were many hands pressed to the container, there were hands touching the photographs and pressed to the metal.

Karen went backwards into the lives of the women, she saw them coming toward the camera in the narrow streets, then back even further to when they were growing up, to when they put on the veil and looked out at the world from the black wrapping, backwards to what it felt like dressed head to foot in black the first time, calling out a name under the burning sky.

The living carried signs and chanted. Khomeini the idol-smasher is with God today. Hours into night, under floodlights, the living beat their hands against their chests in grief.

Early in the park, first thing, she talked to those who were awake. A few people sat huddled on benches with coffee in paper cups and a woman spread a blanket over the pool fence.

Karen said, "We will all be a single family soon. Because the day is coming. Because the total vision is being seen."

Then she climbed onto the bandshell stage and went among the bodies in sleeping bags and burlap and plastic. She talked to people one by one, squatting down flatfooted, her fingers linked an inch above the floor.

She said, "Prepare the day. Be ready in your mind and heart. There is plan for all mankind."

She made her way across the stage, searching for bodies with open eyes.

She said, "Heart of God is only homeland. Pali-pali. Total children of the world."

The sounds of bitter sleep, the moans that rose from untellable dreams. And she talked to those who lay awake. Totally talked. Rough coughing all around her, the nasal scrape, the measure of those bodies breathing, it sounded very much like work. Stale air holding close, the old dead smell of bedding and sweat and pee and slept-in clothes. She talked in the intimacy of first light with sleeping people all around.

She said, "For there is single vision now. Man come to us from far away. God all minute every day. Hurry-up time come soon."

The police minicab scooted past the box huts webbed in blue sheeting, past two men in hooded jerseys sharing a smoke. Past the woman in the broken folding chair sitting lopsidedly asleep.

Past the man on the ground with pigeons moving near his head, poking for food in his hair and clothes. Past the whole population that knows the laws of the nomad encampment, all their bundles tight, bags containing bags, people edged down, reading the space their lives are assigned.

Karen came down from the stage and looked for someone who might listen. She had Master's total voice ready in her head.

13

There were two stories about the ferry. It was hit by shell-fire from gunboats about thirty miles from the Lebanese coast and it turned around and came back to Larnaca. Two dead, one missing, fifteen wounded. Or the ferry was very near the Lebanese port of Junieh when it was struck by land-based artillery batteries or rocket launchers and it turned around and came back to Larnaca. One dead, one missing, nine wounded.

Bill was down at the harbor watching the ferry put in. He counted eighteen holes in the white hull. The ferry was called Zeno the Stoic and held one thousand passengers but the story was that only fifty-five had made the voyage.

Another story concerned the gunboats operating in Lebanese waters. They might have been Syrian, Israeli or Lebanese, and if they were Lebanese the story had it that they might have been operating from a makeshift base controlled by a Christian general who thought the ferry was an Iraqi freighter carrying arms to a rival faction.

But if the ferry was hit by land-based batteries, the story was that Shiites loyal to Syria did the shelling, or Shiites loyal to Iran, or possibly Christians loyal to Israel. The other story said the Syrians themselves were responsible.

Bill watched passengers come out of the opening in the bow

and walk slowly along the pier toward a group of waiting people. It was midday and hot and he thought if he'd arrived a day or two sooner he would now be among them, slumped and trudging or dead somewhere or said to be missing. The story was that the casualties had been picked up at sea by Royal Air Force helicopters and taken to one of the British bases on the island. There were many thousands of Lebanese on Cyprus these days and now fifty-five who thought they were going home were unexpectedly back, if the number was accurate, minus the dead and missing.

He walked along the palm-lined seafront past cafés and shops. The pang in his side was deeper and steadier now, right front upper abdomen. He was getting to know it well. Sometimes a pain feels familiar even as it hits you for the first time. Certain conditions seem to speak out of some collective history of pain. You know the experience from others who have had it. Bill felt joined to the past, to some bloodline of intimate and renewable pain.

He took a table and ordered a brandy. There were lights strung across the promenade and he thought he might sit here all day waiting for dusk, for the sea breeze to freshen and the lights to come on, colored bulbs attached to wires that trailed and looped among the palms. And then sit here some more, sit into early morning with his Metaxa, a medicine dating nobly to the nineteenth century, and come back at noon or so and sit a while longer, waiting for a story to circulate that the ferry was running again.

He didn't really think he would have ended among the dead, injured or missing. He was already injured and missing. As for death, he no longer thought he would see it come from the muzzle of a gun or any other instrument designed to be lethal. This was a thing he used to brood about. Shot by someone. Not a thief or deer hunter or highway sniper but some dedicated reader. He felt a touch of anticipation at times, seeing the bleak thing happen. He had put himself in deep seclusion and a certain forceful logic made it possible that some lonely young man might see a mission here. There were the camera-toters and the gun-wavers and Bill saw barely a glimmer of difference. An undersized kid with pinkish eyes, self-creating, an only child (as Bill began to see him) who lives in full-length mirrors and comes upon a novel that speaks to him in dangerous and radiant ways. Scott was not one of these. He had an enterprise and wit that scattered the darker spirits but it was also true that he'd popped out of a package, gasping for air, showing a need to consume whatever is left after he has read the books and collected the rumors. Then there was the finger Bill had received in the mail. He kept it around a while, a ring finger he guessed, gone mummy-brown, and he used to look at it and wonder what it meant. But that was long ago and he'd lost the feeling he might walk out of the post office and see a slight lad come diagonally toward him, showing the roguish smile he's been preparing for weeks.

He felt like calling up what's-her-face, the photographer, and talking to her machine.

He started back to his hotel. His leg didn't hurt much and his left shoulder, where he'd struck the pavement when the car hit him, felt altogether fine. But there was pain in the other shoulder now. He stopped in the lobby of one of the larger hotels to pick up a Paris Herald and saw a sign welcoming a group of veterinarians from Britain. Among the doctors again. The newspaper said thousands were leaving Beirut to escape the fighting. Coffins were stacked at cemetery entrances because there was no more room for the dead. Outside the city they were burying people in clusters, two or three bodies to a grave. Skulls were spray-painted on the walls of ruined buildings and there wasn't any water and the rats were getting bigger and the power grid was down.

Bill believed he faced no danger there. Isolation only, un-sparing, stony, true, the root thing he'd been rehearsing all these years. And if the ferry didn't run, maybe the hydrofoil would, lifting above the sea chop and maneuvering through the fire of massed batteries. And maybe it wouldn't. But there was a chance the airport would reopen. He'd sit aboard a ghostly flight with six or seven tense Beirutis, refugees in reverse, going home to terror on every level.

On the street he tried to recall the name of his hotel so he could ask someone where the hell it was. The place was small and cheap, a fair distance from the swaying masts in the marina. That's the life he might have had, an answering machine and designer sheets and a racing sloop and a woman he could love and a mess of red mullet grilling in a pit. He realized he was feeling pain every time he took a deep breath.

In his room he noted down expenses on a pad. Then he looked at the pages he'd written and didn't think he could do any more. It was too hard. It was harder than major surgery and it didn't even keep you alive. He looked at a picture on the wall and saw everything that existed outside the room he was sitting in and the one he was trying to write about. It was a picture of fishing nets stowed in canvas baskets and it had sex, memories, cravings, names of old friends, principal rivers of the world. Writing was bad for the soul when you got right down to it. It protected your worst tendencies. Narrowed everything to failure and its devastations. Gave your cunning an edge of treachery and your jellyfish heart a reason to fall deeper into silence. He couldn't remember why he wanted to write about the hostage. He'd done some pages he halfway liked but what was the actual point?

He looked up and said aloud, "Keltner takes his time, tipping a glance at the baseball. Hey what a toss. Like a trolley wire, folks."

He took off his shoes and socks. He slouched in the chair, his feet on the bed, the writing pad flat in his lap. He needed to talk to a doctor and have a drink. First the drink. But it would hurt to get up, it would hurt to walk to a café and sit down and breathe, it might even hurt to swallow, so we have the classic dilemma here. He should have asked Charlie how he'd stopped drinking. He loved his old friend, he felt an unremitting love all those recent hours they'd spent together in New York and London, felt an unremitting need to leave, get going, shake hands goodbye. Charlie used to talk about growing old on Park Avenue, he saw himself a frail old man in a wheelchair tended by some wordless black nurse in subaudible sneakers. She pushed him ever steadily into the sun. He was so old and brittle he could barely issue a breath but they dressed him up like a small child at a party, they made him look helplessly resplendent in an oversized jacket and a shirt collar that hung off the neck. He saw himself bundled in a blanket in the warmest time of day and the sunniest part of the street. Because when the shadows fell across the sidewalk, the nurse pushed him toward the sun, they went ever sunward, slowly, until he was posed totally still at the corner of a prewar building, taking the sun, this was the sun spot for the next quarter hour, and Charlie used to go pink with shame and delight, conjuring his senile end.

That was the death Bill could be having, almond soap and a redone kitchen and a widow with an answering machine. He loved his old friends but begrudged them something and wanted them to renounce it, whatever it was, so they could all be even once again.

Firecrackers were called salutes.

It was a life consisting chiefly of hair—hair that drifts into the typewriter, each strand collecting dust along its length and fuzzing up among the hammers and interacting parts, hair that sticks to the felt mat the way a winding fiber leeches on to soap so he has to gouge it out with a thumbnail, all his cells, scales and granules, all his faded pigment, the endless must of all this balling hair that's batched and wadded in the works.

Ought to do some sightseeing while I'm waiting for the ferry. Did he say this aloud? The Turkish Fort, the English Cemetery. He changed position slowly, testing movement and weight shifts in several directions, his face showing strain until he realized he could get up easily. He went to the bathroom and urinated and there was no sign of blood. He lifted his shirt and looked at the original bruise on his abdomen and it hadn't expanded or changed color. The middle-period pottery, the lace-making village. He looked in the mirror and saw he hadn't shaved in some days. The scrape on his face was no better and no worse. Better if anything and certainly not worse. He thought he would put on his shoes and socks and have a little lookaround if only to hide from the gaping page.

His right shoulder throbbed heavily.

He could have told George he was writing about the hostage to bring him back, to return a meaning that had been lost to the world when they locked him in that room. Maybe that was it. When you inflict punishment on someone who is not guilty, when you fill rooms with innocent victims, you begin to empty the world of meaning and erect a separate mental state, the mind consuming what's outside itself, replacing real things with plots and fictions. One fiction taking the world narrowly into itself, the other fiction pushing out toward the social order, trying to unfold into it. He could have told George a writer creates a character as a way to reveal consciousness, increase the flow of meaning. This is how we reply to power and beat back our fear. By extending the pitch of consciousness and human possibility. This poet you've snatched. His detention drains the world of one more thimble of meaning. He should have said these things to that son of a bitch, although actually he liked George, but he'd never considered the matter in quite this way before and George would have said that terrorists do not have power and anyway Bill knew he'd forget the whole thing before much time went by.

He remembered the important things, how his father wore a hat called the Ritz, gray with a black band, a raw edge and a snap brim, and someone was always saying, "Measure your head before ordering," which was a line in the Sears Roebuck Catalog, and how firecrackers were called salutes.

He thought he'd like to sit in the sun, get away from the gaping page and hail a cab and go down to the seafront and find a bench near a cluster of canvas baskets piled with fishing nets. He finished lacing his shoes but then pulled down the bedcover and eased onto the sheets, just for a moment, to stop the dizziness, the helpless sense that he was fading into thinness and distance.

Hair nuzzled to the edges of the hooked rug, hair that's twirled around the spokes of the tub strainer and snarled in the drain trap and grimed around the base of the sink, pubic hair curlicued on the rim of the toilet bowl, nape hair kinked fast to the inside of his collar, hair on his pillow and in his mouth and on his dinner plate, but it's the typewriter where he notices mostly, accumulating hair, all his lost strands settled in the mechanism, the grayness and tumble, the soft disorder, everything that is not clear and sharp and bright.

Find someone to push him ever sunward.

There's always something you're not supposed to see but it is a condition of growing up that you will see it.

When the boy pulled the hood away the prisoner looked for lizards fixed to the wall. They were small and pale, milky green, so pale and still he had to concentrate to find them.

The room drained the longings out of him. He was left with images.

Time moved tormentingly, carried by insects, all-knowing, if we can say it moves, if we can call it time. It all but talked to him. It had its own despair, it was present in the food and the effects of food, it seeped through his body in the form of fevers and infections, endless watery waste.

But the images were small and closed, time-dimmed. He wanted to think of the city burning, rockets streaking off the launchers. But the only images he could shape were compact and private, small closed moments in a house where things half happened, dimly, somewhere at the end of the hall.

It made the prisoner anxious, not having a pencil stub or scrap of paper. His thoughts fell out of his head and died. He had to see his thoughts to keep them coming.

He thought of the lizards as shards of light, sunlight in the shape of tapered jade. He memorized their positions on the wall and tried to bring them back into the world of the hood.

The boy wore a dark T-shirt under the top part of someone's jogging suit and almost always had fatigue pants and ratty striped sneakers.

There was no more schedule for the war. It took place anytime or all the time and Israeli jets pounded over the city, creating the ancient spacious booms of a detonating sky.

The prisoner thought of himself as the boy's own thing. He was the handy object the boy might tip and shape to his own wandering designs. He was the boy's childhood, the idea of boy-hood shining bright. A young male finds a thing and takes it directly to the center of his being. It contains the secret of who he is. The prisoner thought about this. He was the lucky find that enabled the boy to see himself clearly.

But then he stopped memorizing the lizards. It violated some resentful rule he couldn't quite identify.

His body began to swell up. He watched his legs become airy

white floats and did not accept them as his own. His body was fleeing with his voices.

No one came to interrogate him.

It was hard to stand normally or even shift positions on the mattress and he knew the time was near when he would become the collector of permanent conditions. They would find him and move in. Serous fluid in the tissues, spasms in the chest, all the chronics and abidings.

He wanted a notebook and pencil. There were thoughts he could not formulate without writing them down.

He thought of the no-shirt man alive on the wire.

It was hard to adapt to the absence of sense-making things. He couldn't know for certain whether the rules had changed or been slightly refined or completely and eternally abandoned or whether they had ever existed in the first place, if we can call them rules or even trust the runted memory of a thing called a rule.

He identified with the boy. He saw himself as someone who might become the boy through the effortless measure of the mind thinking back. He thought at times he remembered the boy. There was a moment in some dim summer day when the boy stood by the door in the casual contraction of time.

The prisoner sensed a second darkness under the hood and knew the power was off again. He was just another Beiruti, no power, no water, listen to whistling shells, happens all the time.

There were strip fragments of concrete still attached to the bent steel rod the boy used to beat the bottoms of the prisoner's feet when he remembered.

The war was audible but without the traffic sounds now, the routine honking that rode above the machine guns and mortars. City emptying out. He tried to shape an image of stark vistas down the long ruined avenues, a last sad pleasure, but it didn't work anymore.

Nothing lay behind him but compact snatches. All energy, matter and gravity were ahead, the future was everywhere, all the things people say, stretching unbearably.

The hoods made no sense. Why were both of them wearing hoods? The boy needed only his own hood to protect himself from being identified at some unlikely future time. And if the boy wanted the prisoner to wear a hood, a hood without eyeslits, a punishment, a midair hole, then he didn't need a hood of his own. He could have fed the prisoner through a mouth slot in the man's rag hood.

Two images in the dimness. The grandmother that had to be tied to a chair. The father seated drunk on the toilet, vomit sloshed in his dropped pants.

Only writing could soak up his loneliness and pain. Written words could tell him who he was.

He knew there were times when the boy pretended to leave the room but remained to watch him. He was the boy's discovery, the glow he'd scraped from the earth. He felt the concentrated presence and knew exactly where the boy stood and he remained motionless on the mat and studied a dead stillness all the while the boy stood watching.

Small closed images under the hood.

The only way to be in the world was to write himself there. His thoughts and words were dying. Let him write ten words and he would come into being once again.

They brought him here in a car with a missing door.

A wet scrap of paper and a pencil that a dog has chewed. He could write his terror out, get it on the page and out of his body and mind.

Is there time for a final thought?

He knew the boy was standing by the door and he tried to see his face in words, imagine what he looked like, skin and eyes and features, every aspect of that surface called a face, if we can say he has a face, if we believe there is actually something under the hood.

Bill listened to the voices at the next table and knew he was in the presence of the British vets. Two men and a woman. He looked at the food in front of the woman and pointed. The waiter made a scrawl on his pad and went away. Bill downed his brandy.

He got up, taking the empty glass with him, and leaned toward the veterinarians.

"I wonder," he said, "if you might oblige a writer by answering a question or two. See, I'm doing a passage in a book that requires specialized medical knowledge and as I need a little guidance I wonder if I could trouble you for half a minute."

They looked all right. They looked friendly enough, undismayed, not deeply interrupted.

"A writer," the woman said to the others.

There was a heavy man with a beard who looked closely at Bill while the other two were looking at each other to decide whether this was going to be funny or bothersome.

"Would we have heard of you?" the bearded vet said with a trace of skepticism in his voice.

"No, no. I'm not that kind of writer."

No one seemed perturbed by this remark even though Bill wasn't sure what he meant. The remark satisfied them if anything, set the terms for a quiet and relaxed exchange among anonymous travelers.

Bill looked at his empty glass, then tried to find a waiter somewhere, his glance extending to other restaurants down along the promenade.

"But mightn't we have read something you've written?" the woman said. "Possibly at an airport, where the names don't always register sharply."

The other two looked at her approvingly.

"No, I don't think so. Probably not."

She was small and broad-faced, pleasantly so, he thought, with brown bangs and a mouth that pushed forward when she spoke.

"What sort of thing is it you write?" the second vet said.

"Fiction."

The one with the beard nodded carefully.

"I'm doing a passage, see, where no amount of digging through books can substitute for half a minute's chat with an expert."

"Did they ever make a movie?" the woman said.

"Right. Are any of your books also movies?" the second vet said.

"They're just books, I'm afraid."

The other man smiled faintly, looking at Bill out of the full beard.

"But presumably as an author you make appearances," the woman said.

"You mean on television?" the second vet said.

"I often think, you know, there's another one."

Bill gestured to a passing waiter, raising his glass, but it wasn't clear if the waiter saw him or knew what he was drinking. The colored lights were on and a few people stood on a top-floor balcony of the white building just beyond the far row of palms.

Bill squatted by the table and shifted his gaze among the vets as he spoke.

"All right. My character is hit by a car on a city street. He is able to walk away unassisted. Bruises on his body. Feels twinges and aches. But he's generally okay."

"You do understand," the woman said, "that we diagnose and treat diseases and injuries suffered by animals and animals only."

"I know this."

"Not people," the second vet said.

"And I'll happily take my chances."

Bill jumped up and went after a waiter, draining the already empty glass and handing it to the man and slowly pronouncing the name of the brandy. Then he came back and squatted by the table.

"So then over a period of days my character begins to experience deeper symptoms, mainly an intense and steady pain at the side of his abdomen."

Another waiter arrived with more wine for the vets.

"And he wonders whether he has an internal injury and which organ and how serious and how disabling and so forth. Because he wants to make a journey."

"Is he pissing blood then?" the bearded man said.

"No blood in his urine."

"If you make him piss blood you can do a nice little bit with a kidney. We might help you there."

"I don't want blood in his urine."

"Readers all that squeamish?" the woman said.

"No, you see the pain is frontal."

"What about the spleen?" the second fellow said.

Bill thought a moment and couldn't help asking, "Does a dog have a spleen?"

This was very funny to the others.

"If they don't," the bearded vet said, "I've made a nice career doing splenectomies on furry midgets."

He had a big chesty laugh that Bill liked. Bill's first wife despised him for liking doctors because she thought he was contriving to outlive her.

"Let me add one thing," Bill said. "My character has a tendency to drink."

"Then his spleen might indeed be enlarged," the second vet said. "And a large spleen is easier to damage and might bleed and bleed and cause quite considerable pain."

"But the spleen is on the left side," Bill said. "My character feels pain on the right side."

"Did you tell us this?" the woman said.

"Maybe I forgot."

"Why not change it to the left side and do the spleen?" the bearded vet said. "It would actually bleed nonstop, I expect. Might be a nice little bit you could do with that."

The waiter came with the brandy and Bill held up a hand to request a formal pause while he drank the thing down.

"But, see, I need the right side. It's essential to my theme."

He sensed they were pausing to take this in.

"Can it be upper right side?" the second man said.

"I think we can do that."

"Can we give him some pain when he takes a deep breath?"

"Pain on breathing. Don't see why not."

"Can we make his right shoulder hurt?"

"Yes, I think we can."

"Then it's absolutely solved," the woman said.

The bearded vet poured the wine.

"Lacerated liver."

"Hematoma."

"Local swelling filled with blood."

"Doesn't show externally."

A waiter came with Bill's dinner and put it on the other table. They all watched it for a moment. Then Bill went to the table and got the plate and utensils and squatted at the vets' table, cutting up his meat.

"So it's the liver that's dealing out this misery. As he sort of suspected. What do I do with him next? What does he think and feel?"

The woman looked at the second vet.

"Feel faint?"

"I should think."

"No blood to head," she said to Bill.

"What else?"

"His blood pressure's falling and his abdominal cavity may be on the verge of acute infection."

"But he wants to take a trip," Bill said.

"Completely out of the question," the second vet said.

"What sort of trip?" the woman said.

"An ocean voyage. A cruise or passage. Not very long or trying."

Bill poured some wine into his glass and looked from face to face.

"Completely and totally implausible," the bearded vet said.

"No, we can't have it," the woman said. "Can't let him do it. Stretches the limits. Absolutely no."

Bill drank his wine, caught up in the fun.

"But if he only feels faint? No blood to head? This is why people go on cruises."

"Sorry, no," the woman said.

The bearded vet said, "If you give him the symptoms we've agreed upon, the only plausible recourse is a doctor."

"Or you'll simply have to send him into a coma."

Bill finished cutting his meat before taking the first bite. He stood up and looked for a waiter. The air had a clear and happy tang.

"No offense, people, but we're not talking about a parakeet. This is an otherwise healthy human being."

"Otherwise healthy. That's a cute touch."

"The trouble with healthy humans, otherwise or not, is that they don't let their doctors do the jobs they're trained to do."

"Animals first, last and always," the woman said, gripping the edge of the table and pushing forward in her chair.

Bill caught a waiter's attention and waved his empty glass, pointing into it with the other hand. The bearded vet poured the wine.

"All right," Bill said, "I'm ready to make my character yield to professional advice and wisdom. What exactly would a doctor do if someone in this condition showed up in his office?"

"He'd call a bloody ambulance, wouldn't he?" the bearded vet said.

They were having a great time. The second vet got a chair from Bill's table and dragged it over and Bill sat down and ate another piece of meat. The waiter arrived with brandy and they ordered more wine.

They decided to go to a nightclub along the coast, a place where Lebanese in large numbers took their exile and longing. Bill sat jammed in a corner of the taxi feeling muddled and blurred. Muzzy. This was a word he hadn't heard or thought of in many years. The vets were trying to get the driver to improvise a verse for Kataklysmos, an important local feast in memory of the flood.

The club was large and crowded. A middle-aged woman with a hand mike moved among the tables singing laments in Arabic and French. Bill sat drinking at the end of a banquette packed solid with the three original vets and two others found wandering outside. The original woman let him lay a bent hand on her loamy thigh. A champagne cork shot out of a bottle about every forty seconds. Bill thought he saw his book across the room, obese and lye-splashed, the face an acid spatter, zipped up and decolored, with broken teeth glinting out of the pulp. It was so true and real it briefly cleared his muzziness. Couples stood clinging on the dance floor and a champagne bottle exploded in someone's face, the man standing in a creamy flash of blood and foam and looking down at the damage to his suit. There were fashion references everywhere, women wearing skull jewelry and

several young bravos in camouflage sunglasses and pieces of militia gear. Arguments spread around the room, the champagne
came sluicing with a bang and Bill thought there was a two-
hearted mood in the air, a reflectiveness at the center of the noise
and babble, a yearning for home that had a secret hidden inside
it, the shared awareness that they did not want to escape the war,
that the war was pulling them into it and they were here to join
hands and death-dance willingly past the looted hotels and the
fields of tumbled stonework. And he looked at the weird little
man in whiteface going up on the small stage to sing "Mack the
Knife" in Louis Armstrong's voice, a perfect chilling imitation
of the famous sweet-potato growl, and Bill hated hearing that
sound coming out of a fold-up body that lives in a suitcase, it
was awful, it was damn scary, but the vets were fascinated, not
a whisper or blink, it was the shark song they'd been waiting for
all night, the cataclysmic verse.

It hurt to breathe. He moved his hand along the woman's
thigh. There was something about her hair being cut straight
across the forehead that made him think he was feeling up a
teacher in a storeroom filled with the new-penny freshness of
school supplies. Oh God make her let me do it to her. Later in
the men's room Bill and the bearded vet walked right past each
other without a word or sign. Seemed natural enough in the
episodic course of a long night among strangers in a distant city.
It felt to Bill that a life had come and gone since the segment
on the promenade with a sea breeze and colored bulbs.

When he woke up on the hotel bed he was in his shorts, still
wearing his socks and one shoe. It took him a while to figure out
where he was. Once he had this settled he tried to recall how
he'd made it back. He had no memory of leaving the nightclub.
It frightened him, it made him see himself banging into walls,
stagger-drunk in the dark somewhere. The danger of the world
is immense. He saw it now, how dumb and lucky he'd been,

testing that peril. There was one cigarette in the pack. He took off his shoe and had a smoke. Strange to think of himself in lost time, managing any number of delicate maneuvers, shuffling, trailing the hash of a lifespan. It frightened and humbled him but also made him feel darkly charmed.

He remembered the important things, how the boy who ate grasshoppers opened his mouth to show part of a wing and an eye and the juices of the chomped-up body leaking through his teeth.

He went into the bathroom to spit. He hawked it up and spat it out. He urinated. He shook the last drop of pee off his dick. This was his life. He put the cigarette on the glass shelf and washed his face. He dried himself and went to sit at the edge of the bed, smoking intently, studying the cigarette in his hand, what a sweet idea, a small roll of finely cut tobacco enclosed in a wrapper of thin paper, meant to spring a pleasure in the head. Funny how he'd never noticed.

He'd removed his pants, or someone had, without taking off his left shoe. What serene traces of queerness spelt out across the night. He wanted this smoke to last about four more drags and saw it didn't have but two and felt a mood come upon him of soulful loss.

He slept for some hours. It appeared to be early evening when he got up. He called downstairs and they gave him the name and address of a doctor he might talk to. He got dressed, feeling altogether fine, ready to forget the doctor, then thinking better of it, then ready to forget again, feeling hungry, always a sign of resurgence.

He decided he would see the doctor. Before walking out the door, he called the shipping office on an impulse. They told him the ferry was running again.

He patted himself down for passport, wallet and traveler's checks. He dropped his things in the bag and went down to check out. At the shipping office he stood in a line of exactly three people, himself included. He looked at posters of sunsets and tawny coasts. A man came in with cups of coffee and glasses of cold water on a round metal tray that was suspended from wire struts. It felt like a moment with a history. The clerk made a gesture and they each took a cup and stood around talking.

"Now how far is it to the port of Junieh?"

The clerk said, "Roughly in kilometers maybe two hundred forty."

"And from Junieh to Beirut, what do I do?" Bill said.

"Taxi distance. Take a taxi."

"Will they overcharge me?"

"Of course."

"What about the holes in the boat? All repaired?"

A round of amusement here, the others sharing some joke without a word or glance.

"Don't worry about the holes."

"All repaired?" Bill said.

"The holes are well above the waterline."

"We don't speak about the holes," another customer said.

"The holes are but details," the clerk said.

Bill sniffed the grounds at the bottom of his cup, trying to outfox the pain, maneuver past it.

"Now what about the truce? Does it look serious this time?"

"They're all serious. You can't look at a cease-fire and say this one lasts, that one has no chance. They're all serious and they never last."

"But does the truce affect the safety of the ferry? Do the terms of a truce include gunboats at sea?"

"The sea is nothing," the clerk said.

"We don't speak about the sea," the other customer said.

"The sea is a detail compared to the land."

He paid for his ticket with traveler's checks and the clerk asked him if he had a visa. Bill did not. The clerk asked him if he had a waiver from the State Department and Bill had never heard of such a thing.

"Never mind. There is always a way."

"What's the way?" Bill said.

"When you get to Junieh you go to passport control and you will see a man from the Lebanese Forces. Always there is some-one. He has a uniform, a rubber stamp and an ink pad. Tell him you're a writer."

"Okay, I'm a writer."

"Tell him you would like press credentials. Maybe he suggests some money will change hands. Then he stamps something on a piece of paper and you are now under the protection of the main Christian militia."

"And I don't need a visa to get into the country."

"You are completely free to enter."

"And how much money is changing hands?"

"If you are willing to pay to get into a city like Beirut, I don't think you care how much."

He stood on deck and was surprised to see them come aboard, easily a hundred people, some with children, with infants pouched in sleep across a breast or shoulder. The gulls rocked high in the burning light. He thought it was touching and brave and these people were dear to him, families, cartons, shopping bags, babies, the melodious traffic of a culture.

He thought he ought to formulate a plan, maybe something along the following lines.

Take a taxi from Junieh to Beirut. Bargain with the driver. Pretend to know the area and the fastest route and the standard price for the trip. Find a hotel in Beirut and ask the manager to hire a car and driver. Bargain with the driver. Speak knowledge-ably about the layout of the city and try to give the impression you've done this many times. Show him your map. He had a map he'd bought after picking up his boat ticket but it was odd that he'd been forced to go to three shops before finding a map of Beirut, as if the place no longer qualified, or had consumed all its own depictions. Show him your map. Go to the southern slums, and this is where Bill's plan grew soft and dim but he knew he would eventually walk into the headquarters of Abu Rashid and tell them who he was.

Bill has never walked into a place and told them who he is.

They were still boarding. The light was the kind that splits the sky, a high sulfur spearhead fading into night. He went to find his compartment, which consisted of three wire hangers and a bunk. He grew dizzy again and lay down, his forearm over his face to keep the light out. The boat whistle sounded, making him think it was nice, inside the pain, that boats still have whistles that seem to call a song. He thought he was resting well, having a good rest. He thought the pages he'd done showed an element of conflict, the wrong kind of exertion or opposition, a stress in two directions, and he realized in the end he wasn't really thinking about the prisoner. Who is the boy, he thought.

It was writing that caused his life to disappear.

No blood to head.

He thought of the time, when was it.

Can you wait two shakes.

He fell away from the pain and tried not to return.

He thought of the time, when was it, sitting in a taxi on the way to Idlewild it was called then and the driver said, "I was born," right, and the point is that we were going to get there about two and a half hours before flight time due to some typical personal mixup and the driver said, "I was born under the old tutelage the earlier the better," and he told himself at the time be sure to remember this line to recite to a friend or use in a book because these were the important things, born under the old tutelage, and it made his heart shake to hear these things in the street or bus or dime store, the uninventable poetry, inside the pain, of what people say.

He wanted devoutly to be forgotten.

He fell away again, steeply this time, and changed his mind about not returning but he'd forgotten the line, never told it, never used it, maybe thirty-five years ago, Kennedy was Idlewild, time was money, the farmer was in the dell, so steeply it scared him, made him try hard to return.

His father. Can you wait two shakes.

His father. I keep telling you and telling you and telling you.

His mother. I like it better with the sleeves rolled down.

He could hear his breathing change, feel a slowness come upon him, familiar though never felt before, an old slow monotone out of the history of shallow breathing, deeply and totally known.

Measure your head before ordering.

His father. We need to have a confab, Junior.

He knew it completely. The glow, the solus. And it became the motion of the sea, the ship sailing morningward toward the sun.

The gashed hillside above Junieh was clustered with balconied buildings that looked red-fleshed in the early light. Down by the seafront a few open-sided trucks were parked near the disembarking point, stocked with food and drink. Once the passengers were all ashore the cleaning crew boarded and an old man with a limp took the cabins along the starboard side on the upper deck. When he came to the man lying in the bunk he looked at the bruised and unshaved face and the dirty clothes and he put a gentle hand to the pale throat, feeling for the slightest beat. He said a prayer and went through the man's belongings, leaving the

217

insignificant cash, the good shoes, the things in the bag, the bag itself, but feeling it was not a crime against the dead to take the man's passport and other forms of identification, anything with a name and a number, which he could sell to some militia in Beirut.

14

He heard a car door slam on the gravel road and then the sound of the car driving off and he thought a moment before turning to look out the window behind the kitchen table. Because who could it be coming down on foot? The rare visitor drives in. He was at the sink doing a scouring job on a skillet and couldn't see anyone from this angle but didn't bother changing position because whoever it was would appear in the window sooner or later, somebody selling God or the wilderness or the end of life on earth, or they wouldn't. The rare visitor comes bumping down the dirt trail in a van or pickup to deliver something or repair something and it is usually a familiar face and scuffed shoes.

Scott did three or four more strokes with the scouring pad and glanced again and it was Karen, of course, looking not so different from the first time he'd ever seen her, a cloud dreamer on a summer's day, someone drifting out of Bill's own head, her tote bag dragging on the ground.

He remained at the sink. He ran the water over the skillet, then scoured some more, then ran the water, then scoured, then ran the water. He heard her come up the steps and open the door. She walked into the hallway and he ran the water, keeping his back to the room.

She said, "I took the taxi from the bus station instead of calling.

I had just enough money left for the taxi and the tip and I wanted to arrive totally broke."

"The wind blows the door and look what walks in."

"Actually I have two dollars."

He didn't turn around. He would have to adjust to this. He'd naturally fitted himself to the role, for some years now, of friend abandoned or lover discarded. We all know how the thing we secretly fear is not a secret at all but the open and eternal thing that predicts its own recurrence. He turned off the water and put the skillet in the drain basket and waited.

"Ask me if I'm glad to be back. I missed you. Are you all right?"

"Run into Bill?" he said.

"I sort of kept seeing him, you know? But not really. Did you hear anything?"

"All quiet."

"I came back because I was afraid you wouldn't be all right. And I missed you."

"I've been keeping busy. I've done some things, some organizing."

"You always put a premium on that."

"Same old Scott," he said.

His voice sounded unfamiliar. He thought it was because he hadn't spoken aloud to anyone in some time. But maybe it was the situation. It was dangerous to speak because he didn't know which way a sentence might tend to go, toward one thing or the logical opposite. He could go either way, one reaction as easy as the other. He was not completely connected to what he said and this put an odd and dicey calm in his remarks.

"Of course you might want to be alone," she said. "I know that. I know I left at probably a bad time you were having. But I honestly thought."

"I know."

220

"We weren't the old dependency."

"It's all right," he said.

"I'm not very good at this type conversation."

"I know. It's all right. We're embarrassed."

"I didn't call from New York and I didn't call from the bus station."

"It's not a station. You always call it a station. It's a little ticket booth inside a drugstore."

"Because I don't trust the telephone," she said.

He turned and looked at her and she looked like hell. He walked over and put his arms around her. She began to shake and he held her tighter and then stepped back to look at her. She was crying, making the motion or taking the shape, but without tears, her mouth stretched flat, the animated light missing from her eyes, and he put his hand behind her head and drew it softly toward him.

They went for a long walk in the woods beyond the road, single-file along a path and then out into a glade of lady fern. She told Scott she'd brought the pictures with her, the contact sheets of Brita's photographs of Bill. He said nothing but felt an ease, a redress, the partial payment for damage suffered. She said Brita would not publish the pictures without Bill's, or Scott's, consent.

They held each other much of the night, or lay in wettish touch, haphazard, one prone and the other supine, two legs engaged, and talked and did not, or fell away to clear and periodic sleep, or made choppy laboring love, made heaving breath, converged at some steep insidedness, or Karen talked and Scott laughed, delighted at her imitations of the New York speech machine, they blat and cram, they champ and smash, or Scott told her how the lines of her face were printed in his vision so that he saw her sometimes in the middle of a meal, afloat in her own hair like a laser image of some Botticelli modern.

In the morning they drove twenty-two miles to buy a lightbox and magnifier, and twenty-two miles back.

In the afternoon they cleared the desk in the attic and spread out the contacts. There were twelve sheets, each containing thirty-six black-and-white exposures—six strips, six frames per strip. The sheets were eight and a half by eleven inches and each frame was one and a half inches long and one inch high.

Scott and Karen stood at different ends of the desk. They bent over, careful where they put their fingers, and looked at the strips of developed film but not thoroughly or analytically. It was too soon for that.

Karen's hands were clasped behind her back and after a while Scott put his hands in his pockets and this was how they scanned, leaning deeply toward the desk, moving around each other to exchange positions.

In the evening, after early dinner, Scott carried the telephone table up to the attic. He set it at one end of the desk and placed the lightbox on top.

They took turns looking at the sheets. Because the frames followed each other in the original order of exposure, they were able to see how Brita had established rhythms and themes, catching a signal, tracking some small business in Bill's face and working to enlarge it or explain it, make it true, make it him. The pictures of Bill were glimpses of Brita thinking, a little anatomy of mind and eye. Scott thought she wanted something undesigned and casually come-upon, a familiar colloquial Bill. He took the magnifier to frame after frame and saw a photographer who was trying to deliver her subject from every mystery that hovered over his chosen life. She wanted to do pictures that erased his seclusion, made it never happen and made him over and gave him a face we've known all our lives.

But maybe not. Scott didn't want to move too soon into a theory of how much meaning a photograph can bear.

First came the great work of cataloguing the pictures, making lists based on camera angle, subject's expression, part of room, degree of shadow, head shot, head and chest, hands showing or not showing, visible background and so on. What we have in front of us represents one thing. How we analyze and describe and codify it is something else completely.

Although in a way, and at a glance, the differences frame to frame were so extraordinarily slight that all twelve sheets might easily be one picture repeated, like mass visual litter that occupies a blink.

All the more reason to analyze. Because there really were differences of course—position of hands, placement of cigarette —and it would require time to do a comprehensive survey.

At breakfast Scott said, "There's something I haven't wanted to think about."

"I know what you're going to say."

"We have to be prepared for the possibility that Bill won't return, that we won't ever hear from him again. But I'm not going to be puzzled or resentful."

"Neither am I."

"We can't let our own feelings define his behavior."

"We can't use normal standards."

"Whatever he's done, we have to understand it's something he was preparing for, something he's been carrying all these years."

"He needed to do it."

"And we are absolutely the last people on earth to require an explanation."

"Can we still live here?" Karen said.

"The house is paid for. And he'd want us to live here. And I have money saved from the salary he paid me and this money goes automatically from his account to mine every month and if he didn't want me to keep getting it he would have advised the bank when he went away."

"I can get a job waitressing."

"I think we'll be all right. We're in Bill's house. His books and papers are all around us. It depends on his family. When they find out the situation, they may try to sell the house out from under us. They may try to sell his papers, get the new book published. Every scenario of total disaster I've ever imagined. And there's the question of royalties from the other two books."

"We won't worry now," she said.

"There's the complex question of who's entitled."

"He lived with us, not them."

"He left no instructions."

"We're the ones who made it possible for Bill to devote his whole time to writing."

"We removed every obstacle. It's true."

"So shouldn't they let us live here if we promise to keep things just as they are and do Bill's work?"

Scott laughed.

"The night of the lawyers is approaching. The long knives are coming out. Blood and slogans on all the walls."

"They can own the house," Karen said. "But they should let us live here. And we keep the manuscript and we keep the pictures."

Scott leaned toward her to sing a bit of old Beatles, a line about carrying pictures of Chairman Mao.

Then he sat in the attic alone through the rainy morning, hunched over the lightbox, making notes.

He had the secret of Bill's real name.

He had the photographs, the great work of describing and cataloguing.

He had the manuscript of Bill's new novel, the entire house

filled with pages, pages spilling into the shed that abutted the back of the house, a whole basement containing pages.

The manuscript would sit. He might talk to Charles Everson, just a word concerning the fact that it was finished. The manuscript would sit, and word would get out, and the manuscript would not go anywhere. After a time he might take the photographs to New York and meet with Brita and choose the pictures that would appear. But the manuscript would sit, and word would travel, and the pictures would appear, a small and deft selection, one time only, and word would build and spread, and the novel would stay right here, collecting aura and force, deepening old Bill's legend, undyingly.

The nice thing about life is that it's filled with second chances. Quoting Bill.

IN BEIRUT

H er driver tells her three stories.

First one, people are burning tires. In the midst of car bombs and street skirmishes and the smash of long-range field guns and buildings coming down and whole areas lost in smoke, people are burning tires to drive away mosquitoes and flies.

Second, a pair of local militias are firing at portraits of each other's leader. These are large photographs pasted to walls or hanging from awning poles in the vegetable souks and they are shot up and ripped apart, some pictures large enough to swing from a wire strung over the street, and they are shot up and quickly replaced and then ripped apart again. There is a new exuberance in these particular streets, based on this latest form of fighting.

Last, they are making bombs that contain flooring nails and roofing nails. The police are finding quantities of common nails, nails sprayed and dashed and driven into the bodies of victims of random blasts.

Brita waits for the point of story number three. Isn't there supposed to be an irony, some grim humor, some sense of the peculiar human insistence on seeing past the larger madness into small and skewed practicalities, into off-shaded moments that help us consider a narrow hope? This business about the nails doesn't do a thing for her. And she's not so crazy about the other stories either. She has come here already tired of these stories, including the ones she has never heard. They're all the same and all true and it is sad that they are necessary. And they almost always exasperate her, especially the stories about terror groups that issue press credentials.

They are driving past the rubble of the racetrack's arched façade. Then they are going the wrong way down a one-way street but it doesn't matter. All the streets are right and wrong. She sees cars burnt skinless, water flying gloriously from broken mains. Street life as well, vendors, wooden carts, a man selling radios and shoes from the hood of his car. There are balconies dangling vertically from shelled buildings. Then they are going into the slums near the refugee camps. Cars wrapped in posters of Khomeini, whole cars postered except for a space on the driver's side of the windshield. Sandbagged shops and mounds of uncollected garbage. She sees a street vendor's little homemade city of Marlboro cartons, the neat stacks of cigarettes a wistful urban grid of order and deployment.

Brita is on assignment for a German magazine, here to photograph a local leader named Abu Rashid. He is hidden somewhere deep in these shot-up streets where weeds and wild hibiscus crowd out of alleyways and the women wear headscarves and stand on line, long lines everywhere for food, drinking water, bedding, clothing.

Her driver is a man about sixty who pronounces the second *b* in bomb. He has used the word about eleven times and she waits for it now, softly repeating it after him. The bomb. The bombing. People in Lebanon must talk about nothing but Lebanon and in Beirut it is clearly all Beirut.

A beggar approaches the car, chanting, one eye shut, chicken feathers stapled to his shirt. The driver blows the horn at a guy who carries a bayonet in an alligator scabbard and the horn plays the opening bars of "California Here I Come."

The streets run with images. They cover walls and clothing— pictures of martyrs, clerics, fighting men, holidays in Tahiti. There is a human skull nailed to a stucco wall and then there are pictures of skulls, there is skull writing, there are boys wearing T-shirts with illustrated skulls, serial grids of blue skulls. The driver translates the wall writing and it is about the Father of Skulls, the Blood Skulls of Hollywood U.S.A., Arafat Go Home, the Skull Maker Was Here. The Arabic script is gorgeous even in hasty spray paint. It is about Suicide Sam the Car Bomb Man. It says Ali 21. It says Here I Am Again Courtesy Ali 21. The car moves slowly through narrow streets and up into dirt alleys and Brita thinks this place is a millennial image mill. There are movie posters everywhere but no sign of anything resembling a theater. Posters of bare-chested men with oversized weapons, grenades lashed to their belts and cities burning in the background. She looks through shell holes in a building wall and sees another ruined building with an exposed room containing three stoned men sitting on a brand-new sofa. There are boys tattooed with skulls who work the checkpoints wearing pieces of Syrian, American, Lebanese, French and Israeli uniforms and toting automatic rifles with banana clips.

The driver shows Brita's press card and the boys look in at her. One of them says something in German and she has to resist the totally stupid impulse to offer him money for his cap. He wears a great-looking cap with a bent blue peak that she would love to give to a friend in New York.

The car moves on.

She does not photograph writers anymore. It stopped making sense. She takes assignments now, does the interesting things, barely watched wars, children running in the dust. Writers stopped one day. She doesn't know how it happened but they came to a quiet end. They stopped being the project she would follow forever.

Now there are signs for a new soft drink, Coke II, signs slapped on cement-block walls, and she has the crazy idea that these advertising placards herald the presence of the Maoist group. Because the lettering is so intensely red. The placards get bigger as the car moves into deeply cramped spaces, into many offending smells, open sewers, rubber burning, a dog all ribs and tongue and lying still and gleaming with green flies, and the signs are clustered now, covering almost all the wall space, with added graffiti that are hard to make out, overlapping swirls, a rage in crayon and paint, and Brita gets another crazy idea, that these are like the big character posters of the Cultural Revolution in China—warnings and threats, calls for self-correction. Because there is a certain physical resemblance. The placards are stacked ten high in some places, up past the second storey, and they crowd each other, they edge over and proclaim, thousands of Arabic words weaving between the letters and Roman numerals of the Coke II logo.

A man is standing in a devastated square. The car comes to a stop and Brita slings her equipment bag over a shoulder and gets out. The driver hands her the press credentials. It is clear she is supposed to follow the other man. He is older than the driver and she notes that he is missing half his right ear. He wears slippers and carries a plastic water bottle. There are people living in the ruins among powdery hills of gypsum. Where there are cars at all, parked snug to walls, they either have no plates or are cleanly stripped, going brown in the sun like fruit rinds. She sees a family living in a vehicle that is a cross between a wagon and a pickup but without wheels, sunk to the axle in dust. Her guide carries the water bottle tucked up near his armpit and leads her without a word directly into a collapsed building. She lowers her head and follows in the dimness over fallen masonry. Wires dangle everywhere and the dust smells sour. They exit through the remains of a butcher shop and cross an alley to the next building, which may have been a small factory once. It seems intact except for shell scars and broken windows and they enter through a large steel door complete with cross-bracing.

There are two hooded boys standing watch on the stairs with photographs of a gray-haired man pinned to their shirts. On the second floor the guide stands at a door and waits for Brita to enter. Inside, two men are eating spaghetti with pita bread and diet cola. The guide slips away and one of the eating men gets up and says he is the interpreter. Brita looks at the other man, who is easily in his sixties and wears clean khakis with shirtsleeves rolled neatly to the elbows. He has gray hair and a slightly darker mustache and his flesh is a ruddy desert bronze. He is bony-handed, maybe slightly infirm, and has gold-rimmed glasses and a couple of gold fillings.

Brita starts setting up. She doesn't think it is necessary to ease into this with small talk. The interpreter moves some furniture, then sits down to finish eating. The men sit there and eat in silence.

She looks out the window into a schoolyard. The school building at the far end is a near ruin. In the yard there are thirty or forty boys seated on the ground, arms crossed over their raised knees, and a man in a khaki outfit is speaking to them.

Rashid says something to the interpreter.

"He is saying you are completely welcome to join us."

"This is very nice but I don't want to cause inconvenience or delay. I'm sure he is busy."

She aims the camera out the window, sighting on the boys in the yard.

Rashid says something.

"Not allowed," the interpreter says, half rising. "No pictures except in this room."

She shrugs and says, "I didn't know you were placing restrictions." She sits down, goes through her bag for something. "I was under the impression the reporter does his story and I do my pictures. Nobody said anything to me about avoiding certain subjects."

Rashid doesn't lift his head from the plate. He says to her, "Don't bring your problems to Beirut."

"He is saying we have all the problems we can handle so if you have communications difficulty in Munich or Frankfurt we don't want to hear about it."

Brita lights up a cigarette.

Rashid says something, this time in Arabic, which goes untranslated.

Brita smokes and waits.

The interpreter swabs the gravy with his flat bread.

Brita says, "Look, I know that everybody who comes to Lebanon wants to get in on the fun but they all end up confused and disgraced and maimed, so I would just like to take a few pictures and leave, thank you very much."

Rashid says, "You must be a student of history."

His head is still down near the plate.

"He is saying this is a statement that covers a thousand years of bloodshed."

Brita raises the camera, seated about fifteen feet from the men.

"I want to ask him a question. Then I'll shut up and do my work."

She has Rashid in the viewfinder.

"I saw the boys outside with your picture on their shirts. Why is this? What does this accomplish?"

Rashid drinks and wipes his mouth. But it is the interpreter who speaks.

"What does this accomplish? It gives them a vision they will accept and obey. These children need an identity outside the narrow function of who they are and where they come from. Something completely outside the helpless forgotten lives of their parents and grandparents."

She takes Rashid's picture.

"The boys in the schoolyard," she says. "What are they learning?"

"We teach them identity, sense of purpose. They are all children of Abu Rashid. All men one man. Every militia in Beirut is filled with hopeless boys taking drugs and drinking and stealing. Car thieves. The shelling ends and they run out to steal car parts. We teach that our children belong to something strong and self-reliant. They are not an invention of Europe. They are not making a race to go to God. We don't train them for paradise. No martyrs here. The image of Rashid is their identity."

She puts out the cigarette and moves her chair forward, shooting more quickly now.

Rashid is eating a peach.

He looks into the camera and says, "Tell me, do you think I'm a madman living in this hellish slum and I talk to these people about world revolution?"

"You wouldn't be the first who started this way."

"Just so. This is exactly just so."

He seems genuinely gratified, confirmed in his mission.

A boy comes in with mail and newspapers. Brita is surprised to see mail. She thought all mail ended at the city limits. The boy wears a long hood, a pale cloth with holes cut for the eyes and with the upper corners flopping over. He remains near the door watching Brita work. She thought the concept of mail was a memory here.

"Okay, one more question," she says. "What is the point of the hood?"

She turns the chair around so she can straddle it, facing the men with her arms resting on the chair back, shooting pictures.

The interpreter says, "The boys who work near Abu Rashid have no face or speech. Their features are identical. They are his features. They don't need their own features or voices. They are surrendering these things to something powerful and great."

"As far as I'm concerned, listen, you do what you want. But these boys have weapons training. They're an active militia as I understand it. I've heard killings of foreign diplomats have been traced to this group."

Rashid says, "Women carry babies, men carry arms. Weapons are man's beauty."

"Take away their faces and voices, give them guns and bombs. Tell me, does it work?" she says.

Rashid waves a hand. "Don't bring your problems to Beirut."

She reloads quickly.

"He is saying the atrocity has already befallen us. The force of nature runs through Beirut unhindered. The atrocity is visible in every street. It is out in the open, he is saying, and it must be allowed to complete itself. It cannot be opposed, so it must be accelerated."

She listens to the interpreter and photographs Rashid.

"You're dropping your chin," she says.

He drinks and wipes his mouth with a napkin.

He says, "The boy who stands there is my son. Rashid. I am lucky at this age to have a son who is young, able to learn. I call myself father of Rashid. I had two older sons dead now. I had a wife I loved killed by the Phalange. I look at him and see everything that could not be. But here it is. The nation starts here. Tell me if you think I'm mad. Be completely honest."

She moves the chair up against the dinner table and tilts it slightly and leans forward with her elbows on the table, snapping pictures.

"What about the hostage?" she says. "About a year ago. Wasn't there a story about a man being held?"

Rashid looks into the camera. He says, "I will tell you why we put Westerners in locked rooms. So we don't have to look at them. They remind us of the way we tried to mimic the West. The way we put up the pretense, the terrible veneer. Which you now see exploded all around you."

"He is saying as long as there is Western presence it is a threat to self-respect, to identity."

"And you reply with terror."

"He is saying terror is what we use to give our people their place in the world. What used to be achieved through work, we gain through terror. Terror makes the new future possible. All men one man. Men live in history as never before. He is saying we make and change history minute by minute. History is not the book or the human memory. We do history in the morning and change it after lunch."

She reloads and shoots.

"What happened to the hostage?"

She waits, her thumb on the shutter release. She lowers the camera and looks at the interpreter.

He says, "We have no foreign sponsors. Sometimes we do business the old way. You sell this, you trade that. Always there are deals in the works. So with hostages. Like drugs, like weapons, like jewelry, like a Rolex or a BMW. We sold him to the fundamentalists."

Brita thinks about this.

"And they are keeping him," she says.

"They are doing whatever they are doing."

Rashid raises his glass to drink. She sees his right hand is shaky. She repositions the camera and resumes shooting.

He puts down the glass and looks into the camera.

He says, "Mao believed in the process of thought reform. It is possible to make history by changing the basic nature of a people. When did he realize this? Was it at the height of his power? Or when he was a guerrilla leader, at the beginning, with a small army of vagrants and outcasts, concealed in the mountains? You must tell me if you think I'm totally mad."

She leans across the table and takes his picture.

He says, "Mao regarded armed struggle as the final and greatest action of human consciousness. It is the final drama and the final test. And if many thousands die in the struggle? Mao said death can be light as a feather or heavy as a mountain. You die for the people and the nation, your death is massive and intense. Die for the oppressors, die working for the exploiters and manipulators, die selfish and vain and you float away like a feather of the smallest bird."

She moves toward the end of the roll.

He looks into the camera and says, "Be completely honest. I want to hear you say it, so I'll finally know. Living in this filth and stink. Talking to these children every day, all the time, over and over. But I believe every word, you know. This room is the first minute of the new nation. Now tell me what you think."

The interpreter drinks and wipes his mouth with a napkin.

"He is saying very simple. There is a longing for Mao that will sweep the world."

Eloquent macho bullshit. But she says nothing because what can she say. She runs through the roll, leaving a single exposure. On an impulse she walks over to the boy at the door and removes his hood. Lifts it off his head and drops it on the floor. Doesn't lift it very gently either. She is smiling all the time. And takes two steps back and snaps his picture.

She does this because it seems important.

It takes the boy a moment to react. He gives her a look of slow and intelligent contempt. He wants her to see every muscle moving in his face. He is very dark, wearing the picture of his father safety-pinned to his shirt, and his eyes are slightly murderous, this is the only word, but also calm and completely aware. He knows her. He wants her to think she is someone he has thought about and decided to hate. His hair is matted and sweaty from the hood and he hates her not because she has humiliated him but because he knows who she is, there is pleasure in his knowing, a violence in the eye that shows how hate and rage repair the soul.

She sees his eyes decide, the little flash of letting go, and he attacks her now. She protects the camera, turning a shoulder toward the boy, and she thinks it is only seconds before the interpreter will step between them. The boy hits her hard in the forearm and reaches in for the camera and she throws an elbow that misses and then slaps him across the face.

There is a pause while everyone reflects on what has happened. They see it again. Brita feels it beating in her chest, happening again.

She waits for the boy to look at his father for an explanation. But he stares at her evenly with new contempt, new indulgence in his hatred, and she sees him get ready to come at her once more.

Abu Rashid says something. There's another pause. The interpreter repeats the remark and then the boy picks up his hood and leaves the room.

Brita takes her time putting things back in the equipment bag. She hears the boys in the yard reciting a lesson together. Feeling detached, almost out-of-body, she walks over to Rashid and shakes his hand, actually introduces herself, pronouncing her name slowly.

Downstairs the guide with half an ear is standing with the water bottle cradled to his chest.

. . .

Brita is staying in East Beirut in a flat that belongs to a friend of
a friend. The hotels are crushed or ransacked or occupied by
squatters and the flat has been empty for over a year, so here she
is, back out on the balcony again. It's late and she has eaten and
taken a bath and read a magazine piece about Beirut because
what else can you read or think or talk about in a place like this.
She doesn't especially want to sleep. Not that sleep would be easy
in any case. All night intermittent bursts of machine-gun fire
and many dark rumbles to the immediate east that sound like
mountains ringing. And the odd round fired now and then, some
despond of the heart or a drug deal gone slightly sour, and she
doesn't like being in bed when the shooters are about. Even in
the periodic stillness she finds herself scrutinizing the silence,
waiting uneasily for the boxy clatter to begin again. So out she
comes one more time, half dressed, wanting to stand within it,
feel the cordite wash of the city against her skin.

She sees streaky lights bolting from the coast and making long
bodiless arcs over the roofscape and down through scuds of dark
smoke that roll across the low sky. A black van goes by right
below and there's a curly-haired guy sticking out of the sunroof
wearing an iridescent track suit and shouldering a rocket-
propelled grenade launcher that's about seven feet long. He is
the Phallic Master of the Levant, at least for now. A radio plays
voices calling in, several radios perched on balconies, people
talking about Beirut because there's no other subject.

She wants to stand inside it. It is wrapped all around her like
some computerized wall of enhanced sensation.

She goes inside and finds a bottle of Midori melon liqueur.
She can hardly believe there is such a thing. She has seen it
advertised at airports and convention centers, the walk-through
places of the world, but never thought it was more than a gesture,
a billboard that rides the skyline in streaming light. And now she

finds an actual bottle of the stuff in someone's abandoned flat. Where else but here? Everybody's nowhere. She pours some into a glass and takes it out to the balcony. Sirens going in the distance. On a wall across the street there are layers of graffiti, deep deposits of names and dates and slogans, and she sees in the dim light that Ali 21 has made his way into the Christian sector. He is here in French and English, newly and crudely sprayed.

Ali 21 Against the World.

A silver flare sails briefly over the streets, bits of incandescence trailing away. Radio voices calling all around her. Beirut, Beirut. They crowd in toward her, pressing with a mournful force. People calling from basement shelters, faces in shadow, clothing going dark with heavy sweat, sleeping children curled around their war toys. All the hostages, pray for them stashed in their closets and toilets. All the babies, pray for them lying in rag hammocks. All the refugees, pray for their dead and wait for the shelling to subside. The war is so fucking simple. It is the lunar part of us that dreams of wasted terrain. She hears their voices calling across the leveled city. Our only language is Beirut.

She drinks the scummy green liqueur and goes inside to get some sleep. She has to be up before seven and on her way out of here.

About an hour later something wakes her. She comes out on the balcony again, telling herself to be alert. It is nearly four a.m. and she has a sense of some heavy presence, a grinding in the earth. She leans over the rail and sees a tank come chugging around the corner into her cratered street. Mounted cannon bobbing. She feels the beat of adrenaline but stays where she is and waits. She thinks it's an old Soviet T-34, some scarred and cruddy ancient, sold and stolen two dozen times, changing sides and systems and religions. The only markings are graffiti, many years of spritzed paint. The tank moves up the street and she hears voices, sees people walking behind it. Civilians talking and laughing and well dressed, twenty adults and half as many children, mostly girls in pretty dresses and white knee-stockings and patent-leather shoes. And here is the stunning thing that takes her a moment to understand, that this is a wedding party going by. The bride and groom carry champagne glasses and some of the girls hold sparklers that send off showers of excited light. A guest in a pastel tuxedo smokes a long cigar and does a dance around a shell hole, delighting the kids. The bride's gown is beautiful, with lacy appliqué at the bodice, and she looks surpassingly alive, they all look transcendent, free of limits and unsurprised to be here. They make it seem only natural that a wedding might advance its resplendence with a free-lance tank as escort. Sparklers going. Other children holding roses tissued in fern. Brita is gripping the rail. She wants to dance or laugh or jump off the balcony. It seems completely possible that she will land softly among them and walk along in her pajama shirt and panties all the way to heaven. The tank is passing right below her, turret covered in crude drawings, and she hurries inside and pours another glass of melon liqueur and comes out to toast the newlyweds, calling down, "Bonne chance" and "Bonheur" and "Good luck" and "Salám" and "Skål," and the gun turret begins to rotate and the cannon eases slowly around like a smutty honeymoon joke and everyone is laughing. The bridegroom raises his glass to the half-dressed foreigner on the top-floor balcony and then they pass into the night, followed by a jeep with a recoilless rifle mounted at the rear.

It is over too soon. She stays outside, listening to the last small rustle of their voices falling. It is still dark and she feels a chill in the smoky air. The city is quiet for the first time since she arrived. She examines the silence. She looks out past the rooftops, westward. There is a flash out there in the dark near a major checkpoint. Then another in the same spot, several more, intense and white. She waits for the reciprocating flash, the return fire, but all the bursts are in one spot and there is no sound. What could it be then if it's not the start of the day's first exchange of automatic-weapons fire? Only one thing of course. Someone is out there with a camera and a flash unit. Brita stays on the balcony for another minute, watching the magnesium pulse that brings an image to a strip of film. She crosses her arms over her body against the chill and counts off the bursts of relentless light. The dead city photographed one more time.